Jill Paton Walsh was educated at St Michael's Convent, North Finchley, and at St Anne's College, Oxford. She is the author of three previous adult novels: *Lapsing* (1986), *A School for Lovers* (1989) and *Knowledge of Angels* (1994), which was shortlisted for the 1994 Booker Prize. She has also won many awards for her children's literature, including the Whitbread Prize, the Universe Prize and the Smarties Award. Her latest adult novel, *The Serpenti* now available as a Doubleday hardb

She has three children and live

Praise for *Goldengrove* and *Un*

'A beautiful novel and an enduring one'
New York Times Book Review

'An extremely good story, marvellously told. As the story gathers momentum, the deeply understood characters, the golden atmosphere, the small change of everyday pleasures and ageless tragedies are all put over with such newly seen immediacy and such controlled mastery that the reader is carried along like a surf rider on the crest of a wave, knowing it must soon break'
Times Literary Supplement

'Written with an intensity of feeling and care, with a Woolf-like awareness of the instant's sensation: a story all in the present tense but with a remarkable sense of an overshadowing past'
Guardian

Also by Jill Paton Walsh

KNOWLEDGE OF ANGELS
LAPSING
A SCHOOL FOR LOVERS

and published by Black Swan

Goldengrove Unleaving

Jill Paton Walsh

BLACK SWAN

GOLDENGROVE UNLEAVING
A BLACK SWAN BOOK: 0 552 99655 6

GOLDENGROVE © Jill Paton Walsh 1972
UNLEAVING © Jill Paton Walsh 1976

Goldengrove originally published in Great Britain by
Macmillan Ltd

PRINTING HISTORY
Macmillan edition published 1972
Macmillan edition reprinted 1975
Bodley Head edition published 1985
Black Swan edition published 1997

Unleaving originally published in Great Britain by
Macmillan Ltd

PRINTING HISTORY
Macmillan edition published 1976
Bodley Head edition published 1985
Black Swan edition published 1997

GOLDENGROVE UNLEAVING Copyright © Jill Paton Walsh 1997

Set in Linotype Melior by
Phoenix Typesetting, Ilkley, West Yorkshire

Black Swan Books are published by Transworld Publishers Ltd,
61–63 Uxbridge Road, London W5 5SA,
in Australia by Transworld Publishers (Australia) Pty Ltd,
15–25 Helles Avenue, Moorebank, NSW 2170
and in New Zealand by Transworld Publishers (NZ) Ltd,
3 William Pickering Drive, Albany, Auckland.

Reproduced, printed and bound in Great Britain by
Cox & Wyman Ltd, Reading, Berks.

FOR MARNI
and
FOR J.R.T.
in several ways

MÁRGARÉT, are you gríeving
Over Goldengrove unleaving?
Leáves, líke the things of man, you
With your fresh thoughts care for, can you?
Áh! ás the heart grows older
It will come to such sights colder
By and by, nor spare a sigh
Though worlds of wanwood leafmeal lie;
And yet you wíll weep and know why.
Now no matter, child, the name:
Sórrow's spríngs áre the same.
Nor mouth had, no nor mind, expressed
What heart heard of, ghost guessed:
It ís the blight man was born for,
It is Margaret you mourn for.

Gerard Manley Hopkins

Author's Note

Goldengrove and *Unleaving* were written in the 1970s and published in the then-new category of 'young adult' novels. I am glad to offer them to a wider readership. I was and am deeply interested in the strange light cast on adult life seen with partial understanding by young and vulnerable minds. Though originally published separately the books are, as the titles imply, a pair. They concern the same characters, themes and settings, and it seems natural to put them in one volume.

Goldengrove

Rhythmically, like a runner, the train gasps and pants as it pulls up the long rise. Hearing its heavy breathing, looking at azalea, and rhododendron, and gloriously improbable palm trees growing wild along the verges of the line, the passengers can tell that they are nearly there. Sitting near the end of the train, looking and looking through the window – it has made his nose dirty – for the moment when the line turns suddenly and you can see the sea, Paul knows it is nearly there. Madge is somewhere, looking for it too, Paul tells himself. Somewhere in the snake of carriages ahead, she is riding, looking for the sea. They get me to the train in time, just in time, for Daddy to kiss me once, on my left cheek, and for me to just leap into the last carriage as the train draws breath, and the platform starts to jerk sideways. They are so jumpy they can hardly bear to wait to slam the door on me. And it's always a non-corridor train, I suppose it has to be a thin train to fit through the tunnels or something, and so here we always are, together and apart, going there together, and meeting when we get there. Of course, my people don't want to meet her people, that's why it is, of course . . .

'There it is!' he interrupts himself, for now the train is turning, and suddenly the sea is there, Oh, wider than you ever expect, though of course, thinks Paul, I know it is, and a fantastic blue, like the ultramarine in my paintbox when I first touch the brush over it and wet it, and all frisky with windy white horses galloping shorewards to smash and leap on the broken, black, rocky, petering-out-here edges of the land. So round we go now, running at the foot of the cliff, beneath Goldengrove, with white puffs of smoke ascending to signal in the garden to Gran that we are coming, and as we come, just here – yes, there it is! – we can see the lighthouse in the bay.

Getting up, Paul pulls his holdall down from the luggage rack, steadying his rocking body in the diddlidum swaying of the train.

Madge, looking through the window, leaning her head back into the crown of her straw hat, thinks about Paul. I suppose he's on the train somewhere. I suppose he nearly missed it again. He's awfully bad at catching things. Except fish. We'll see the lighthouse soon. She looks for it. There it is in the bay, standing on its rocky island. It is a cleft island, through which, when the ocean is angry, the white surf surges and boils, but today the sea is only playing. She looks at it, and names it to herself. Godrevy . . . Godrevy . . . a dream upon the waters . . . no, that's Byron on Venice. No wonder I got through that exam. I've got a really English examination mind, through and through. And it's all very well being fussed over, and being hurried forwards, and being the youngest girl they've ever let take Matric, but I wonder if it marks you for life? I mean will I wake up when I'm married saying 'Busy old fool, unruly sun (Donne)' to myself? Will I always be quoting in my head, and telling myself where the line comes from? Oh, hell! I won't think school yet, it's still holiday for a while.

And we're nearly there. I got here, in spite of it all. It's always the same; they always try to stop me. Always take me off somewhere else, and say it's instead of coming here. And then they try to fix it so I won't be here at the same time as Paul. 'You can go if you

14

really must,' says Mother, coldly. 'But it will have to be in July. We are going to Berne in August.' I wonder what it's all about, I really do. She *will* ask about Paul, and then whatever I say she hates it, and gets all upset . . . but I'm here now, or nearly, and it will be the same as ever. That's the thing about Goldengrove, it's always the same as ever . . . though I suppose it will be different this time because of being later in the year. 'If you had gone in July, as I suggested,' Mother said, 'you wouldn't have had to miss the beginning of term.'

'Miss Higgins said I had to read widely for the sixth form curriculum,' I said, 'and I could do that anywhere.' It had to be September, because that's when Paul could come. But September is the only difference there will be to Goldengrove, which is always the same. Can the time of year cast a difference over everything?

The train jolts to a halt, and lets out a long dying sigh of steam. Madge gets up, allows the elderly gentleman who got into her carriage at St Erth to lift down her suitcase for her, and gets out. The bright-smelling sea air washes over her, and she raises a swift hand to hold onto her hat. Running from the back of the train, leaning sideways to counterbalance his bulging holdall, hopping in and out dodging the other passengers, Paul is hurtling towards her, shouting 'Madge!' and eyes shining.

At Goldengrove their grandmother sits in the garden in a wicker chair on the terrace, with the windows behind her open to the drifts of lavender ringing the lawn. The seven beech trees and five chestnuts after which her house is named lie to the right of the grounds, with a September colour just creeping over them. In front of her the lawns slope away to the rose garden, and, beyond, the land drops steeply to the garden wall, with the little gate to the path to the beach, to the sea. She hears the train striving, chuff, chuff,

15

below the garden, and sees cotton wool puffs of cloud rising from behind the roses and dispersing through the garden, bringing a sudden smutty smell to interrupt the lavender for a moment. They are here, she thinks, my dear Madge and Paul, together. Their parents make me so angry . . . no, I won't think of that. They are here now. Amy has sent Mr Arthur to fetch them up to the house in the car. I shall have their fresh young faces, their bright smiles around me now for a little while.

'I have put you in the best spare bedroom this year, Madge,' says Gran, when the kissing on the doorstep has been done. To Paul's crestfallen face she says, 'You are getting too big to share a room, you know. Look how big you are, Paul! You've grown six inches since last year.' But standing up against the notched door-frame in the kitchen shows it to be not more than two inches, really. The tea tray is ready on the scrubbed deal table in the kitchen, and, while Gran is measuring Madge, Paul manages to stuff home three of the paste and cucumber sandwiches. The cake plate looks too finely balanced to steal from. Madge isn't much taller. It's round her middle somewhere Gran ought to measure her, thinks Paul, looking at Madge critically. It's somewhere there she's gone different. Narrower, and bendy-looking.

'Oh, Paul, dear!' cries Gran, looking at the inroads on the sandwiches. 'And you haven't washed your hands from the train yet!'

Upstairs, with her suitcase open on the foot of the bed, Madge is trying the best spare room. It doesn't look towards the sea, she finds, but into the trees. It is large and square, with long windows, and a dressing-table. Thoughtfully, she puts her hair-brush down on a lace mat. She is divided, partly trying in a pleased way what it feels like to be a best spare person, with glazed chintz

16

curtains, and a moon-shaped mirror, and lots of mats and little boxes beneath it laid out ready – what for? – and roses in a silver bowl beside the bed. But part of her is sick with disappointment, because it is not the same, after all, as every year till now, and there will be no whispering to Paul from under the starched arc of sheet raised by her thin shoulder as she lies facing him across the room, not seeing him in the bedtime, lights-out-now-dears of Gran's attic.

Madge throws her clothes out of the suitcase, and pushes them hastily into the drawers, empty except for little muslin bags of dusty dried lavender. She doesn't bother to hang anything up. She sits down on the bed. What is it about Paul I like, anyway? she asks herself. He makes me feel like doing the last pieces of a jigsaw puzzle, or that time I mended the Worcester cup Mother broke, he makes me feel that things are where they ought to be, in their right place. But it's stupid of me, really it is, he's only a boy after all, and younger than me. It would be much more fun if he were older. She imagines to herself a scene at the school garden-party, in which Sophia, the snobbiest girl in the fifth, can be heard saying 'Who is the handsome boy you were talking to?' and Madge says, 'Oh that's my cousin, Paul. He's taking me to the dance tonight!' But then she sees at once that if he were older, and likely to take her to a dance, there would have been no long sandy days playing with the boat on the beach down there, and her disappointment wins and she races up the stairs to the attic to talk to Paul.

'Will anyone have remembered to put the boat out for us?' says Paul, looking down towards the sea.

'I don't know. Now it's Amy, instead of Mrs Arthur, perhaps not. It was Mrs Arthur who always remembered.'

'Mr Arthur still does the garden, though. Perhaps he'll have thought of it.'

'Tell you what, though, Paul, if anyone has re-membered at all they're sure to remember to forbid us to put it in the water.'

'Worse luck!'

'Oh, I don't know,' says Madge. 'It probably would be dangerous. And it's fun to play with anyhow.' And they stand for a moment, looking pleased to be here at each other.

The attic is painted white, with sloping angled ceil-ings, and a big dormer window, with a window-seat beneath it, that fills the room with a view of the sea. Madge casts a rueful glance at the patchwork counterpane of the bed that is not now hers, and the funny bamboo bookcase with only Paul's things laid on it, and then goes to sit on the window-seat, and watch the view. And from here she sees the sweep of the bay, and dark Godrevy with its white tower of a lighthouse, and looking the other way the harbour, with the town around it, and behind the harbour the domed grassy hill called the Island, for island it once was, before the fishermen's houses edged out along the sand bar to reach it, so Gran says. It is green below the little chapel on top, and squared with white sheets stretched out to dry and bleach. Nearer lies the long golden beach with the little railway line behind it – the beach that has bathing huts made of coloured canvas, and always lots of people on it, and is quite unlike their beach, which is small and lonely, for the only way down to it lies over Gran's land, and so it is their very own.

'Look, Madge,' says Paul, coming to sit beside her on the sun-faded cover of the window-seat. 'There's a wisp of smoke from over the trees. Someone must be in Gran's cottage.'

But looking, Madge cannot see it, and the brassy noise of the tea-gong tells them that new, redhaired Amy is carrying the tea-tray out to the terrace, and they race down the stairs.

*   *   *

18

Gran is sitting in her chair, pouring tea, with a shawl spread over her knees. 'What's that for, Gran?' Paul asks her.

'I feel the cold so, nowadays,' she says, while Madge, taking her place in a deck chair, feels only the sun.

'It's warm,' says Paul.

'I'm all skin and bone these days,' says Gran.

After tea Madge says, 'Let's go and look for strawberries in the wood.' But Paul says, 'Let's go to the beach.'

Bother, why can't he want what I want? thinks Madge, crossly. 'I want to look for strawberries first,' she says.

'There won't *be* any in September, will there, Gran?' says Paul, but Gran has gently dozed off to sleep in the sun which she declared only a moment ago was not enough to keep her warm.

Off goes Paul at a run, down through the rose garden, to the garden gate, to the path, to the beach. Madge walks into the grove that gives the house its name, thinking: it is just beginning to turn gold, and I have never seen it gold before, only green, always green, hundreds of variously-lit little floating boats of green and lizard-spotted light. Below these trees, especially here round the huge chestnut tree – I was here once when it was in flower, like huge candles – the wild strawberries grow. They spread like wild-fire, Gran says. They all come from six plants Grandfather put here once, long ago when he was alive, Gran says. And I want to eat some, I want them to be here, I don't want it to be September and I shall hate my mother for *ten years* if there aren't any just because trying to keep me from Paul she made it be September instead of August, and I didn't like Berne anyway! Well, not much. Oh, strawberries, be here!

Miraculously, the strawberries are still there. Not many; not like full summer, when the little plants are speckled scarlet that you can see at a glance, and Mr Arthur can go out for an hour and bring back a bowlful for dessert, even though it takes heaven knows how many to fill a kitchen bowl, and there are enough even though Madge and Paul have been happy with mouth and fingers stained with them for hours beneath the trees the day before. Now Madge has to look and look, gently turning the leaves, and finds them one by one, few, late, and last ones. They are no bigger than her little fingernail, as though they were for fairies, and they taste very delicate and clear, like an ordinary strawberry, she thinks, just after you've eaten it, when you are full of the pleased feeling, and your tongue remembers it. 'I shall find twelve before I go in,' says Madge, aloud.

Paul is standing on the beach, looking out to sea. You can see the lighthouse from here, but not the harbour, nor the house, nor the trees of Goldengrove. But behind him rises a grassy, wild-flowered slope, rather steep, with a little path descending diagonally; to his left and right the cliff becomes steeper and rocky, and in a broken staircase steps down to run out as a rocky promontory into the dancing sea. A half-moon of sand lies between. A little cove, with no name, and why should it need one, for it is private; it is Gran's, though she never comes down here now. The path is too much for her, she says.

The boat is there, he sees, his first moment down there, but not because it has been remembered, he sees next moment, but because it has been forgotten. No-one put it away after last year; no-one heaved and hauled it up the path to the shed at the bottom of the garden, and it is half full of sand, and swathed in seaweed, and tied up to a ring in the rock with a rusty chain. Paul decides to leave playing with it till Madge comes. Instead he takes off his shoes and socks, and walks in the surf, jumping in the bolsters of froth, but keeping clear of the great hills of green, white-crested water, rolling in, smoking as they break, for the sea is high here, being ocean, and having come a long way; 'A long fetch, these waves have,' said Jeremy the boatman last year. They are high enough to knock you down, and drag you under, thinks Paul. And it's cold, I'm feeling it too, in this thin shirt flecked with sea-water, and a small cloud crossing the sinking sun. Time to go in.

In the garden again he meets Madge. 'I found some,' she says.
    'Don't believe you!'
    'Smell them!' she says, and opening a purple-pink cavern of mouth full of white teeth and arched tongue, she breathes strawberry breath in his face, enough to make him feel jealous.
    'I'll find more than you tomorrow!' he says. 'The boat's there. It's been left out.'
    'Still in one piece?'
    'More or less. I didn't look till you came.'
    'Tomorrow,' she says.
    Now the little glasses of tonic wine, and the dish of raisins and almonds, and a radio symphony concert turned down low to go with their Grandmother's evening gossip will come next, before bed, and tomorrow.

*   *   *

In darkness Madge wakes up, hearing her bad dreams. A storm has blown up since nightfall, and wind and rain now rattle on the shut panes of glass. The curtain bellies and tugs in front of the window she has opened; as she props herself on one arm the wind sucks it out through the window into the rain. She runs to close it, and finds it jammed. A gale of cold air clutches her nightdress round her as she pulls. The sky outside is black and broken silver with storm and moon. Gran comes in, holding a lamp. She cries, 'Oh dear, my dear, you'll catch your death!' and with

21

surprising force – she looks so frail now – she closes the window.

'I'm going to close Paul's now,' she says. 'Come and look out to sea, Madge. My eyes do let me down so.' Madge follows her.

Paul's window is shut already. He has not woken up, and only a hump in the bed and the familiar tuft of hair sunk in the pillow can be seen of him by the lamp in Gran's hand. Madge looks out to sea, and sees patchy, interrupted moonlight on dark tossing water.

'Are there any ships there?' says Gran, in a low voice, not to wake Paul.

'I can't see any, Gran,' says Madge, and I don't think I'd see them from here even if there were any, she thinks. They'd show like a shadow on the water at most, a black patch among all these shifting blacknesses.

'Won't they all be in the harbour?' she whispers. The wind sounds fiercely up here, whistling on the roof tiles, and keening down the drainpipes of the house.

'The Frenchmen won't, dear,' says Gran. 'Can you see no lights in the bay?'

'Only Godrevy light, Gran.'

'All's well, then. Come down,' and they go down, closing the attic door gently on sleeping Paul.

'Why wouldn't they be in the harbour, Gran?' asks Madge, at her bedroom door.

'It's the French trawlermen, Madge dear. The war stopped them coming, but they're back again these last few years. They don't know this coast well enough. They come round Land's End, looking for shelter, and the bay here looks safe enough. They don't want to pay harbour dues. And then, well, there's no love lost between them and the local men. The men here say the foreigners use fine-mesh nets, and ruin the fishing for others. So the Frenchmen drop anchor in the bay, and when the wind gets up northeasterly, that's not good enough. Sometimes someone goes out to them,

22

to warn them, and try to make them come in, but they don't always heed it.'

'What happens then?'

'They can drag their anchors, poor fellows, and run onto the rocks. Every year, somewhere hereabouts, a few men lost. A trawler on the rocks, or a man washed overboard. Such a pity; such a waste. But when they're in trouble they show lights, or send up flares. You would have seen something. The lifeboat goes out to them. But there's nothing amiss tonight,' and I mustn't frighten her, thinks Gran. I shouldn't have let her see I was concerned. 'All's well tonight,' she repeats. 'Sleep well, Madge.'

So back to the now cold hollowed bed, and listen to the wind again, closed out by the four walls of the house, and Madge sleeps without knowing she has slept, till she opens her eyes again on the bright morning shining all round the room. Finding where she is she wakes thinking first 'Not Goldengrove!' and then, Oh, yes it is, it is Goldengrove's best spare room, and Paul waking up without me up another flight of stairs, and perhaps it is after all better to sit up – she sits up – and stretch – she stretches – than to double-up winded and fighting while Paul jumps on my tummy to wake me! Getting dressed she stares briefly at her naked reflection framed like a Regency portrait in a round of mirror, for it has not escaped Madge's own attention that she is changing somehow around the middle, and she keeps a regular eye on herself to see how she is shaping up. Looking out, she sees that Paul is up and out already – she can see his tracks marked in the dew on the lawn.

No mackerel for breakfast today, for the fishing fleet, says Gran, stayed safely tucked up in the harbour last night, and Paul who slept through every sound of it, and slept through Gran walking with a lamp in her hand, trembling at the thought of death in the

23

watery darkness, clearly thinks that the storm cannot have been excuse enough to miss the sweet firm pink and grey flesh flaking off the web of thin translucent bones on his morning plate. Amy has provided kippers instead, and I like kippers quite a lot, thinks Paul, but they're not the same because we eat them at home, and mackerel only here. And I've brought my six spinners in a chipped blue metal box, and a pair of lines, and Jeremy will take me fishing in his boat, and I will let Madge have the red and silver spinner which always catches the largest fish, and we will bring mackerel gleaming, hanging by the gills in a loop of string, for Amy to cook. I will carry them, and they will brush against my bare leg all the way, and leave a shiny scaly patch on me, like a terrible skin disease, which will wash off in the bath. He grins to himself.

'Nice kipper, dearie?' says Gran.

'Fine, thanks, Gran,' and, 'Do hurry up, Madge. We'll be late down to the beach,' says Paul.

'How can we be late,' asks Madge, 'when there isn't a time we should be there by?'

'We ought to be there as soon as we can!' says Paul.

'Well, it isn't as soon as we can yet, because I can't eat any quicker than I am eating,' says Madge. 'Gran, is there anything we can do to help in the house before we go out?'

If I asked her to pick roses and put them in bowls for me, thinks Gran, they would stay a little. I would watch them going to and fro from bed to bed, and bringing the flowers in. But they would rather be gone. Paul is so eager he can hardly sit still. 'No thank you, Madge,' she says. 'Nothing this morning. Another day perhaps.'

And at once the children are up and away, through the open French windows to the terrace, and over the lawn, and out of sight though their voices rise up to her like birds' voices from the path below. She smiles over the half-drunk coffee cups and the kipper bones.

24

'The beach felt different last night,' says Paul to Madge, as they run down the path, dead-nettle and Ragged Robin leaning to brush against their legs all the way.

'How different?' asks Madge.

'I didn't feel alone there,' he says.

As he says it they are there, leaping from the little platform of squared stones that once made a mooring, or a landing-stage, at the foot of the path, and landing ankles-under in soft sand that slides on their dry skins like silk, and rises to every puff of wind. One or two steps further, and a dry black crackly line of seaweed marks the top of the tide, like the lacy edge of an old black petticoat, and beyond it the width of the beach is golden sand, firm with the sea, that holds every toe-mark, every battlement of a sandcastle, Paul remembers, and they run across it hand in hand to go surf-hopping in the eternal rolling coming-and-going edge of the sea.

In a little while they are both wet through. I always mean to be careful till I get my dress off, thinks Madge, and I never am, and I never learn, and I'm not sorry. She peels off her wet dress, and drops it in the sand, thinking, I'll spread it on a rock to dry in a minute. Paul is putting his shorts and aertex shirt to dry on a rock straight away. Like her he has his swimming things on underneath the accident-prone top layer, and then they are back in the water. Playing in the waves like a dolphin Madge once saw in a documentary film – how sleek and wet and shiny, and supple and intelligent they were, Paul reminds her – Paul simply thinks sea. Pull back, foaming, gather, rise, break, crash in white waterfalls! he thinks. Run, jump, swim in that one, oh, there's a high one, can I stand steady in that one? No, help! Here I go, head-under, struggling, and come up with my hair full of sand, and gritty trickles, oh it tastes of salt! running down my face.

'Are you all right, Paul?' calls Madge, over the waves.

'No! Drowned, drowned!' he shouts back, and not seeing the big wave come, goes under again. He rises to Madge, wading, struggling with deep heavy legs towards him. Seeing him all right she pretends at once that she was only coming to chase him, but he knows. 'Fusspot!' he calls.

Later they lie in the soft sand to dry, and look at the great cloud-castles wheeling by, and the gulls drifting circles in the depths of the sky. 'You are right about it feeling different, Paul,' says Madge. 'I feel watched.'

'There's nobody here,' he says. 'Shall we look at the boat now?'

'Yes, now,' Madge says. We always have to come round to it slowly, she thinks, I wonder why. It has something to do with liking it so much. I don't understand me.

The boat lies tilted slightly, slightly submerged in the sand. Sand has washed inside it, and settled there, giving it a smooth beachy floor. Its sides are festooned with the necklace-of-beads sort of seaweed that pops when you squeeze its bubbles. Lower down it is livid with the bright green weedy slime that covers the sea-washed rocks. And yet it is all in one piece, and still riding on its rusty chain, though it is the slope of the beach it rides now, not the tilting sea. But the winter has left its mark. Most of the boat is bleached grey, weathered down. Deep cracks run along every grain of the once living wood, and it has a pale worn smoothness, like leprosy. Running fingers over it finds ups and downs like bones. A little paint still holds on it. It was turquoise blue paint, all crazed along the cracks in the wood, and mostly flaked away, so that what remains are little lines of it, curling at the edges, and bright against the pale wood. Madge scratches at the raised edge of a piece with her fingernail, and at once the whole flake lifts off.

'Could we paint it blue again, Paul?' she asks.

'We'd have to empty all the sand out, and scrape off all the seaweed,' he says. 'The bottom will be rotten as hell with all this wet sand in it, but we could paint the upper bit blue again. It would be as good as ever to play in.'

'Let's. Let's paint it just exactly that blue-green, green-blue colour it must have been when it was new. I'd like that.'

'Girls!' says Paul. 'Paint your boat sky-blue-pink, this year's fashion colour!' Madge punches him in the ribs, and he continues cheerfully, 'We could paint it. It would be a lot of work before we got to the coloured bit. You'd jolly well have to help.'

'I don't want to start today,' says Madge. 'I feel watched.'

'Yes,' Paul says. 'And now I know who's doing it. Look up there, Madge!'

Looking up she follows his pointing finger. On the cliff overlooking the cove is Gran's cottage — a little, low, snuggling-into-the-slope, white-washed, slate-roofed, tiny house, a fisherman's once, then the servants' in the days when Goldengrove had more hands than Amy's to run it, before the war, that time which the adults all remember so much, and the children hardly at all. The trees mask the cottage from the house, and it looks out to sea, with a path of its own branching from the other path, and a crazy cliff-top garden that is walled for safety and where only sea-pinks grow. Only from here can the cove be seen. And in the garden of the cottage a man is sitting and staring at them.

'What cheek!' says Madge, indignantly.

'Of course,' says Paul, very slowly, in his voice of lordly anger, 'Gran must have rented the cottage to him. So, therefore, he has every right to *be* up there, in his garden. But he jolly well doesn't have to spend all his time *staring* at us!'

'He'll have to stop, or he'll spoil our beach for us!'

27

'I'll make him stop,' says Paul. 'All we have to do is stare back.'

'Well, we have been,' says Madge. 'He must have seen by now that we've stopped playing, and are standing here side by side, looking at him. And he's still looking straight at us.'

Paul jumps up and down and waves his arms. He puts his thumbs in his ears, and waggles his spread-eagled fingers. Joining in, Madge thumbs her nose vigorously at the distant figure. Unflinchingly, and without moving at all, he continues to fix her in his gaze. Perhaps he *isn't* looking at us, she thinks, but what else can he be doing, just sitting there like that? She turns round to see the thing behind her that might be drawing his eyes. Nothing but sand and rock. It *is* us! she thinks, exasperated. 'Yah!' she yells at him, fists clenched. '*Stare cat, stare cat, whatdye think yer looking at!*' but her derisive chanting falls short of him, at his distance, lost in sea and bird calls. Paul picks up his spade, and begins to run, trailing it at an angle behind him, scratching huge wobbly letters in the sand. BUZZ OFF he writes, SCRAM! Madge takes a stick and writes SPY! LOOK AWAY. THIS BEACH IS PRIVATE runs Paul. There is hardly any smooth sand left to scrawl upon, and they stand, out of breath, panting, and looking up, and still, over the low stone wall of his garden, they can see the man staring at them, steadily.

'Come on, Madge,' says Paul. 'I'm going to spy on *him*, and see how *he* likes it!'

She runs after him. They scramble up the path, doubled-over as they run, so that they are hidden as in a tunnel by the encroaching flowery weeds. Madge's heart is beating, as though she were playing hide-and-seek, or 'It'. The clever children, good at catching spies who have eluded the police, the brave dauntless children who capture dangerous criminals single-handed – not that she has ever met any, but she has read about them – come back to her, and she tries them on for size. She begins to laugh. Looking back, Paul lays a hushing finger over his answering grin.

They run past the gate to Gran's garden, and on, further along the path. It takes them to the front of the cottage, or rather to the front door, which nestles in a sprawl of overblown roses in the side of the little house. The door is standing open. Ducking down again, Paul leads the way round the outside of the garden wall. It is only some three feet high, so they have to stalk, still doubled-over, Indian fashion. The wall is nearly at the edge of the cliff, and the grass they are creeping on slopes dangerously, and then drops away altogether to the rocks below. Every few yards as they go, Paul bobs up to spy on the staring man, and when he does so, Madge does too. The man is sitting – they can see his back – in a wooden garden chair. A dog lies on the grass beside him, a black Labrador. The dog's front legs are stretched out very straight and crossed one over the other; he looks as though he had just keeled over sideways from standing up, and lain there. He is asleep, sun-drunk, but still has one black ear cocked towards them. They move, and his ear lifts. They stand still, and very slowly the ear subsides again. But what is the man doing? wonders Madge, for surely he is still staring at the beach, and we are gone from there. She looks down, and sees the scrawled words written in the sand. They edge further round the wall. Next time they bob up she can see he has a book on his knee. But he isn't looking at it! she tells herself. He isn't even pretending to read it, thinks Paul. 'Madge! Madge!' he hisses, waiting for her to wriggle up to him, and breathing urgently in her ear, 'I vote we work round to just in front of him, and then stand up suddenly, and just stare back. Don't flinch, don't speak.' They hear the dog growling sleepily, like an undecided snore, and he hastily finishes, 'Just give him a bellyful of what he's giving us, right?'

'Right,' murmurs Madge, though I am not very good at staring, she thinks. Jenny Martin can out-stare me any day of the week. She wriggles further and further along behind Paul. The grass margin they are on grows narrower, and the grass is that fine and only-beside-the-sea kind that is round and fine, like hair, and very slippery. I hope it's soon, thinks Madge. Oh, Paul, be careful!

Paul stands up suddenly. She stands up, too. Dog cocks his ear. They face the man, and stare straight into his wide-open eyes. Steadily he stares back at them. It takes Madge a long second to understand what is wrong. She is looking at a man with dark hair slightly grey at the temples, wearing an open-necked shirt. A book lies open on his knees, and he does not look at it. His hands are held out straight over the page, fingers downwards, like a piano-player's. His fingertips travel steadily, brushing the paper. His head is held rather high, like a man looking at the distance, but when Madge and Paul pop up right in front of him, his eyes do not change focus at all. In the brilliant sunlight of mid-day he turns skywards eyes so dilated that you cannot see what colour they are at all. And oh, he isn't staring, thinks Madge, oh poor man, poor man, he's blind, and we are wicked, wicked, to have mocked and jeered and ambushed him!

'Is there anybody there?' says the man, but how does he know, Paul wonders, since we've been so quiet the dog hasn't even woken, only rumbled a bit, and my shadow doesn't fall as far as where he is sitting? 'Who's there?' says the man more sharply. Nobody answers.

But overcome with remorse, Madge grabs at Paul to pull him away, and he slips, and she grips onto him, and goes too. Silently they fall together from the grassy ledge, and hit another tuft of grass, and then another, and then they are not quite falling, but hurtling from one bump to another on the way down. They find themselves lying on a grass-topped outcrop half way down, clinging together, gasping. 'Are you all right?' and 'Are you all right?' they ask, but it seems to be only bruises. 'Could have been nasty, though,' says Paul.

'Can we climb down from here?' asks Madge, but it looks as if they can. Overhead the blind man's dog, woken at last, is barking. 'Who's there?' he shouts.

Slithering down and down they reach the beach. At once Madge begins to run, scuffing the letters on the sand with her heels and toes, rubbing them out.

'What are you doing that for?' asks Paul.

'Oh, it's horrid of us,' says Madge.

'But he can't see it,' Paul says.

'He wasn't staring at all,' says Madge, shuffling round the great S of SPY with tears in her eyes.

'He wasn't seeing, but he jolly well was staring,' says Paul, and, 'Come on Madge, we'll make the lunch late for Gran if you don't come now.'

Madge hasn't remembered her dress, of course, till the moment she needs it again, so she has to go home clammy and crumpled, and scratchy with clinging sand.

* * *

'The beach again now, dearies?' says Gran over her coffee cup. Madge glances swiftly at Paul. 'I thought I might pick some flowers and arrange them for you, Gran,' says Madge, because, she thinks, I certainly don't want to go back there till the sea has washed out those words. Paul says, 'Madge found strawberries yesterday, and I'm going to look for some now.'

'Yes, yes, we do need more flowers,' Gran says. 'The petals are dropping.'

Madge goes for the flower-basket and the secateurs, into the green-and-cream painted kitchen, with its huge windowed dresser, and Amy elbow-deep in dishes in the sink. 'That was a super pudding you cooked, Amy,' says Madge. 'What was it?'

'Queen Mab's pudding, Miss,' says Amy. She sounds sulky, thinks Madge, but I would be too if I got left with all the dishes every day. 'It's a lovely day, Amy,' she says. 'Will you have time to go out later on?'

'I've the evening off, Miss Madge, thank you. Walt is coming for me.'

'Who's Walt?'

'He's, well, a friend. A soldier off the American base.'

Amy is blushing. Madge grins. 'Your boyfriend? Oh, have a good time tonight, Amy!' And she goes to join Gran in the rose garden.

'A bowlful of Peace, and one of Rosa Mutabilis, I think,' says Gran, sitting on the stone bench at the edge of the rose garden, while Madge cuts the prickly stems and lays them in the basket. They are good children, thinks Gran. They are staying with me now without my asking. Was I as kind at their age? I can't remember . . . she is falling asleep. Seeing her nodding, Madge smiles, and goes to cut sweet peas.

The kitchen table is covered with vases, all shapes and sizes, and crumpled chicken-wire, and little lead lumps with spikes on, like heavy hedgehogs. Amy has gone, and the buzz of the Hoover is heard faintly from an upstairs room. Madge fills the silver bowl first, the one with the domed lid full of holes for the stems to go through. That's for the living-room. Then sweet peas – for Gran's dressing-table, and some for me, thinks Madge, for the best spare me that likes sweet peas as much as grown-ups do, and now, I think, these extra roses for Amy's room, because really she has so much washing up to do. Madge goes up and down, carrying the vases upstairs one by one. Amy's room is close, with a heavy smell of scent. A photo of a soldier in American uniform stands beside the mirror on the chest of drawers.

Now, thinks Madge, as she gently stirs the roses in the sitting-room vases to look their best where she has put them, I'll make a cup of tea, and take it to Gran. She comes down the steps to the rose garden, carefully balancing the tin tray with a cup, and a little brown teapot on, and the tinkle of cup on saucer wakes her dozing Gran with a jump. Madge sets the tray down, and pours tea. 'How sweet of you, dearie,' says Gran, smiling. I was not as kind at their age, she decides. How deeply she wrinkles when she smiles, thinks Madge. I suppose she is still nice to look at because all her wrinkles are on smile lines. Shall I smile enough to grow like that, I wonder? As a start, she smiles now.

'Madge!' Paul calls from the terrace. 'Do you want to go fishing?'

'Off you go then, Madge,' says Gran at once. 'Jeremy asks after Miss Madge and Master Paul all summer, every time we send down to him for mackerel. He'll be glad to see you.' Madge runs off, leaving behind her a sense of peace. How good to have them with me, thinks Gran. She has noticed, but is trying not to notice, that really very little of having them with her is enough; they are so bright and restless. She loves them more contentedly when they are not with her, but somewhere off a little way, when she can, without missing them, simply see them in thought. She sips her tea. Madge has forgotten the sugar.

Jeremy's boat, the *Amulet*, is lying at anchor in the harbour, with her faded blue sail furled.

'Why, you've grown again, young Paul,' he says. 'You'll be after having a boat of your own any day now, and then who'll help with my lines? And Miss Madge here is quite the young lady now I see. Well, well.'

'Are you taking the boat out today?' asks Paul.

'Maybe I am,' said Jeremy, smiling, 'if I can just find someone to see to the lines, while I mind the sail. Wind's pretty.' He hands them down into his little rowing-boat, and begins the gentle haul out to mid-harbour, to reach the *Amulet*. Hanging over the side

33

of the boat, Madge watches through glassy water the sandy harbour floor falling, falling deeper and deeper, till the height they are floating at goes to her head, and makes her dizzy. Still she can see the rippled sea bottom, and the shoals of little fish swarming half-way down the clear green depth.

The open sea is different. *Amulet* rises and falls, leans in the wind, breasts the slopes of water. Beneath her feet Madge feels the tremulous, living movement of the wood. The wind blows so steady and cool you would think it is a different day from the breathless heat on land. Madge goes to the prow to be showered with beads of spray. Paul opens his chipped blue box, and shows Jeremy his new set of spinners. Jeremy takes the red and silver one in his brown gnarled fingers. 'Here's the best one,' he says.

'Madge is having that one,' says Paul.

Madge is singing, *Speed bonny boat like a bird on the wing, over the sea to Skye!* and over the sea there is sky, she thinks, you can see where they join, and it looks as if you could sail there, and it would be just about as far as Godrevy, for over there Godrevy stands, just on the line where sea meets sky.

'Shall we go round Godrevy?' she asks Jeremy.

'Fish are further in,' he tells her, and Paul gives her a line to hold, that trails out behind the boat. 'I wish we could come out sailing, and not fish,' she says.

'Why, what'd be the point of that?' says Jeremy. So holding her line Madge sits and waits. She looks with distaste at the spinners in Paul's box – little fish made of tin, with hinges and joins in them, so they will spin and flash in the race of water like living things, and for fins and tail they have hooks, sharp little murderous barbed ones. So cruel, thinks Madge, so cruel. I hate to see them die. She feels the jerky tugging begin on her line, and pretends she doesn't.

'Madge, Madge, you've got a bite!' cries Paul, and so she has to haul in her line, while he jumps and cries

34

with joy, for they have sailed over a shoal, and all his lines are dancing. Jeremy puts a loop of rope on the tiller to hold them on course, and helps pull the fishes in.

It takes Jeremy's strong hand to tear the spinners from their throats. He throws them into the cockpit. Gasping for water there, drowning in cruel air, they thump and flap, flailing their strong lithe bodies, beating like trapped birds from one wall to another of the boat. How dark their sea-blue spines! And on their sides dragon markings, electric blue and green, bright and splendid from the water! Blood flies from their exploding gills and spatters round the boat. And when you think they are finished at last, and they lie still on the decking, suddenly they lift their strong tails, and beat – thump – once more. All the while cringing, nearly whimpering with pity and terror, Madge shuts her eyes and winces, and shudders from top to toe as a frantic fish hits into her and slithers down her legs. Spots of blood freckle her legs and arms. When the wild thumping ceases she opens her eyes and then startles and flinches again as the largest fish beats one last dying flap against the floor. Jeremy casually brains it with a wooden pin, while Paul checks the spinners, and runs them over the side again. I suppose girls can't help it, he thinks disgustedly about Madge. I suppose if any girl could, Madge would, he admits to himself, grudgingly. After all, she does like eating them! he adds, exasperated.

Oh I don't mind so much once they are still, thinks Madge, recovering, though she knows well enough that she will mind when it comes to threading string through their gills. Jeremy brings the boat about to sail over the shoal again, and she watches the hazy shore swing round them, and idly tries to pick out Goldengrove, hanging on its perch on the cliff that looks small and insignificant and doesn't tower over the sea at all, from the sea's point of view.

Three times more the death-throes have to be lived through, and then there are fish enough – enough for breakfast at Goldengrove, and enough for Jeremy to sell to landladies on the quay and make it worth his while to have come out. 'We must go in now,' he says, before Madge has time to ask about sailing round Godrevy. 'Weather won't hold.'

'*Won't* it?' says Madge, astonished, looking up at the blue, blue sky. But Jeremy points to a black cloud, sun-rimmed, hovering out to sea, and look, thinks Paul, all the other ships are making for harbour now.

So back they go, tacking, leaning in the wind, and mind your heads now! as the boom comes over, back towards home. The harbour stretches out its two stone arms to enfold them, and behind it on the hill the women are taking the sheets in from bleaching, ready to tuck up their men. So, landing, climbing the steep weedy steps to the quay, they go, Paul carrying a stringful of fish, and sending the women who ask him how much, to Jeremy coming just behind him with a boxful.

'Look, Jeremy, what about that boat?' says Paul, pointing at the bay, across which the water has darkened under the spreading cloud, and over which the white horses are beginning to gallop for the shore. For one boat hasn't come in.

'Frenchy,' says Jeremy. 'Won't be told.'

Up the path then, the shining fish fading in the dry air, though still beautiful, swinging against Paul's leg. I'll wash the scales off in the bath tonight, he thinks.

*   *   *

Next morning they come down to mackerel for breakfast. All the roses Madge picked yesterday have unlaced themselves, and are open-heartedly lavishing their scent around the room. The garden is deep in dew, smelling of moisture in heat. The trees of Goldengrove are quietly baking brown. A soft morning haze wreathes the garden.

'A real Indian summer,' says Gran.

'Why Indian?' asks Paul, but Gran does not know.

And after breakfast, they go running over the lawn, getting their sandalled toes wet in the grass, and then down the path to the sea. 'Look, I brought this to tackle the boat with,' says Paul, unwrapping a rusty scraper from his beach towel. It has made a rust mark on the worn white towelling.

'He's not there today!' says Madge, with a lift of the heart.

And neither, she thinks, are those scrawls we made. How clean and entire the sea leaves its beach!

'It's very early. He might come out later,' says Paul.

'But he's not there *now*,' says Madge. 'Come for a swim?' For the sea is very gentle and quiet this morning, and only baby waves are breaking on the shore.

'Too cold just yet,' says Paul, but Madge has to find it so with her own toes, and then her knees, before she suddenly decides not to go further, and runs back to Paul. Paul has discarded his shirt, and is busy sharpening his scraper, holding it at an angle against a piece of rock, rubbing it to and fro. Rust powders off it.

'OK now,' he says, trying the edge gingerly with his finger. Madge looks up, and he says, 'He's not there. I just looked.'

Then they start to strip off the weed. Madge pulls away great handfuls of black snakes, like the locks of Medusa. Where it is still wet it is very tough, and she borrows Paul's penknife to sever it. He loosens its grip with his scraper, slicing off the suckers where they grip the wood. There are little clusters of tight-fisted barnacles to be shifted too; soon Paul is sweating with the effort, and he wraps his handkerchief round his hand to guard against blistering his palm.

Madge, though, is soon tired of hacking at weed, and carting away prickly handfuls; she soon wants to swap with him. 'Let me have a turn with the scraper, Paul,' she says.

He gives it to her straight away, though she won't be able to use it, he thinks, and he is quite right, for a red sore place on her hand seems to come almost at once where the round handle of the scraper pushes when you drive it along the surface. So Madge puts the scraper down, and begins to dig sand out of the boat, and the charm of that too fades very fast when she feels how high you have to swing the loaded spade to clear the sides, and toss the sand over and away. Soon she is thinking, surely it is time for a rest, and a swim, and our orange juice, but looking at her watch she finds, astonished, that they have only been working twenty minutes. 'I think I'll go and put the orange bottle in a pool,' she says to Paul. 'To keep it cooler.'

'I'll come too,' says Paul. For I don't see why I should keep at it longer than her, he thinks. It's her idea to paint it after all.

At the rocky corners of the beach, where the sea covers the stones at high tide, it leaves abandoned pools when it ebbs. Here is one with a sandy floor, and three fishes, very small, catch-and-keep-in-jam-jar-size, and some of the bright green weed, all feathery and leafy-looking, and two sea-anemones, like pustules on the rock. Paul dips a finger in, and gently swirls the water, and it opens groping fronds, looking like a garden pink, and it's really hard to believe, thinks Madge, leaning over the pool to look at it, that it's really searching for meat. But the fishes swerve away from it as they swim.

The bottle of orange stands on the floor of the pool, with only its neck above the surface. 'Let's swim now,' says Paul.

After swimming they go dripping wet back to the boat. 'He's not there yet,' says Paul, taking up his scraper again. Perhaps he won't come, he thinks. Madge is thinking, perhaps he won't ever come again.

'Damn!' says Paul sharply. Swift-falling gouts of blood spot the sand in the boat. He claps one hand round another, and blood oozes between his fingers. He has gashed himself with the scraper.

'Give me my handkerchief, Madge,' he says.

'Oh, it's dirty, Paul, you can't put it round a cut,' she says. 'Is it deep? Is it bad?'

'It doesn't hurt much, but there seems to be a lot of blood,' says Paul. 'Do give me that handkerchief.'

'No, really Paul, it isn't clean enough. Come on, we'll have to go up to the house for a plaster and some iodine.' She wraps his towel round his hand, and leads him away.

As soon as they enter the house, they hear voices coming from the drawing-room. Gran has a visitor; his deep voice is clear and surprising in that house. Madge calls for Amy, and pulls Paul, who is still saying, 'What a fuss!' into the kitchen.

They were hoping to creep away to the beach again, with Paul's hand neatly bandaged and cleaned, but looking up from her favourite armchair Gran sees them through the open door, and calls them in.

'Professor Ashton, these are my grandchildren,' she says, 'Madge and Paul.' Sitting opposite her is the blind man. He is holding his head at that unnatural angle, as though he were looking at the join between ceiling and wall.

'Hullo,' he says, and smiles, but he does not move his head. His smile is directed over their heads.

'Hullo,' says Madge. And I wonder if my father was like this man? she thinks, as she always thinks, meeting any man older than twenty. Of course not, it doesn't seem likely. But how do I know, when everything they tell me is so vague? Even his death, for 'Missing in the war' is a very vague way to die.

Gran is saying, 'This is Professor Ashton, dears. He is a famous professor of English Literature. And he was a good friend of your grandfather's.'

'Hullo,' says Paul. He can't think of anything to say.

'So yours are the voices I can hear below me on the beach. Your grandmother has been kind enough to let me take her little cottage for a while,' says the Professor. 'I won't keep her from you for long. I have just called to pay my respects.'

Does he mean pay his rent? wonders Paul. What does one say to him? I'm sure Gran wants us to say something.'It must be rotten to be blind,' he offers.

'Paul!' cries Gran, horrified.

But the Professor, tuning in to the direction of Paul's voice, turns his strange, fixed face towards them. Seeing him from near enough, you can see round the huge black pupils of his eyes a tiny rim of blue iris of unchanging width. 'Yes, it is,' he says. 'I find it hard to get used to.' Unlike Gran's his voice is not shocked.

'I mean,' Paul plunges on, 'what do you do all day?'

'I was just going to ask you if you find you can still work, Ralph,' Gran breaks in hastily.

'I have some books in braille. But it certainly is difficult to do anything worth while. In London some of my students were kind enough to come and read to me, but down here . . .'

'I'll come and read to you,' says Madge.

The Professor smiles again. 'My books would bore you very quickly, Madge, I'm afraid,' he says.

'Well, as long as they don't bore you, I'll read them to you,' says Madge. 'I'll come this afternoon.'

'Thank you,' he says. 'But you mustn't change your plans for me.'

'We weren't planning anything,' she says. Bloody girls! thinks Paul. Well, I'm not sweating on that boat if she's not. I'm going fishing.

*　　*　　*

Paul, out in the bay, with the arc of wind-stretched canvas curving above him, looks at the sleek fish, jumping and dying at his feet, and thinks of Madge cringing. He looks shorewards, and sees the white cottage, framed by golden treetops, and thinks where she is. Then his line tugs again.

Sitting in a wooden chair in the window bay of the cottage, draped in sunlight, Madge is reading. Bright drifts of sea-air float past her, intermittently wafting across the dusty smell that hangs on the inside air. Books lie in piles on a dusty table beside her. Her listener sits in an armchair by the empty hearth, facing her, with his dog at his feet. You can stare at him as you never could at anyone else, Madge finds. His face is crowded, full of events, for all the blankness of his eyes. Paul's face, by comparison, or her own, is empty as the open air. It's not that he is wrinkled, like Gran; but lines as fine as spider thread are there; you wouldn't see them unless you really stared, but they crowd his face with the ghosts of expressions absent now, with joy and pain.

'*Weep me not dead' means: 'Do not make me cry myself to death'*, reads Madge, '*do not kill me with the sight of your tears; do not cry for me as for a man already dead, when, in fact, I am in your arms,' and, with a different sort of feeling, 'do not exert your power over the sea so as to make it drown me by sympathetic magic;' there is a conscious neatness in the ingenuity of the phrasing, perhaps because the same idea is being repeated which brings out the change of tone in this verse . . .* Her voice is flat and expressionless, and full of tiny un-punctuated hesitations, as she tries to make out what she is reading.

'Are you bored?' the Professor asks her.

'Yes, I mean no, of course not.'

41

'You mean yes. You should say so. You should always say what you think.'

'Should I? My mother is always telling me not to.'

'No conversation is possible otherwise. You never get to grips with what people are like, if they hide it from you. If people just make polite noises when they talk, then talking's hardly worth the effort.'

'You're right, I suppose,' says Madge. She is astonished. Talking to grown-ups, she had thought, would always be like one of those trick party-games where you have to try all the time not to make a mistake, and uttering what comes naturally to your lips gets you three black marks at once.

'Now, are you bored?' he is saying.

'Yes – I mean no – I mean yes, I am bored with this horrible book because I don't understand a word of it, but no, I am not bored with being here reading to you, even if the book is horrible.'

He smiles. 'Nevertheless, let's put the horrible book away, and read *Alice through the Looking Glass* instead,' he says.

'Oh, no, don't let's!' says Madge. 'This is the book you need, isn't it? And I didn't come for you to be kind to me, I came to be kind to you!'

'I don't know that I like people being kind to me,' he says.

'Whyever not?' she says, astonished again. 'I like it lots.'

'Well, for lots of reasons, but mainly because they usually stop, sooner or later, just when you have got used to it.'

'But I'm not stopping,' she says, indignantly, 'I'm trying to go on!'

He pauses, then 'You go right on then,' he says, smiling again. But his smile is very funny, thinks Madge, as she mouths . . .'*What it may doe too soon,' since the middle line may as usual go forwards or backwards, may be said of the 'sea' or of the* '*winde*'... It doesn't go anywhere. I suppose it's because his face has no direction, but it's a very inward sort of smile. Like the difference between hugging oneself, and hugging someone else, and his smile hugs himself. And how good I am being, she reflects, as she ploughs on and on through the thicket of words, when I might be out fishing with Paul, or working with him on our boat. I suppose it's my goodness and kindness this afternoon that makes me feel so warm and glowing inside. It must be true that virtue is its own reward. She reads on and on.

'You may stop now,' he says in a while. 'You need not say you are willing to continue. I have heard all I can take in for today.'

'All right.' Madge thankfully puts the book down. 'But I'm not going yet. I'm going to dust this room before I go home for tea. It's terribly dirty. You should see it!'

'I don't mind what it looks like,' he says.

'But it smells of dust!' she protests.

'Really? Does it?'

'That dry tickly smell is dust. Surely you'd like me to get rid of it for you.'

'You are being kind again,' he says. 'But all right, only please don't move anything, or I won't be able to find it.'

Madge dusts. She lifts each pile of books in turn, and dusts away the outline of the bottom book on the table, and slaps them together before putting them back. They release a cloud of grey specks when she bangs them against each other. She finds a broom to sweep the floor. The dog growls at it, and she has to sweep round him. The Professor has got out of his chair, and is making tea in the kitchen. Taking the broom back she watches him. The kitchen looks very untidy, but he puts his hand on each thing he needs, just by reaching for it. 'You see why things mustn't be moved,' he says. He pours out the tea, feeling first with his left hand

43

for the rim of the cup, to judge where he should pour. But the kitchen is full of scattered tea-leaves, crumbs, small spills and a stale smell, because he can't see his accidents. Madge wipes, and tidies, and picks up the dropped peeled potato that is stinking quietly in a corner by the stove. He shouldn't have to live like this, she thinks. Nobody should, and especially not an important and clever man like him. She sits down and drinks her tea. It tastes funny, a bit like tar smells, but she doesn't like to say so. She gulps it down.

'I must go now,' she says, standing up. 'But I'll come again.'

'Thank you very much, Madge,' he says, 'But you must remember that I don't need kindness.'

'Oh, bother kindness!' says Madge crossly. 'I shall come to read to you, that is all, Professor Ashton.'

'Don't call me Professor,' he says.

'Is it wrong? I thought Gran said it.'

'I am a professor, but my name is Ralph. I'd rather, if you really are coming again, that you called me that.'

'Goodbye, then,' says Madge. She was going to say 'Goodbye Ralph,' but, suddenly embarrassed, she cuts herself short.

Running up to the house she meets Paul, strolling in the garden, with a palmful of tiny strawberries from the grove.

'Done your good deed for the day?' he asks her. 'I got enough fish for breakfast all by myself. Look, I think these are the very last of the strawberries, you'd better have some.' He counts seven little red heart-shaped seed-studded fruits in his palm. 'Three for you,' he says, 'and four for me, because I found them.'

*   *   *

'Could I borrow a mallet from the carpentry box in the shed?' asks Paul, over breakfast.

'What are you doing, dear?' asks Gran.

44

'You know that boat, down on the beach? Well we're cleaning the weed off it, because we're thinking of painting it.'

'You have the mallet, then, by all means,' says Gran. 'That's a nice little boat. Your grandfather used to go fishing in it.' And it hasn't been used for years now, she thinks, except for the children to play in, high and dry on the shore. So long since it floated. When was it, I wonder, when would it have been? I remember my son taking Madge out in it, on a still calm day . . . he sailed all the way to Godrevy, with Madge fallen asleep, I think he said, most of the way, with her head on a coil of rope, and then he had to rest there, and have tea with the lighthouse men. That was before the bitter quarrelling began. . . . Madge was only a child then, a tiny child . . . so long ago . . .

'Good morning Gran,' says Madge, with a soap-scented kiss.

'Good morning, dearie. Eat up your fish before Paul fusses to be out and away.' But with 'See you down there,' Paul is off anyway.

'Gran,' says Madge, with a mouth full of toast, 'I was wondering if I would go again to read to Professor Ashton. Do you think I should?'

'Not if you don't want to, dear. After all you're on holiday here. I'm sure Ralph doesn't expect it.'

'But I do want to. And I know he doesn't expect it; he said I wasn't to be kind to him. But I thought, if he's such a clever man, what a waste if he doesn't work. And he could work if he could get the books read to him. I thought I might keep going till I've finished the one he needs now. What do you think, Gran? Is it true one shouldn't be kind to him?'

'Stuff and nonsense, dearie!' says Gran. 'One should always be kind to people. If you don't mind going, then it would be very good of you to give him a helping hand. But you won't forget about Paul, dear, will you? You know how he looks forward to playing with you.'

'Oh, Paul won't mind,' says Madge. 'He keeps wanting to go fishing, you know, Gran. And I'm not going till after lunch. I'm going down to the beach with Paul now.'

The beach is cooler when they reach it. There is a keen freshness in the wind, though the sea is still mellow with yesterday's warmth. Little puffy clouds scud rapidly overhead, casting patches of shade. Paul shows Madge how to use the mallet; instead of pushing the scraper with your palm, and getting sore, you hold it against the weed and strike it with the mallet, forcing it along the wood. The weed falls off in swathes, and lies like my hair, thinks Madge, when Mummy had it bobbed last year, and great heavy locks fell to the floor round the hairdresser's chair. But the bright green slimy weed is still difficult – the scraper slips on it instead of dislodging it. Madge works very hard, keeping on while Paul goes swimming, trying hard for his approval.

'You don't have to kill yourself over it, Madge,' he says, coming back beaded with salt water from his second dip. 'There's more time this afternoon.'

'I was thinking of going and reading to Ralph this afternoon,' says Madge, cautiously.

'But you've done that,' Paul says. 'You did that yesterday.'

'It isn't the sort of thing that stays done,' she says. 'It's like brushing your teeth; having done it yesterday is no reason for not doing it today.'

'But Madge,' he wails, dismayed, 'you can't mean that! It'll be like fagging for someone, on and on and on.'

'Not and on and on. Just some each day. I didn't think you'd mind. I thought you'd quite like to go fishing without a cowardly girl along.'

And it's quite true, thinks Paul, pulling on his aertex shirt, which sticks on his salty skin, that I'd go out with Jeremy every day if she didn't hate the fish flapping so.

46

But she's crazy, all the same. What is it to do with us, if the man's blind? *She* can't make it all right . . .

And it's quite true, thinks Madge, that I hate the bloody bit, but I do like the wind and the push, and the rise and fall of it, and I would really rather like to go too . . . 'I was just going to finish what I was reading yesterday,' she says.

'Oh, I see,' Paul says. 'All right. I'll go out with Jeremy.'

* * *

She goes through the open door, cat-walking, in bare feet. He has drawn his chair into the window recess, to feel the sun, and opened the windows. She has picked a handful of sweet peas in the garden on her way down – 'More you pluck 'em, longer they grow,' says Mr Arthur. 'They keep coming till the frost down here.' She goes to find a jam-jar to put them in.

'You did come again,' he says, hearing her quiet movements, putting aside his blank-paged, embossed book in braille, and smiling over her head.

'Yes. I said I would,' she says, putting the jam-jar on the table, and coming to sit down.

'This book today, please.' He runs his fingers over a pile of books, feeling the spines, and picking one out.

'That's a novel,' Madge protests. 'Can't we read the horrible book again? I do so want to be useful to you!'

'It doesn't have to be a horrible book to be useful,' he says, grinning. 'Thank heavens! And the book you are rejecting is a masterpiece of literature. Can you start on page 91?'

A woman, reads Madge, *especially if she have the misfortune of knowing anything, should conceal it as well as she can. The advantages of natural folly in a beautiful girl have been already set forth by the capital pen of a sister author; and to her treatment of the subject I will only add, in justice to men, that*

47

though, to the larger and more trifling part of the sex, imbecility in females is a great enhancement of their personal charms, there is a portion of them too reasonable – Ralph was smiling gently – *and too well-informed themselves, to desire anything more in a woman than ignorance.* 'Oh!' cries Madge, indignant.

'Go on, go on,' he says. 'The next bit is delicious.'

But Catherine did not know her own advantages; did not know that a good-looking girl with an affectionate heart, and a very ignorant mind, cannot fail of attracting a clever young man, unless circumstances are particularly untoward. In the present instance, she confessed and lamented her want of knowledge; declared that she would give anything in the world to be able to draw; and a lecture on the picturesque immediately followed, in which his instructions were so clear that she soon began to see beauty in everything admired by him; and her attention was so earnest, that he became perfectly satisfied of her having a great deal of natural taste. He talked of fore-grounds, distances, and second distances; side-screens and perspectives; lights and shades; and Catherine was so hopeful a scholar, that when they gained the top of Beechen Cliff, she voluntarily rejected the whole city of Bath, as unworthy to make part of a landscape . . . Madge begins to laugh, and he laughs too. Like a double wave the two laughters swell each other, and she can't stop.

'Oh, but listen,' she says, when she does get her breath back, 'This isn't work. You just chose this to amuse me, Ralph, didn't you?'

'Well, it amuses me too,' he says. 'And I miss reading for fun quite as much as I miss working. But your suspicions, Madge, are quite without foundation. Go and look at the dark blue file on the desk.'

She wanders over and opens the file. *The novels of Jane Austen* it says, in typescript. *A critique, by R. Ashton.* 'Oh!' she says, 'Can I borrow this?'

'Is it the sort of thing you read?'

'Well, it's the sort of thing on my reading list.'

'Yes, you can borrow it,' he says.

'Oh, thank you! I've never *seen* a manuscript before, let alone read one.'

'Did you bring me some flowers?' he asks. 'Will you put them within reach?' I couldn't smell them from across the room, thinks Madge, bringing the flowers. He's awfully good at that.

He takes the jam-jar, and buries his face in the flowers. He brushes their multicoloured little butterfly wings across his face, to and fro, and draws breath like a sigh. A gust of their sweetness reaches Madge, standing beside him, as though his touch had set it free. 'They're sweet peas,' she says.

'Yes, I can tell,' he says, and Oh, how awful of me, thinks Madge, wincing; of course he can. 'Shall I read some more?' she asks hastily.

'Do you want to read more?'

'Oh, yes . . . *You know what you ought to do* she reads. *Clear your character handsomely before her. Tell her that you think very highly of the understanding of women.*'

'*Miss Morland, I think very highly of the under-standing of all the women in the world, especially of those, whoever they may be, with whom I happen to be in company.*'

'*That is not enough, be more serious.*'

'*Miss Morland, no-one can think more highly of the understanding of women than I do. In my opinion, nature has given them so much that they never find it necessary to use more than half . . . *' and Oh, thinks Madge, how happy he looks now, smiling all the time at this lovely stuff, and basking in sweet peas. I have made him happy. I read, he laughs. I brought him the flowers. They have done him good. I have done him good. I am happy, reading this, with the sun on the nape of my neck, and the fresh air blowing through the window here, and I hadn't really noticed till now, but when you get used to his eyes, he's really quite handsome, in an aged sort of way. He'd do for Mr Rochester, almost. It's getting late, and I don't want to go. He is Mr Rochester, and I am his Jane. I will come and see him in plain grey alpaca – whatever sort of cloth *was* alpaca? – and call him Sir.

'You've stopped reading, and you haven't moved,' he says. 'What were you thinking?'

'I was thinking of calling you Sir,' says Madge.

'Good grief!' he says, looking really amazed. 'Whatever makes you say that?'

'You asking me what I was thinking made me say it.'

'I asked for that, in short,' he said, smiling.

'I must go now, or I'll be late for tea, and Paul might be cross with me.'

'Might he, indeed? You seem very close, for cousins of a different age.'

'We have lots in common.'

'You both like the beach, you mean?'

'No, I mean we understand each other very well. He has a stepmother, and I have a stepfather, and we know without ever having said anything what we feel about that. You know what I mean; if I didn't see Paul for twenty years, and then I met him suddenly, in the street, I would know at once what sort of mood he was in. I wouldn't have to think about it; I'd just know. There must be somebody like that for you.'

'There was once,' he says. 'But I shall never see her again. Off you go now, or Paul will be cross! And Madge, thank you for coming.'

'Gran,' says Madge, finding Gran alone in the drawing-room, when Paul has been sent off to bed, slowly putting a green stitch into the chair-seat she is making, 'why is Professor Ashton all alone like that? There ought to be someone. You should see his kitchen; it's positively squalid . . .'

50

'Oh dear,' says Gran, sighing. 'I'd better find someone to come in once a week and do round for him.'

'No, but, I mean, why hasn't he married someone?'

'He is – was – married, Madge,' says Gran. 'It's a sad story. He has had a lot to suffer. First he lost his sight, fighting in the war. When he came home his wife left him. That is why he is alone. I wonder if Mrs Paine has time to spare? She could do with a little extra money, I dare say . . .'

'Oh!' cries Madge. 'But how terrible! But his wife – she must be wicked, vile, to be so cruel! How *could* she?'

'Now, Madge, dear, you mustn't talk like that. She was a nice enough woman; I liked her. And it may not have been because he went blind that she left him – we don't know that. Quick to praise and slow to blame – that's the way to be. We never know what another person feels,' and best that way, far best not to know, she thinks. This child alarms me.

'But to be left alone . . .'

'Yes, it's hard. Life is hard. That's why I let him have the cottage, though I usually don't like someone so near. I'm tired of neighbours, and getting on with people. They always want you to make egg-cosies for bazaars or something. . . . But I thought the sea air would do him good. Take him out of himself a bit.'

'Yes of course, but Gran . . .'

'It's getting late, now, dearie. Late. Off to bed with you. Sleep well.'

Coming warm and powdery from the bathroom, and shutting the bedroom door, switching on the little lamp with a rose-spotted china base and scalloped peach-coloured parchment shade that stands beside the bed, she eagerly opens Ralph's manuscript, as though it were a box of chocolates, and props her head on her arm on the pillow to read it, expecting it to prolong the remembered afternoon. But it is all about the Mysteries of Udolpho, whatever those may be, and the metaphysics of irony. How clever he must be, thinks Madge dreamily, I can't understand this at all. But there isn't any laughter in the book, and she is very soon asleep.

*   *   *

Madge sits cross-legged in the sand, working the scraper round the curved boarding of the boat, hacking at weed. Paul comes from the sea to lie on the sand beside her. He looks at the sky. 'I suppose you're working so hard because you want to go playing goody again this afternoon.'

A cloud falls over Madge's thoughts. 'Aren't you going fishing?' she asks.

'Jeremy's going to Newlyn today,' says Paul, and oh, hell, he thinks, I'm jolly well not going to *say* I'd like her to stay here with me. He feels angry. She ought to know that.

'I was thinking,' Madge lies, for she has only just thought of it, 'that it would be nice to walk along the cliffs today. Do you remember the lizards we found last year?'

'Oh yes!' says Paul, and the clouds roll away from him. 'And the tails came off in your hand when you tried to catch them. Yes, let's do that, Madge.'

'Good, that's fixed then.' She goes on working, making a deliberately long pause. Then, 'Paul,' she begins, 'if we are going for a walk we could perfectly well ask Ralph to come with us, couldn't we?'

Oh lord! thinks Paul, Oh hell! He rolls over abruptly, and watches his hands angrily jabbing into the sand. The sharp grains driven under his fingernails prick and hurt.

'. . . He wouldn't make any difference to us, we could still go where we like, and catch lizards. He can't go by himself, in case he falls, he said. His dog is trained

52

for roads, not cliffs. What do you think, Paul? Shall we ask him?'

I shall look pretty beastly if I say no, thinks Paul. Being beastly to the blind – what a part to play! And why do I mind so, anyway? I haven't got anything against the geezer, have I? He rolls over again, and looks up, and sees the Professor sitting blankly, all alone in his garden. His darkness hangs over Paul like a cloud. 'Oh, all right then,' he says. 'You can ask him. I like his dog,' he adds, in an attempt to be nice about it.

The dog, relieved from duty for once, and off the lead, races and gambols like a puppy on the path ahead of them. Paul runs and shouts, throwing a stick for the dog. 'What's he called?' he asks Ralph, wanting to yell the name. 'I just call him Dog,' says Ralph. 'Or sometimes Hell-hound.'

'How foul of you!' says Paul. 'Hey, Dog!' he yells, running after it again.

Madge walks beside Ralph, leading him. She has to be shown how to do it, since her first thought had been to put her arm through his. But he needs instead to rest his hand over hers, while she, elbow bent, keeps her arm steadily pointing in the direction they are going. He can be steered, as with a tiller, that way.

His hand is very heavy and hot over mine, all the time, thinks Madge. I would like to run with Paul. He walks very slowly.

'It is good to stretch my legs again, and be about in the open air,' says Ralph. 'I used to come here when I was one of your grandfather's pupils. He held reading parties sometimes in the summer.'

'It's very nice up here,' says Madge. 'Always fresh, however hot the day. The grass is very glossy, and there are sea-pinks, and sea-carrot growing,' and oh, the view, she thinks, the things you can see from here! The wide sea, filling and frilling the great bight of the bay, and the fishing fleet scattered over the dreaming water – purple shadows in the haze, and the sky so drenched in sunlight that it looks lilac, and the town, and the hill above the town, no sheets pinned out today, and beyond, again beyond, again more sea, and everywhere distances, great distances. Oh, oh, look at me, how far I can see! And I had better not mention anything about it to Ralph. It wouldn't be kind, just as it wouldn't be kind to leave him, and go running after Paul and Dog, and it's an awful pity how being kind doesn't always make you feel warm and glowing, but sometimes, like now, makes you feel hot and cross, and I don't think Paul should have left me with Ralph *and* the picnic box . . . for the wicker handle of the little tea hamper is irking her free hand.

'I like to hear the waves below,' Ralph says, and he does hold his head at a silly angle, thinks Madge. Why can't he *pretend* he's looking, so he looks like normal people?

They are nearly at the lizard den, a remembered-from-last-year place with a tumble of rocks and flat stones topping the cliff, with scrubby heather, and gorse growing, and the fleshy-fingered sea-carrot, smelling of school dinner salad, and the tough-stemmed clumps of wiry thrift, and the little butter-yellow bird's-foot- trefoil growing bright against stone and grass. The bees hum loudly here, and the lizards bask and blink on the lichen-blotched sun-baked stones, and then scurry away into dark crevices with a dry scuttering rustle on the stones. Ralph has some difficulty stepping down to the place they want, but with Paul's hand to hold on as well, he manages it. They choose a wide flat stone for him, and as soon as he sits down Madge runs away, breaking free of her hour-long duty, and races, leaping from ledge to ledge, up to the crest of the hilltop behind the stony hollow at the cliff's edge, and then sprinting, forcing her muscles to their utmost possible speed, she careers down the inland slope beyond, wheeling round in a great circle to run

54

halfway up again before collapsing, gasping for breath, in the grass, with a burning feeling in the back of her throat. She lies still for a moment, and then picks herself up, and goes back.

Ralph has got himself propped into a crook of the hillside like an armchair within moments of Madge's flight, and is leaning back in the sun.

'I like that!' says Paul, watching her go.

'She's had enough of my snail's pace, that's all,' says Ralph. Dog comes and lies down at his feet, and he nudges the furry flank with his toe. 'What does Madge look like, Paul?'

'Oh,' says Paul, 'she's quite tall. Not thin, not fat. Brown hair, greenish eyes. She has a very absent-minded look most of the time. That what you wanted to know?'

'Some of it,' says Ralph. 'Is she like her voice, do you think?'

'*I* don't know,' says Paul, and what am I supposed to make of a corny question like that? he asks himself. I suppose he means is she pretty, and I know what I think about that, but I'm not telling anyone; I'm certainly not telling *him*. 'She's coming back,' he says.

Madge sits down and opens the tea-basket. She sets out the bakelite beakers in a carefully balanced row, and pours out the tea, sweet and milky, just how Paul likes it. Then she unfolds the white damask napkin Amy had done up for her, with the ghosts of roses shining in its polished starch, and brings out a pile of cheese scones with blackberry jam. 'Yummy!' says Paul, contentedly. He watches Ralph taste his tea, and wince faintly. He grins, and looks out to sea. Calling gulls wheel overhead, and then fly away. The sun feels hot. A droning bee, hanging in mid-air, attempts to share Paul's scone. 'Bzzzzz!' says Paul.

'You know, I used to come here as a boy, and then later as a young man,' says Ralph. 'I can remember this view very well. I can see it in my mind's eye.' His voice sounds contented, thinks Madge. What does it matter if he walks slowly and holds his head too high? 'Tell us!' she says. 'Pretend *we* can't see it, and you have to tell us.'

Smiling he says, 'Well, starting at the left, you can see the town from here, with the harbour, and the hill called the Island behind the curve of the harbour, with sheets spread out to dry, and then a beach; it has coloured tents for changing in. Behind it is a little green grass – that's the putting green – and behind that the railway runs along a low viaduct, with more houses behind that on a steep rise of the land.'

'Oh, yes!' cries Madge, delighted.

'Then the land curves; you can make out, I think, the trees in your grandmother's garden, but not her house. The land curves on, towards us, and you can see back the way we have come. You can see the cliffs, and the promontories of rocks, and the waves breaking over them. And there's nothing else to be seen but the open sea.'

'Oh, Ralph,' says Madge, 'you remember jolly well. You really might be looking at it, for you remember it just as it is!'

'He's forgotten the lighthouse,' says Paul.

Madge flinches. But looking, she sees there, undeniably solid and real, the crag of Godrevy, standing out of the swirl of breaking water, with the lighthouse upon it, tall and white, and streaked with salt and weathering. And he, thinks Madge, has lost the lighthouse, for ever and ever, and can never get it back, because he cannot see it, and he cannot remember it, and oh! how much I like it, standing there, not because it is beautiful, but because it is real, and I can see it.

'Lighthouse?' says Ralph. 'Oh, yes I seem to recall . . . out to sea somewhere?'

Suddenly Godrevy seems to melt, and waver, like a reflected image in moving water. Madge's eyes have filled with tears.

When she has rubbed them away, she sees Paul's hand crawling over the platform of rock beside him, very quietly, walking on its fingers towards a lizard, a small scaly dragon, that has come out to sun itself. A little forked scarlet tongue flickers in and out of its crocodile mouth. It is a golden green colour, spotted and mottled.

'Oh no, Paul, don't!' cries Madge, seeing again, in her mind's eye, from last year, the shed tail in Paul's hand, and the truncated creature scurrying away, maimed, and unbalanced, lurching forwards, its broken end bobbing grotesquely upwards as it tried to run without the weight of its tail. Paul makes a grab, and misses. But the lizard, convulsed with fright, breaks in two, and wriggles to safety, leaving its tail behind, anyway.

'Crazy brute!' says Paul, picking up the tail, and looking at it curiously. 'I hadn't even touched it!' He thrusts his hand into the crack where the lizard had disappeared, a dark groove running up the rock beside Madge's head, for she is leaning back now, looking idly at the sky.

There is a sudden hiss, like an engine letting off steam. A snake sleeks out of the hot stone, with a silken rustle, and arcs its head, drawn back to strike, beside Madge's cheek.

'Don't move, Madge,' says Paul, the colour draining from his face as he sees the black V-marking on the creature's head. It sways, rocking its head to and fro, and 'Oh, what is it?' Madge says, and as she speaks it hisses again, louder.

'What is it?' says Ralph.

'Stay still, everyone, and quiet,' says Paul, and the tremor in his voice betrays his fright. Oh, bloody stupid snake, it was me who disturbed you, not Madge, he thinks. I shall have to reach out and get you. It would be my legs only, if only you would hit back at me, but it's her face you are aiming for. I must catch you like a lizard, but you won't drop in half and run –

you'll twist round swiftly to strike at me, and oh, I'm afraid, he thinks, there ought to be someone to help, there ought to be a grown-up, and thinking of Ralph, just sitting there, looking worried, and what good did that do? he adds, *he's* useless!

Madge lies still. Paul's fright has frightened her, but he doesn't seem to be moving, and she turns her head, very slowly towards whatever it is, till she can see it, narrow, like the bend in a whiplash, and so near she almost screams. From the slope behind her she can hear Ralph's dog, coming back from a foray, beginning to rumble with growl. Oh no, he'll frighten it, she thinks, terrified.

Paul grabs suddenly. He seizes the snake just behind its head, and holds it tight, squirming, in the air. Oh it feels dry! he thinks, not slimy; I'm surprised at its feel. It curls round his wrist, getting a purchase, and with astonishing strength tries to tear free its head. Paul goes to the cliff edge.

'Oh, be careful, Paul, be careful!' cries Madge.

'What is it? What's going on?' says Ralph.

Paul unwinds the viper. He draws it out straight, tail in one hand, head gripped in the other, then he lets it go, with both hands at once, and it falls, twisting and hissing in the air, to the wave-tossed rocks below. 'Phew!' says Paul. Running to the cliff edge, Dog barks loudly after the event.

'What is it? What is happening?' says Ralph again.

'It was a viper hissing at me, and Paul threw it over the cliff,' says Madge.

Paul looks down at the rocks and waves. He shudders, and rubs his hands on his khaki shorts, trying to get rid of the feel of snake on his palms. I triumph, he thinks, executing a slow, turning war dance on the cliff edge. I am brave, I am swift and sure, I knew what to do, I did not flinch, steady of nerve and hand. I, I, Paul, saved her. I am a knight in armour, I am Perseus with dragons, she owes her life to *me* – it might have killed her, mightn't it? I mean they are very poisonous, I think – how pleased I am, and what use was *he*, may I ask?

'It was probably a grass-snake,' says Ralph.

'Grass-snakes,' says Paul, sitting down, and with great deliberation knotting a stem of grass, 'don't, I think, have black V-markings on their heads. Grass-snakes are a golden colour, and vipers have markings all the way down, and are also rather smaller.'

'There. It was a grass-snake,' says Ralph.

'I am speaking to show you that I am quite well able to tell them apart,' says Paul.

Madge thinks, oh, how it hurts me to be able to see the things I can see at the moment. I know why Ralph doesn't want to believe it – he doesn't like to think he was just sitting there while danger threatened that was averted by someone else. And I know why Paul is so pleased with himself; it is because he did it, while a grown-up sat by and did nothing. I wish I did not see. I liked it better when people were like rocks or waves to me; they did what they did, and I understood nothing about it.

'But did it bite you, Madge?' says Ralph, suddenly urgent. 'I mean, if it was really a viper we have to cut the wound, cut it deeply, and suck the venom out.'

Madge's fingers fly swiftly to touch her smooth cheek, where it curves over her cheekbone at the point the snake had threatened. Pain, blood and a scar! she thinks.

'It *was* a viper,' she says firmly, thanking Paul with all the looking she can do. 'But it didn't bite me. Paul threw it over the cliff.'

'Good for Paul, then,' says Ralph, 'whether it was a viper or not.'

Paul makes a face at him, and thumbs his nose. And Madge, instead of frowning, as he really expects, grins. For a long moment they exchange conspiratorial smiles under Ralph's unseeing eyes. Then, leaning towards each other they mouth soundlessly, in unison, the words IT WAS A VIPER.

'Perhaps we had better start back,' says Ralph, 'since I take so long over this rough ground.'

Hopping along behind as they go, Paul mimics Ralph. He looks – head in air – not where he is going, and puts his feet down tentatively, and stumbles a little, and makes joyful faces. A great affection for Madge fills him. You soppy goose, Madge, he tells himself, grinning. But Madge, with Ralph's arm over hers again, feeling his every step, in forced sympathy with his difficult walking, soon finds Paul unkind – though unseen he does no harm – and frowns him off. In a little while Paul comes and takes Ralph's other arm, and helps her help him home.

'Thank you very much for a delightful afternoon,' says Ralph at his door.

*   *   *

Alone in the best spare room, which is filled with soft evening light, Madge wonders what it is like to be blind. She looks out of the window, and sees that the trees are now golden, rust and beautiful. They must turn earlier down here, she thinks, for surely everything was green at home still. Perhaps home is changing while I'm here. If I were blind all seasons would be the same. No, they wouldn't. They each have their own smells. You can feel mist as well as see it. You can hear leaves underfoot when they have fallen. Only sight has gone. I wonder what it's like.

She closes her eyes tightly, and begins, hands outstretched in front of her, to move across the room. About three paces, she thinks, and then I'll reach the bed. She takes three, four, steps forward, and gropes for it. It isn't there. She opens her eyes, and finds herself facing in the wrong direction. She has missed the bed by yards. Oh, but looking is cheating, she tells herself.

I must keep my eyes quite shut. She begins again, moving towards the bed. Something under foot. She probes with her toes, wriggling them in her sock. My shoes, she thinks, pushing them away with her foot. It's really quite easy: you have to know what's in the room; that's why he asked me not to move anything. There is a sharp pain on her shin, and she trips up, and falls headlong. She finds herself sitting on the floor, eyes wide open, looking at the dressing-table stool, over which she has fallen. Oh, I mustn't open my eyes, she scolds herself. That's no good, that's not what it's like at all. I would have to find out by feeling what it was I had tripped on. She rubs her shin furiously, gets up, closes her eyes, and begins again.

She crosses the room, and is on her way back before she trips again. And as soon as she stumbles she finds her eyes open again. She hasn't looked down to see what it was, but the moment the unknown something tangles her feet her eyelids spring apart, and she finds herself looking at the opposite wall. 'Oh damn!' she cries. It's my dress that tripped me, of course. I just dropped it on the floor as usual. A punishment for slovenly habits – gosh, I bet you have to be fiendishly tidy if you're blind, and you can't even see where you are putting things! I am going to start again. I am going to do something with my eyes shut, instead of just blundering around. She moves towards the little wooden stand on which her towels hang. I shall get my things, and go and wash without looking, she decides. First my towel. She goes towards it, hands outstretched, until she finds herself touching the wall. I'm facing the wrong way again, she thinks, and at the thought her eyes flutter, and a little grey light, filtered through her lashes, gets in. She shuts it out again at once, but it has already leaked to her what is wrong with the towel-hunt: she hasn't come in the wrong direction, but is groping too high. She reaches down, and takes the towel. Now for my sponge-bag, she thinks. Where did

I leave it? Hanging on the brass bedpost at the foot of the bed. She rotates, and begins towards the bed again. She finds the bedpost, cool, shiny-smooth in her hands, but the sponge-bag isn't there. I wonder if I hung it on the other one? she thinks, and at once claps her hand to her eyes to stop them cheating her. She gropes for the other bedpost. An image of the bag she is seeking fills her mind; it is made of green rubber-backed canvas with a drawstring through the top, and a little worn Cash's tape saying *M.FIELDING* sewn in a loop round the string. But the look of it's no good, she knows; it's the feel of it I need to find it by. Her hands run up and down the second bedpost, from the round, palm-filling knob on the top to the place where the soft swelling of the bedclothes presses against it. No bag. Madge sits down, and presses her fists into her disobedient eyes while she tries to remember where she has put the beastly thing. Her eyelids are fighting her now, fluttering upwards, and when she grits her will and defeats them they let through not light, but the feel of light, telling her with a colourless brightness which way the window is. She feels herself tugged by the light as though she were a moth, hating to face away from it, empty and useless though it is. But I didn't know till now that eyelids aren't solid, like black-out, thinks Madge, punishing them with the pressure of her knuckles.

Suddenly she smells it. The bag is quite near. The smell of rubber and old soap that it emits has come clearly to her nose. She understands at once what has happened – the weight of the bag has pulled it down past the mattress and blankets, and it is hanging lower than she has been feeling for it. Triumphantly she reaches out and gets it. She jumps up, and recklessly speeds towards the door, so that it smacks her face just as she is reaching out a hand for the doorknob. Out onto the landing, across and a little to the left – would it be about three paces? – to the bathroom door. But on the second pace she bumps into something. Better-disciplined at last, she stands still, eyes tight shut, and tries to feel over whatever it is, instead of looking. It is large, and warm, with a knitted surface. It is Paul.

'Whyever can't you look where you're going, Madge?' he yells. 'And what the hell are you doing standing there with your eyes shut and that dopey look on your face, waving your hands?'

Madge opens her eyes, and blushes. Paul is standing on one leg, rubbing the toe she has trodden on. That's why he's cross, I hurt him, she thinks. 'I was trying to see what it would be like,' she admits, shamefaced.

'You can't do it like that,' says Paul. 'You keep opening your eyes. It doesn't work.'

'I know,' she says. 'It isn't working.'

'You need a blindfold,' says Paul. 'Hold on, I've got just the thing.' He hurtles away up the attic stairs, taking them two at a time. He comes back quickly, holding something behind his back. 'Turn round, and I'll tie you up,' he says.

Whatever it is he has put round her eyes feels silky; his school scarf perhaps. He ties it very tightly with a firm hand. 'Hold on,' he says. 'That's not good enough yet. You can always see a bit squinting downwards, where your nose pushes it away from your cheeks.' He stuffs something underneath the blindfold, little pads of something, smelling faintly of mothballs, tucked in either side of her nose. 'There you are,' he says, 'that should do it.' He sits down on the stairs to watch Madge negotiate the landing. It's not like closing your eyes, because you always open them a bit, he is thinking, and it's not really like being blindfolded either, because you know you can always take the blindfold off. I know what, I'll fix that for her, too!

Safe from cheating, enfolded in her black silk, Madge explores the bathroom. She finds at once that she can't wash her teeth – there's no way of telling her tooth-brush from Paul's just by the feel. Gran's on the other hand is easy: its bristles are splayed out sideways in a flattened tangle. She ought to get a new one, thinks Madge. Somehow the game is easier with the blindfold on. She can concentrate on finding her way instead of spending half her energy on her eyelids. She returns to the landing, confident now, needing only a swift touch on the door-frame to find her way. She is almost enjoying the soft darkness; it has a melted feeling to it, all distances dissolved, near and far, everything reduced to what you can feel.

Paul's voice says, 'See if you can find your way to my room.' Then she hears his steps, going up ahead of her. She reaches out for the bannister-rail, and sliding her fingers up it, slowly climbs the stairs. At the top she takes a big step, as though there were an invisible extra stair, and stumbles. She goes along the narrow landing, trailing a hand on either wall, and reaches for the door. Paul's voice, very close to her, and somehow tight and cold says, 'No, you've got the wrong one. To your right.'

'You mustn't tell me,' she says.

'All right, I won't,' says Paul, but now her hand is on the doorknob, and she goes in. But I've got it wrong again, she thinks, for I was sure I needed to go further for Paul's door. His room feels hot and heavy, and smells of dust. Amy can't have been up here all week! thinks Madge. Funny. She moves to where the bed is, the one that used to be hers, and sits down on it. It seems to be covered with things – she feels over them – in cardboard boxes. Whatever had he been collecting? she wonders. 'Paul?' she says, but she knows before she says it that he has gone, or rather that he did not enter the room with her. It is not only that she has not heard him, but something else – the feel of him is not here. And funny she thinks, that people have feels around them, like magnetic feels, magnetic *fields* I mean, and you don't notice when you can see them, because you think it's the sight of them that you feel, when all the while it is this other thing, like a ghost, and that of course, is how Ralph knew there was somebody, and kept saying 'Who's there?' the day we ambushed him. And I'm tired of this now. It feels so hot and heavy and hard to breathe – it really does smell dusty in here, and as though no window has been opened for weeks – and the darkness is choking me.

She reaches up and tries to untie the blindfold. Paul has tied it very tightly in a double knot, and she cannot undo it. She gets up and goes towards the door, to find Paul to help her. She falls over something at once, and, groping around on hands and knees where she has fallen, her hands find other things too, funny things, whose shape she cannot fathom. The door is beyond the end of Paul's bed, she thinks, so if I find that – but she can't find that – it seems not to be there, and oh, what *are* all these things she is falling over? She remembers her dress, and the dressing-table stool, and the mysteriousness of them when they tripped her. But even so she is beginning to feel scared, blundering and tripping around in the bright uncluttered attic room that seems suddenly full of strange bulks and lurking shin-breakers, crowding in on her, lying in wait with malice. I must see! and with a sudden lurch of panic, painfully tweaking the strands of hair that are knotted into the scarf, she tears off the blindfold.

It is still dark!

Of course, she says to herself, a flash of terror dying out in relief, I forgot to take off those pads Paul put beneath it! Her fingers go to her eyes, and find nothing but naked lids and lashes. A knot of something, like a swallow down a dry throat, presses on her neck and chest. She feels as though the floor were falling, like the first downward plummet of a descending lift. She can't see. Her mind will not accept the darkness as distance without light – instead it seems a solid thing, a something, like the blindfold, a thick curtain, a cloud, that wraps her, and closes her in, and cuts her off from

65

light that lies beyond. She strikes out blindly, and begins to run, falling over, and leaping up, and crashing into something else, and screaming with fear.

On the landing Paul stands between the open door of his room, in which the clear evening shines, reflecting brightness off the view of the sea, and the usually-locked door of the lumber room, through which he has misguided Madge. He waits and waits and then he hears Madge scream. Well, she wanted to *know*! he tells himself. But he is taken aback by the horror-film note in her scream. From below in the house he hears Gran calling, 'What's the matter? Oh, whatever is happening?' He hears her labouring up the stairs, and Amy's running feet coming too, much faster. Hell! Hell to pay, he thinks.

Madge's screaming dies away in sobs. She stands stock still, wide-eyed, staring, and the darkness flows into her, and overwhelms her, like water in death by drowning. A grey line divides the wall of blackness. A vague, furry line, like a chalk mark on a blackboard. Her eyes cease swimming, and narrow to a focus on it so abruptly she can feel them doing it. She is looking at light leaking through a crack. Like a great receding wave the darkness draws back out of her, and belongs to its true place, in the room around her. She is in a dark room, with light leaking round the door. The lumber room, of course! She reaches out a hand for the door catch, and opens it.

Gran and Amy reach the top of the stairs, Gran red-faced, panting for breath. Madge opens the door, and appears, blinking, white as a ghost, with a strained and tear-marked face.

'What is going on?' asks Gran.

'It's my fault, Gran,' says Paul. 'I locked Madge in the lumber room.'

'Whatever has come over you, Paul?' says Gran, and her voice is angry, so that with a small surprise Paul thinks, she can be like other grown-ups if one has been

66

bad enough. 'That's not like you. That kind of trick is neither clever nor funny, just unkind. You will go to bed now, without supper.'

'Yes, Gran,' says Paul, feeling at once how hungry he is. And it's not fair! he tells himself sitting in the attic window, looking at the sea, I wasn't playing tricks. She wanted to *know*, didn't she?

Downstairs Madge eats small bites from her loaded plate. Her napkin, spread out on her lap is ready for anything she can slip onto it. The buttered roll that went with soup, for instance, and one small slice of her roast pork, to put into it, and the fluffy meringue from the dessert. She is ashamed of having screamed loudly enough to have got Paul into trouble, and her heart aches for him, upstairs, alone and hungry.

I only did it for her, and she's downstairs pigging herself, thinks Paul. Bloody girls! But he knows he had not meant it kindly.

In a while there is a tap on the door, and Madge's voice saying, 'Paul'. She comes in with her napkin-ful of loot, and spreads it out in front of him. She had the impression that she was sacrificing all the nicest bits of her own meal, but it looks rather woebegone and tatty now, and she says apologetically, 'This was all I could get, I'm afraid.'

'Better than nothing,' he says, tucking in. When he has mouth-room for words he says, 'Madge was it really scary?'

'Horrible!' she says, shuddering. 'Worse than anything. If it had really gone, I would have done anything, given up anything, to get it back.'

'I read a story about that once,' says Paul, licking a scoop of pink tongue round his meringue, in a long pause. 'The Valley of the Blind, and this man gets into it over the mountains. And he thinks he will lord it over them, and be king, because he can see. But they just think he's seeing things – you know, they think he's mad, and their doctors say that the two round swellings in his head are pressing on his brain, and giving him illusions, and he'll be all right if they operate, and take them out. And he wants awfully to stay, because he's gone soppy about this blind girl, and he wants to marry her, but just the same, when it comes to it, he funks it, and starts to climb out of the valley, even though he knows he won't possibly make it.'

'Ugh!' says Madge. 'Yes, I bet he would, though. He'd just have to.'

'Well, when we had to read it last year in class, I didn't really believe it,' says Paul. 'I thought he'd have taken what he could get, and done without eyes, just to stay alive. But you know, Madge, you did scream most terribly *awfully*.'

'It was terribly awful,' says Madge, and her face goes suddenly sad as she thinks, no grey lines appear, and no doors open ever, to let *him* out!

'Hey, listen, someone's coming,' says Paul. Madge gets up and opens the door to listen. Someone is coming slowly upstairs. Madge slithers through Paul's door, and scurries down to her bedroom, closing the door on herself there just as the footsteps reach the main landing. They go on past her, up to Paul. Whew! she thinks, thank goodness I made it. It's bad enough having anger and punishments at Goldengrove, anyway, but if I'm caught breaking the quarantine it will go on and on, instead of stopping at this.

There is a tap at Paul's door, and Gran comes in. She is carrying a tray, which she puts on the bed. 'You are a very bad boy, Paul dear,' she says, and she still sounds upset, 'but I can't really let you go hungry. Now eat this, and then go to sleep. Good night.'

Paul lifts the cloth off the tray. He expects to find bread and water, but Gran has relented further than that; there is a cold pork and chutney sandwich – he can see from the rough cut of the bread that Gran has made it herself, for Amy cuts neater squares – and a little bowl of raspberry jelly with meringue. I bet I'd have got only one meringue if I'd have been having proper supper, thinks Paul, grinning.

Later, when he is already sleeping, a tap on the door disturbs him. Amy comes in, with her best coat and hat still on, and a little paper bag in her hand. 'Wake up a mo, Paul,' she says. 'I've brought you something. Your gran's quite right, mind, but she hardly eats a thing herself these days, she's forgotten what a growing lad needs. I brought you this, look.'

She gives him a little bag of hot chips, and a small bar of chocolate, American chocolate, Paul notices, so it has come from Walt. 'Oh, thanks, Amy,' says Paul, trying to sound as if he means it, and already wondering where to get rid of the chips, so that Amy won't find them when she clears up next day. But when Amy has gone Paul finds that he has in fact plenty of room for the chips, and more than half the chocolate too.

'You pig! You absolute *hog*!' says Madge when he tells her about it. 'And to think I gave you my meringue!'

*   *   *

That morning Madge, getting up, puts on a white organdy dress, one that her mother bought her for going out in. Amy has found it stuffed and crumpled into the dressing-table drawer, rescued it and pressed it and hung it up in the wardrobe, as if she hadn't better things to do, Madge has thought, for I shan't wear it, and it will get crushed again in the suitcase going home. But now she is wearing it, and looking into the mirror to see why her mother likes it. She looks fresh and crisp in it; a high round collar gives her a controlled look, and its soft, see-through-to-the-lining, tissue-paper material looks misty and dreamlike. Madge notices with astonishment how her image flirts with her eyes, has the smug, guess-what look, the something-beautifully-wrapped look of a birthday present. Doesn't go much with matted hair, she thinks, seizing a brush to torment herself into smoothness. And why does Mummy like it? It isn't at all the sort of thing *she* wears. Never mind, I like it too. And I want to feel nice today. I want to be good to be with. It's the least one can do for him, poor him, locked in the lumber room for ever! Oh, how terrible. And oh, *hell*! what with all this dressing I've forgotten to wash! She gets out of the dress again, struggling with the tiny translucent buttons, and grabbing towel and sponge-bag, runs for the bathroom.

Seeing her come down late for breakfast, chocolate-box-pretty, and very careful how she sits down in her chair, Paul scowls. Not even the morning for me, he thinks.

And oh, it's beginning again, thinks Gran, I see it beginning again. Only a dress this morning, at first only dresses and smiles, and then will come longing and yearning, and wanting too much of someone, and raging, raging, against what cannot be. It is always the same. Where does it come from, all this? All over long since for me, now, and not yet begun upon for them, and in between, such storms! She remembers the storms, not wanting to, so that her mind skitters rapidly through years like moments – her son marrying, and the children being born, and the misery she never understood, for why couldn't they resign, accept, and what was the use of either her son or her daughter-in-law complaining to her, accusing each other? I didn't want to hear, thinks Gran, I didn't want to know. And in the end, when they each went their own way, quarrelling about the house, the books, and whose is the grandfather clock, and whose are the children, and dividing them, like so much furniture, Madge with her mother, and Paul with his father, for 'I must and will have the rearing of my own son', and, but for me, they would never meet again . . . shocking, shocking. She hears her son saying, 'Paul's all right – better with his new mother.' She hears her daughter-in-law saying, 'Madge doesn't miss her father – not in the least. She can't even remember him.' And it never occurs to either that the children might need each other, she grieves, brother and sister, they belong together, together, see how happy we all are together at Goldengrove. Old I may be, but I'm cunning, cunning enough for them. I'll pretend all that stuff and nonsense about cousins if pretend it I must – do they *realize* it makes my one son two, and I have to keep on and on, lying and inventing whenever the subject comes up, and oh, what a tangled web we weave – but as long as death spares me, I'll bring the children together here, and heal the breach, and right the wrong . . .

'Oh Gran, *please* can you pass the butter?' says Madge, obviously for the third time of asking, and startles her Gran back to her here-and-now grand-daughter, crisp in white organdy, wanting butter on it, and, Gran thinks, oh, it's beginning again . . .

'You look pretty this morning, dearie,' she says.

'She doesn't, she looks wet,' says Paul. 'People don't wear that kind of dress for the morning.'

'Well, I've only got one best dress,' says Madge unshakeably pleased with herself, 'so it must be all right for any time. I've never heard of having three different bests for morning, afternoon and evening.' Though Jenny Martin did say she had two, she thinks.

Not even the morning for me, thinks Paul, but it's my fault, I suppose, for I made her feel like this, when I made the Valley of the Blind in the lumber room . . . There might be conkers in the grove this morning, with the wind last night, and there's sure to be Jeremy fishing, and the sand and waves and the shining light on the shore, but I'd better be nice about it all, to make up for last night, and 'I think I'll come with you, if you're going to read this morning, Madge,' he says.

Oh *lord*! thinks Madge, dismayed, the shine going off her morning at once, he *would*! 'You don't have to, Paul,' she says, 'if you'd rather be on the beach.'

'No, I want to come,' he says, lying, for her face has betrayed her.

'We read awfully difficult books, you see,' she says. 'You won't understand a word.'

'That's all right,' he says, grimly. 'I won't mind that.' The more I don't want him to come, the more he will come, sees Madge, resigning herself.

'Have we time to look for conkers?' asks Paul, as they go down through the garden.

'Oh, yes, I expect so,' says Madge, but there are none to be found, though the tender green spiky globes can be seen all over the tree. It is tight-fistedly hanging on to them. There is a mist in the air; the day is suspended, uncertain whether it promises a chill, or a hazy heat. The weather is wearing organdy too, thinks Madge.

'How good of you to come, how good of both of you,' says Ralph. 'I was just wondering how to pass the time. I would like some poetry; I almost need it. Will you mind reading poems?'

'No,' says Madge.

'Not as long as they're not about daffodils,' says Paul.

'I want one particular thing,' says Ralph, 'and daffodils don't come into it. Can you find the Milton, Madge? Will you read from *Paradise Lost* — the beginning of Book Three?'

Hail, holy Light, offspring of Heav'n first-born,
Or of th' Eternal Coeternal beam
May I express thee unblamed? . . . reads Madge.

And settling to listen, Ralph turns towards Madge, towards the window, and leans back into his chair. Paul sits on the floor, and traces patterns in the dust on the unswept boards. She reads, he listens, and this

72

leaves me out, he thinks. And she was quite right, I don't understand a word of it. Not a word. But it reminds me . . . what of? he wonders, as the words roll on and on . . . He wonders till he remembers being taken to Winchester by his father, one winter's afternoon, and when they heaved open the slow and heavy door, and stepped inside, the gloomy, unlit, stone-cold space was full of organ music. He remembers the sound now; it was huge and grand, but jumbled somehow in the echoing arches and fluted vaults, so that he could not make out the tune. Now Madge's voice, gone solemn, as in church, rolls out a magnificence in which he cannot find the sense.

> . . .*Thee I revisit safe,* she reads,
> *And feel thy sovran vital Lamp; but thou*
> *Revisit'st not these eyes, that rowle in vain*
> *To find thy piercing ray, and find no dawn* . . .

and something has gone wrong with Madge's voice, which is shaking and trembly, and the music stumbles. *So thick a drop serene hath quenched their Orbs,* she quavers, helpless, as the tears get into her throat, and she cannot see the lines, and sniffs desperately, and says, 'Oh, Ralph, surely you don't want *this*!'

'What's wrong? What's the matter?' says Ralph, with the peaceful and absorbed expression fading from his face. 'But I do want it. Won't you read on?'

'I can't,' she says, tears flowing freely. 'Ralph, how *can* you?'

'Oh, give it here, Madge, do!' says Paul, very cross, grabbing the book from her, 'I *can*!' And of course it's what he wants, he thinks, he wants to wallow in it, as he looks for the line. Then in his best, reading-the-lesson-in-the-morning-assembly voice, he goes steadily on.

> . . . *Seasons return; but not to mee returns*
> *Day, or the sweet approach of Ev'n or Morn.*

73

Or sight of vernal bloom, or Summer's Rose,
Or flocks, or herds, or human face divine;
But cloud instead, and ever-during dark
Surrounds me . . .

His clear, cold voice is interrupted by Madge, sobbing.

'Thank you, Paul, leave it,' says Ralph.

'Yes,' says Paul, 'I will. I'm going down to the beach. Right away!'

He leaves a long silence behind him, in which Madge, wiping her hot cheeks with the flat of her hands, wishes that she were the sort of person who remembers to have a handkerchief.

'What upset you?' says Ralph at last.

'That did.'

'Why? Why should it?'

'Oh, but how can you bear it? How can you bear to rub salt in your wounds like that?'

'Rub salt? It doesn't rub salt, it helps. It objectifies.'

'I don't understand,' says Madge, leaving off wiping her cheeks, as the tears at last dry up. Her hands are sticky with salt like the sea.

'No, indeed you don't,' says Ralph, dryly. 'But then, why should you, after all?'

'Oh, but I want to, I really want to! What does "objectify" mean?'

'It means it puts things outside me. Makes them into objects, external to the mind.'

'I understand that,' says Madge, confidently, for she is remembering the crack of light round yesterday's door, and how it made the darkness flow out of her terrified mind, and become instead just darkness in the room around her, 'but I don't understand how it does it.'

'Another man's pain, against which to measure one's own. A scream to put against one's own silence. It helps me to grasp how much of what I am is blindness,

74

and how much is me . . . really, this is ridiculous. I never talk like this. It fails. Don't worry your head about it. Change the subject.'

Madge suddenly feels like going and putting her arms round him for comfort. She is remembering running to someone with a cut knee, long ago, sometime long ago, arms outstretched, needing the hug to comfort herself. It is an insubstantial sort of wanting, a thin ghostly sort, that fades swiftly in the reality of standing in a dusty room, looking at a dignified middle-aged face, with the eyes stretched open eternally.

'I can't help worrying my head about it,' she says.

'My dear Madge,' says Ralph, getting up, and groping his way to the window, standing there not-looking out, back turned on her, 'I don't want your worry. I don't want your kindness. I am well able to look after myself. I don't want your tears. They spoil your reading voice. And I did want your reading voice.'

'Oh, I'm sorry, Ralph, truly I am!' she cries, seizing the book from the table where Paul tossed it as he left. 'I'll begin again, and I'll do it properly this time.'

'No,' he says. 'Another day, another book will do. Leave it now. Go with Paul; go and play.'

'Can I come back this afternoon?'

'I am going out this afternoon.'

'Tomorrow?'

'You can if you want to. I am not asking you to.'

'No,' she says, 'no. All right. Goodbye then.'

Leaving, she walks out into open air that is blue with distance. She sees the harbour, and the grey, beige, yellow, tiled and lichen clad houses of the town, and behind them over the roofs the sea again, and she takes the path going down, over the little bridge over the railway, onto the grassy and flowery cliff, and down to the beach and Paul, where the water rolls and piles up layer upon layer, and shines and jumps and breaks and booms on the resounding stretched yellow drum of the shore. Paul looks up smiling, pleased to see her, thinking she has come because of him, and hands her a scraper and she joins in attacking the boat.

'Ugh!' he says. 'It's jolly stuffy up there. And if we keep at this till lunch we'll have all the weed off, and we can begin to paint.'

*   *   *

This is the ninth day, thinks Paul, picking up his chop by the bone and hoping Gran won't notice. But we didn't start the boat till the second day. It's taken eight days, and there are three days left to go. If we painted it this afternoon, it would be dry by tomorrow – wouldn't it? How long does paint take to dry? I think it would. There would be tomorrow and two more days to play in it. It will be super fun, he tells himself, doubtfully. For he is rather vague about what they will do with it when it is painted and finished. Madge wanted it painted, he reflects. She will think of a game for it. There would have been a lot more days for games if she had helped me more with the work. How many times has she helped on it? Not more than three or four. She isn't such fun as she used to be.

'Paul, dear, what a way to eat a chop!' says Gran mildly.

'Cave man!' says Madge, grinning. But I like her just as much, he tells himself, suppressing his disloyal thought, and another thought adds painfully – or more.

I promised Higgy I'd read while I was down here, Madge is thinking. It's funny, I always think I'll have masses and masses of time when I'm down here, and then there doesn't seem to be a single moment to spare, and the time goes by so fast, I can't bear to count how little must be left. In a way I *have* been reading. We have read nearly all the way through the horrible ambiguity book, hours and hours of it, and *Northanger Abbey*, and quite a lot of *Through the Looking Glass*, and we wasted this morning on Milton. She colours slightly as she thinks of it.

The fresh sea air puts roses in their cheeks, thinks Gran, contentedly. They come and go in my house. Soon they will be gone. I shall miss them. I shall go to sleep after lunch, and to bed earlier in the evening. I shall think about them, and buy postcards to send to them at home. Then they will return. They will come back every year. Like the swallows, like the storms.

*　　*　　*

After lunch they go running down the hill into the town, with holiday money clenched in fists in pockets, hot, and smelling metallic and promising chocolate as well as paint. Through narrow streets they go, to the quay, where gulls and shoppers drift along the waterfront from window to window, and a row of boats lies high and dry along the quay beside the railing, ready to ride out the winter earth-bound. Laity's shop is there, opposite the green harbour water which slops and rocks, and cradles the anchored boats. Stopping, they peer in, past the rows of stem ginger pots, tied up with straw, past the blackboard with the prices of different kinds of tea chalked up on it like a cricket score, to stare at the rows of green tins, faded with time, on which the battered white clipper ships lean and race across painted panels. 'Can I help you, young lady?' says a voice within the shop.

'I was just liking your tins,' says Madge. 'But perhaps Gran would like some of your tea.'

'We try to be different,' he says. 'Your grandmother drinks Orange Pekoe. Half a pound?'

Then, clutching the dark green and shiny gold packet with a dragon and a crunchy feel, Madge returns to Paul, outside, and they go on towards the Fishermen's Co-operative. That, too, has a fine window, full of copper ships-lights, and brass bells, and waxed twine on spools for fishing lines, and boxes of spinners, and dark green glass balls to float the fishermen's nets. They go into the shop, brushing past hanging oilskin jackets and sou'westers, and find themselves in cavern-like gloom. The roof is covered with stalactites made of pendant clusters of sea-boots and fishing rods; all around them rise stalagmites of piled-up socks and sweaters, and bales of netting, and new lobster pots. They consider the colour card for paint, with little sun-faced squares to choose from.

'Which colour is sky-blue-pink?' asks Paul, and pointing at bright sea-green, Madge says, 'That one.'

'I'll order it for you,' says the man behind the counter.

'Oh, haven't you got them?' says Paul, disappointment showing all over him. 'We wanted to do it this afternoon.'

'Too many of 'em,' says the man. 'We can't keep them all. But it only takes a day or two to get them. You'll have to have patience. Unless you'd like to use something I have got.'

'Well, what have you got?' asks Madge.

'Black and white, of course, and a few oddments. Plenty of cream – lots of people like that. And Lincoln green. And chocolate brown. That's all. How about green and cream?'

'Ugh!' says Madge.

'Just like school corridors,' says Paul.

'It's not even the right sort of green,' says Madge.

'It's an 'orrible sort of green, I grant,' says the man. 'Funny you wanting that other colour, for I have got some of that put by, though I can't let you have it. We had it ordered for a Frenchy, said he'd come for it next time he was this way. That was last year, and he's never been back. Can't heed a word they say, that lot. They lie like flatfish!'

'Perhaps he wasn't telling lies,' says Paul. 'Perhaps he's been shipwrecked, and drowned, and he doesn't like to collect his paint in case you're unkind to ghosts!'

'What's that?' says the man. 'Here, don't you go joking about shipwreck round here, young man, because t'idn't funny. Be off with you!'

Outside the shop, resigned to waiting for the paint, they stand undecided.

'I say, Madge,' says Paul, his eyes drifting over the harbour to Smeaton's Quay, festooned and cobwebbed as usual with nets hung out to dry, where he can see Jeremy, at the foot of the steps, putting tackle in his dinghy, 'If we can't put the paint on today, anyway, might it be a good day to go fishing?'

'Well,' says Madge, closing her eyes against the image of wild fish, flapping blood, 'yes, why not? Except, would you mind awfully, Paul, if I didn't?'

'Would you mind awfully being left on your own?'

'No, not a bit. Catch a big fish for me, I'm ravenous in the morning. And you could use your red spinner yourself, then.'

'Great, see you later,' says Paul, beginning to run. Madge watches him go. She wanders over to lean on the harbour rail, and sees the shoals of little fishes swarming in the water, and the wavy sand on the bottom. The foot of the harbour wall has a fringe of submerged weed that waves in the moving water like hair in a slow-motion wind. Soon she can see Paul, very little and far away, climbing into Jeremy's dinghy. She sees the dinghy pull out to the *Amulet*, sees the sail flapping, running up the mast, sees Paul casting off from the big rusty buoy, and watches the *Amulet* tilt on the wind and sail out into the bay.

Now I am alone, she thinks, what shall I do? And for a while she does nothing, but simply stays where she is. Then, I'll climb the Island, she thinks, and sets off up a steep crooked cobbled lane to reach it. Up the green slope she climbs, and gains the little chapel on top. It has a stone cross at each end of its roof, and a little low wall like a gunwale all round it, and it looks like Noah's ark, grounded. An old man in a dark blue sweater is leaning on the wall, looking seawards, smoking a pipe. Madge looks too, at the white horses dancing all over the dark blue bay as far as Godrevy, at the lines of great surf rolling onto the beach beyond the Island, that faces ocean, not bay.

'It's windy today,' she says.

'But there's no wrath in the weather,' he answers, and she goes on, clambering down to the path round the foot of the hill, to watch the rocks playing lacemaking with the tossing sea. Nothing happens to me when I am alone, she thinks. Miss Adams went on and on when we were reading Wordsworth, about how good for you it was, and Jenny Martin said you were only truly yourself when you were quite alone, and Miss Adams said Yes, good girl, Jenny, how true, so I ought to be really myself-est right now, at this very moment, and am I? What am I? A great wave explodes in her attention, and casts a swift lace coverlet over the naked rock. I'm just not like that, that's all. I'm a mirror; I just reflect. And all sorts of things happen in a mirror when there are people moving around it, but when it's alone it's empty, glassy and still. When I'm alone I'm just a weather-watcher. Who would I be with no weather, all alone in the dark? She shudders. I just don't like being alone. I think I'll go home now, and have tea with Gran!

She turns back, and scrambles homewards over the sloping clumpy grass, till she can see the town curved round its bay, clinging to its up-and-down hillsides, stretching out towards her along what was once a sandbar, to this hill that was once really an island. She can see her grandmother's house, high on the hill overlooking; a distant four-square outline against the green-gold misty wood that caps the cliff. She settles into swift strides, and makes homewards, and so is just too late to see the *Amulet*, with Jeremy and Paul, sailing past the Island, close inshore, going to lift lobster-pots off Clodgy Point.

*   *   *

Looking up from hauling lobster-pots up their length
of sodden rope, Paul sees the hazy shore. Above the
golden sand he sees the green field of the cemetery,
crowded with white headstones. There lie the ancient
mariners, like a landed shoal, each with a marble
marker-buoy anchored above his head. They must like
to lie there, within sound of the sea, he thinks. And
from out here you can see the headlands of this tall
coast, stretching away east and west, shadow beyond
shadow against sea and sky. And Godrevy stands out
seawards, how clear and near! 'Oh, couldn't we go
round the lighthouse?' he says to Jeremy, though
even as he says it, he struggles with the thought
that he ought to wait for Madge, ought to say,
keep it for another day when Madge will come
too.

'Not straight from here, we can't,' says Jeremy,
'because of the Stones.'

'The Stones?'

'That's a rock reef. Runs north from Godrevy three
mile. Look, you can see the waves on it over yonder,
breaking white; and that lightbuoy marking the end of
it.'

But Paul can only see cormorants, floating like hooks
out of the water, and then a seal, that surfaces and stares
at them with huge sad mermaid eyes, then submerges
in a suck of bubbles that looks like the cloudy spiral
in the heart of a green glass marble.

'We'll go in with these lobsters,' says Jeremy, 'and
then I'll take you round it.' And I can find Madge on
the quay, and tell her, thinks Paul, happily.

Madge walks along the quayside, round the harbour,
past the custom house, and the lifeboat in its shed,
and the church, and up towards the railway station.
On the railway platform, suspended above the beach,
people are waiting for the train. Right at the end of

the platform, leaning against the notice that says *ST IVES* stands a soldier in khaki, with a girl in his arms. Her head is against his shoulder, with her bright red hair wrapped round him by the wind, and he leans his cheek down against the crown of her head, and holds her loosely, hands joined behind her back. How still they are, thinks Madge. Oh, I wonder what they feel like, standing so still! They look like a statue, or a famous painting, or a war photograph from *Picture Post*, or the last shot in a sad, sad film; yet they are only Amy, and Walt, who blushes and stammers when I speak to him, and they will be ordinary again very soon, for I hear the train puffing, coming to disturb them. She watches them stand, unmoving, while everyone else picks up cases, moves them nearer the edge of the platform, and waves, and flutters; she watches them not move till the rattling train pulls in front of them, and blocks her view.

Then she takes the short cut across the beach to reach the cliff path home. The beach is empty, except for two boys swimming, and a dog, and a man sitting alone on a bench by the changing huts. She knows both man and dog. The dog is chasing the plovers and gulls on the rocky end of the beach, barking in the distance. Ralph is sitting, head leaning back, his stick planted upright in the sand in front of him, and his hands crossed upon the handle. Very quietly Madge goes and sits down on the other end of the bench beside him. She mirrors water, rock, sand, sky, and says nothing. After a while he says,

'You are better to be with when you are happy, Madge.'

'Oh!' says Madge, so startled that she jumps. 'How did you know someone was here?'

'I heard you come. I felt your weight as you sat down on the bench.'

'But however did you know it was me?'

'Ah. By your aura. I know it quite well by now.'

82

'I didn't know I had one of those,' says Madge. 'What is it?'

'It's a sort of essence, emanating from all living things; a kind of atmosphere.'

'You mean a *feel* about me?'

'Yes, that's it.'

'And you really can feel it, and mine really truly is different from anyone else's? Oh, tell me about it! What do I feel like?'

'Aha,' he says, smiling. 'Why are you so pleased? Do you like having a secret essence?'

'Oh, yes, I do,' says Madge, drawing her knees up to her chin, and hugging them. 'I'd much rather be known by my aura than by the other way – by how I look.'

'Why?' says Ralph, smiling really deeply now, turning towards her. 'Aren't you pretty enough for yourself?'

'Oh, it's not that. It's just that looking is so shallow – you know, one glance, and you can tell what sort of a person *she* is; horrid! But there's Gran now – she looked so beautiful in old photographs, and now she's gone very small, and wrinkled, especially round the corners of her eyes, like gulls' footprints in the sand, but she feels just the same to be with.'

'So you like your aura for its keeping qualities?'

'Yes, if it's a nice aura to begin with!'

'Rest assured that it is. It makes me feel perfectly at peace. You may safely hope for it to remain unchanged.'

As the *Amulet* glides in beside the little pier by the lifeboat shed, Paul gathers her painter in one hand, and throws it upwards, unwinding in jerky flight, to one of the ageless, sunweathered, blue-clad men who linger for ever, smoking and talking on the quay, ready to catch ropes, and make a turn with them round the bollards, in return for 'Good Morning' or storm-talk, or a fish or two. Paul loops his end round the post at *Amulet*'s prow, the wooden post that is scooped and grooved and sculptured with the run of the rope at a thousand landings, and, leaning back on his heels, heaves hard and slowly draws *Amulet* in towards the quay. Looking up the flight of weedy steps he sees straight overhead the tower of the church, standing so near the shore that it might almost be on the quay itself. It has four little bomb-shaped turrets, tapered top and bottom, projecting from the sides of the top of the tower; in outline against the sky it looks like a lobster claw, raised skywards.

Leaving Jeremy to unload his living lobsters, Paul scurries up the steps and looks for Madge. I must find her, he tells himself, or I shall have to ask Jeremy to go another day instead, and honestly, we've asked so often before, and he's never said yes, that I don't know how long it might be before he says yes again, so where is she, where is she now? Madge is nowhere handy, that's clear. He half-expected her to be sitting having cream tea, but she isn't, not in the nearby little shop with its cloam-oven scones, and cream-pots, and strawberry jam. Is that her, he wonders, walking along Smeaton's Quay, across the harbour? I know what! and running, groping in his pocket for sixpence, he races for the money-in-the-slot telescope perched on the harbour wall. It starts to buzz as soon as it has eaten his sixpence. He fumbles with the focus, and rakes the harbour round, searching. Oh, please, Madge, be there, he begs, for it was always Madge who wanted the lighthouse so badly, and asked to go round it, and wanted to know for certain whether it stood on one rock, as it looks from here, or two, as it looks from the beach. But though he scans all round the harbour he cannot see her. The beach – perhaps she has gone to the beach – he swings around. He can only see half the beach from here, for the nearer end is masked by houses on Pedn Olva Point. There is nothing but a dog running on it – yes, there, on a bench, two people, and surely one is a girl in a white dress. He tries to make the focus change – and then, click, the sixpence runs out, and a black shutter closes across his sight. But not before he has guessed who is sitting with Madge. Oh, all *right* then! he tells himself. See if I care! and he saunters casually back to Jeremy, and says, 'Ready when you are.'

Looking back, as Jeremy sets a course east-north-east across the bay, Paul sees the great bulk of Rosewall Hill, purple with dying heather, rising slowly and solemnly behind the town as they draw away seawards.

Madge watches vaguely as a boat sails out across the bay.

'I don't think what you say can be true,' she says thoughtfully to Ralph.

'That your aura is a good one? Why not?'

'No, that it makes you feel perfectly at peace.'

'Again, why not?'

'Well, I don't think you can feel quite like that with anyone. You're so good at knowing when people move, sensing what they're doing. And people never sit still, do they? Heads move, or maybe just eyes, but people are always looking. I should think you'd always find people restless, fidgety with seeing.'

Ralph suddenly puts his hand over his eyes, as though they were capable of being seen through.'I wonder how you know that, Madge,' he says, in a quiet voice. 'I wonder how you guessed that.'

'I was thinking about you, then I guessed it.'

'You are right. When people turn to look, it feels as though they were jiggling or tapping to some tune I cannot hear. But you are stiller than most.'

'I try to be,' says Madge. 'I really try.' But in spite of herself she looks up to see how far the boat has gone, and now she sees that it is the *Amulet*, going where no fishes are, far out, and it seems to be going towards Godrevy. They are going without me! she cries inwardly, overwhelmed with a sense of time spent, chances lost.

'We are going on Saturday,' she says. 'I can come and read to you twice more.'

'The devil keep me from people's kindness!' says Ralph harshly. 'I shall miss you.'

'I haven't been kind,' she says. 'And there's twice more.'

'You live in the present, I see.'

When else is there? wonders Madge. Don't we all? In a while Ralph says, 'Well, Madge, since you've brought your keen looking to haunt me, will you share it with me? Tell me what the waves look like.'

'Oh, I can't,' says Madge. 'How can I? There aren't words for that sort of thing, not easy ones, and I'm not John Keats, or William Shakespeare.'

'Try.'

Madge watches first. The waves rise and run towards her in glassy straight ridges, and break, spilling froth and diamond-bright flying droplets, and spending and exhausting themselves in creamy foam; then they fall back, sleeking and glossing the yellow slope of the sand . . . 'Well,' she says, 'the waves rise up along the edge of the sea, and run forwards, and break all frothy on the sloping sand. They make it wet and smooth.'

'Thank you Madge,' he says, after waiting as though she might say more.

'Oh, but I feel so bad about it!' she cries. 'I feel as though I'm cheating you, selling you short. I mean, when I'm reading, you are actually getting the book; but words for waves . . .'

'And now who's rubbing salt, Madge?' says Ralph. 'I'm getting cold sitting still in the wind; I must go in. Goodbye till tomorrow, Madge. Keep your lovely aura shining bright.'

And scrambling up the steep cliff path, hugging the thought of her aura, like a new toy, a new dress, a promised holiday, Madge meets Paul, running, laughing and jumping towards her from below, crying, 'Madge! Madge! I've been to the lighthouse!' And a voice inside Madge that she very seldom hears, from something coiled up and hidden, deep down, wails 'Too late! Too late!'

They find Gran in the kitchen, trying to cut up cheese.

'It's Amy's night out, tonight, dears. Bread and cheese for supper.'

'I thought she went out the other night,' said Paul. 'Bread and cheese will be fine.'

'Here, let me do that, Gran,' says Madge, taking the knife from her, and beginning to slice the block of cheddar.

'Well, she has more nights off than Mrs Arthur used to,' says Gran. 'Thank you, Madge. I'm such a lot of trouble to look after nowadays, she has to work very hard. And she must see Walt, her young man, you know. He hasn't *asked* her yet, and he'll be going home to America soon.'

'What's so difficult about you, Gran?' says Paul, giving her a sudden one-armed hug around the shoulders, that nearly throws her off balance.

'I'm getting old. I'm very forgetful. I forgot to ask Amy to cut up the cheese for me. I can only remember things from way back . . .'

This is where I should ask about my father, if I were going to, thinks Madge. But whenever I ask she gets so unhappy. It must be she minds so much about 'missing in the war' it has spoiled thinking about what went before. That must be it. I won't say anything . . .

'. . . there used to be much nicer cheese before the war, for instance,' Gran is saying. 'It wasn't always so hard. But there, there, we have to take what we can get nowadays, and be thankful.'

Sitting quietly after supper, while Gran threads up a row of needles with coloured wools for her tapestry,

Madge nibbles the satin-white almonds, and leaves the raisins unpartnered in the glass dish. She is curled up in the window-seat, with a great purple prospect of deepening evening and dark sea behind glass behind her. Lights shine, jewels in velvet. Two green lights on Smeaton's Quay glow out there, one at the end, one halfway along, and the sapphire-blue flare on the little quay, windows and lamp-posts between, and looking the other way the lonely golden spark of Godrevy, suspended in horizonless distance. You count to ten slowly between each flash and the next. Paul is curled in his grandfather's huge empty armchair, with his favourite book, *Clipper Ships Round the Horn*, full of finicky grey steel engravings, showing the great fine ships exactly, to the last sheet and belaying pin.

'When these ships sailed into Bristol, they must have come right past the mouth of this bay,' he says.

'And perhaps a pilot went out from here to take them up-channel and home,' says Madge.

'And the pilot boat would have taken unsalted meat on board, and fresh bread, and cabbages . . .'

'And brought back green-painted tins of tea, that set up the first Mr Laity in business, long ago!' They laugh.

'Find me the Home Service, for the news, dear,' says Gran. But Paul finds a shipping forecast. '. . . Fastnet, Sole, Lundy, Irish Sea. Storm warning. Gale force nine. East North East. Imminent . . .'

'That's here, isn't it?' says Paul.

'Oh dear,' says Gran. 'Are there any ships in the bay, Madge?'

'No, Gran.'

'I really thought I saw a light when I looked up at the end of my last row.'

Madge looks, but sees nothing.

'It must have been the lightbuoy on the end of The Stones, Gran,' says Paul.

'Ah well. You have sharp eyes then, for I can't spy that from here.'

'Jeremy says it's a poor light, for what it warns of,' says Paul, yawning, turning the knob again for the news. And by the end of the news he has fallen suddenly and deeply asleep. 'How nice to be young,' says Gran. 'I never sleep like that nowadays. Can't seem to lie still.'

Madge takes the book from Paul's slack hands, and rocks him in the chair to waken him. 'Goo'night, Gran, Madge,' he mumbles, and staggers unsteadily towards the stairs. 'Drunk again, you pirate!' Madge calls after him.

Gran lays her work down on her knees, and looks at the fire. 'I met Professor Ashton in Fore Street today,' she says. 'He was looking much better in himself, I thought. He says he has stopped mouldering away, and is thinking of beginning on another book.'

'Good,' says Madge, looking at the clippers, to hide her glowing with joy.

'But Paul – do you think he has enjoyed himself as much as usual?'

'Oh, yes, I'm sure he has.'

'I just wondered what he does with himself while you're reading to Professor Ashton.'

'Oh, he fishes, and swims . . . look, Gran, don't *worry* about it. The whole point about Paul is that you don't have to think about him.'

'Now, whatever do you mean by that, dearie?'

'Well, some people – my friend Jenny at school, for instance – if you just happen to want to do something different one lunch-hour, or if you just happen not to have gone and found them at break for a day or two, or you didn't keep a peppermint humbug for them, suddenly they're less friends than they were; you have to keep looking after your friendship with them. But Paul's more like a brother – I mean like I imagine a brother would have been if only I had had one – he's just there, and he doesn't go away whatever you do. I mean, we just don't have to keep together all the time to be in with each other.'

'Oh, I see,' says Gran, taking up her needlework again. 'As long as you're sure, dearie.'

'Oh, listen to the wind getting up,' says Madge. 'There really is a storm coming. How quickly the weather changes here! I sometimes think I'd better wait till Paul's old enough, and marry him.'

'Oh?' says Gran, looking up at Madge, really startled.

'Well, because I know where I am with him. Anyone else would need so much — what's that that houses need done to them? — you know, so much maintenance work.'

'Go along with you!' says Gran, crossly. 'Stuff and nonsense! Time for bed, dearie.'

Madge goes to bed quicker than to sleep. A wind is buffeting the house, roaring. Through her shut windows it pokes cold fingers, and billows the curtains. Madge remembers, words and tune together, the morning assembly hymn: *Virgin most Pure, Star of the Sea, Pray for the Mariner, Pray for Me* . . . Oh, do that, will you, if you're really there? she says. For truly, there is wrath in the weather now. Even from her room, looking into the trees, surely she can hear the sea! How it roars! Slipping from her bed, lifting the curtain aside to look out, she sees the branches of the great chestnut tree flailing and tossing like willow. Is it waves I hear, or only the agony of the leaves? she wonders. Oh, I'm glad to be indoors! Up beyond Tregenna Hill lightning shows, as though the dark wall of the sky had quaked, and cracked for a moment, and shown the fire beyond. Snuggling back into her warm bed she murmurs, *Blow wind, and crack your cheeks!* I'm safe, I'm warm . . .

*   *   *

Not the wind, but silence wakes her. Rising she opens the curtains upon a sky windswept and rain-washed, pale, fresh with the first new light. The ground below the tree is covered with newly-fallen copper and

90

gold. Surely I am awake before Paul *this* time! she thinks, and pulling on her blue dressing-gown she goes barefoot up the stairs to see.

He is there, a hump in the blanket and a tuft of fair hair on the pillow, unstirring. She sits on the other bed to wait for him. Out of his high window she looks at the sea, dark, rolling smoothly and washed with shifting pools of silver reflected from the pale sky. But she is very soon cold, sitting in her thin nightdress under her worn dressing-gown. She begins to shiver, as though all that cold brightness outside had chilled her. Turning back the quilt on the spare bed, she slips into it, and pulls the covers round her chin, and watches for Paul to wake. And sleep creeps up on her again.

Opening her eyes suddenly, she looks into Paul's. 'You're here,' he says, propping himself up on one arm, looking and smiling. For a moment she has forgotten that it isn't last year, and she doesn't wake every morning under the whitewashed eaves with him. Then, 'I woke up before you, for once, and came for you,' she says, proudly.

'Coming out?' says Paul, getting up, throwing off his pyjama jacket.

'I'll get some clothes,' she says, going.

They have to throw back the bolts on the door, and unlock the chain, having beaten Amy downstairs this one morning. The garden is cool and dewy, and chills their sandalled feet. 'The wind will have brought down some conkers now, Paul, surely,' says Madge, and off they run to the grove to look. In a thick crunchy carpet of leaves lie hundreds of the green spiky globes. They try to prise them open, with blunt fingers. Treading on them gently squeezes open the reluctant shells, but the conkers inside are not ready yet; they have creamy patches, like those glossy brown and white cows. It takes Paul a little while to find one that is brown all over, dark and polished, and finely-veined with lines of deeper brown, like contours on a map. He pockets it.

'Shall we go to the beach?' asks Madge. This morning air is cool like water, she thinks, nearly but not quite shivering. Walking is like swimming now, with an is-it-too-cold-or-isn't-it, well-when-you've-been-in-a-few-moments-it's-nice sort of pleasant chill all over me.

They let themselves out through the gate in the garden wall, onto the zig-zag path. At the second turn it branches, going one way to the wide sands of the public beach, and the other to their own small cove with its little shelf of sand. They stop to pick watery blackberries from the crowded brambles along the path. Looking back at the big beach, and the town, Madge sees the seaward side of Smeaton's Quay, with the waves breaking on it and bursts of foam climbing up it. In a great sweeping half-circle the waves are rolling onto the beach and harbour, as though the sea remembered the storm, even if the morning weather had forgotten. She notices that there is a lot of driftwood on the beach. Then they turn to go down to their own beach, and seeing the crag of Godrevy standing out deep and clear against the more shadowy headlands beyond, Madge says, 'Paul, what was the lighthouse like?'

'Great,' says Paul.

'Oh, *tell* me!' she says, 'please.'

'It isn't round,' he says, 'though it looks it from here. When you get there it has eight sides. It looks very solid, sort of standing eight-square. And there are two rocks. You can see right through the cleft, with the water boiling between them. And there's a garden on the lighthouse rock.'

'A garden?' says Madge, astonished.

'Yes. There's a wall thrown round it, like a loop of rope on the steep slope east of the lighthouse, and inside it is a garden.'

'What kind of a garden?' says Madge entranced. She tries to imagine it. 'Oh, it must be beautiful!'

'Well, with flowers and things,' says Paul. 'What else would there be? And then round the other side there's a little quay, and a breeches-buoy, and a scatter of rocks.'

'But the garden . . . ' Madge begins, her inward eye flowering like the rock with the thought of it, but then she realizes it is no good asking Paul. He can't tell me what *I* would have felt to see it . . . I would only get words for waves . . . and she runs after him down the path.

'Oh, look!' says Madge. 'The sea has made a cliff of sand.' The storm has bulldozed the beach, and raised a precipice knee-high all along it. They run; the edge of the sand steep crumbles and collapses under their feet.

'Hey, look at the boat, Madge,' says Paul as they come up to it. It lies now tilting steeply, for the storm waves have lifted it out of the sand. From the twists in the chain, and the distance it has moved, they can see it has been rolled over and over, emptied of sand, freed from the wet weight and gritty clasp of it. Had the high tide washed only a foot or so further the boat would have smashed on the rocks, being wave-handled like that. Instead, it perches on the shore at a rakish angle, with the smug look of a survivor. 'Great!' says Paul. 'It's free!' He grips the stern and heaves, and the boat slides a little on the firm wet sand. 'We can paint it all over now,' he says. 'We'd never have dug it right out ourselves.' But Madge isn't looking or listening. She is staring at the far end of the beach, under the lee of the point, for beside the cliff of sand there, something is washed up, lying.

'Oh, what's that?' she murmurs.

'It's a drowned man,' says Paul.

'Oh, it can't be!' Madge says. 'He's resting, that's all. He's swum so far he's resting, isn't he?'

'Come on,' says Paul.

'No, I don't think . . .'

'We have to go and see,' he says, starting.

I'm afraid to see someone dead, thinks Madge. What will it be like? She reaches for Paul's hand at the same moment as he reaches for hers. But when they come up to the man she is not frightened. He is as empty and silent as a shell. The sand has washed into the creases in his clothes, and into his hair. His arms are thrown up beside his head, as though the beach were his pillow. He has lost one shoe. His eyes shine with emptiness, like those of a fish. They are open and blind. And remembering when the fish seem to be dead they suddenly flap and thump, Madge shudders and whimpers, and clings to Paul, hiding her face in his shirt.

'Oh, let go, Madge, do!' says Paul, 'Look, there's the lifeboat, and we ought to wave to it.'

The lifeboat is chugging past the beach, near inshore, with everyone aboard her scanning the line of the coast. Taking off his shirt, and instantly goosey in the sharp morning air, Paul shouts and waves it like a flag. Madge shouts too. 'Here he is!' Paul cries, 'Here!' and the boat turns, and noses towards them, and comes aground with a crunch, and the lifeboat men jump out. One of them is Jeremy, Madge sees, half-hidden by the brim of his sou'wester, and wearing thigh-boots that make him walk with a roll. They are all just the fishermen, dressed for storms. They stand round the body.

'He's a goner, then,' says the coxswain. 'Anyone know him, just for the book?'

'I do,' says the man from behind the counter in the Fishermen's Co-operative. ''E's that Frenchy, come back for his paint.'

'That makes the eight of them, then, all found,' says the coxswain. 'Let's have him, boys, and then we can go in for a bite of breakfast.' Four of them lean down, and pick up the dead man, head and foot. 'You know what 'is name was, Tom?' says the coxswain as they heave the man's floppy weight over the gunwale of the lifeboat.

'No. It were gobbledygook to me, that's for sure. But it'll be in my order book, like as not.'

'After breakfast then, you'll look it out for me,' says the coxswain. 'And you, young feller, you did well to wave us in. We couldn't see him from out there, with the waves breaking between. You saved us hours of beating to and fro.'

He puts a hand on the boat, but Jeremy says, 'Hold it. They're troubled maybe. They're only childer.'

The coxswain comes over to Paul and Madge, and says, 'Now don't you be fretted by seeing of him. He were a trawlerman, and for the most part fisherfolk don't ever learn to swim, that the drowning if it come may be quick and easy. Nothing terrible to it.'

'But what happened?' asks Paul.

'They wouldn't come in to shelter last night,' says the coxswain. 'They dragged anchor, and went onto the point. Ship broke up at once. We got most of them out of the water alive, which is more than they deserve, but then we were all ready to come out for them when we saw they were meaning to ride the storm out in the bay. Now you make off home, the pair of you, and get a bite to eat to cheer you; the lass looks in need of it, and so am I.'

And Madge does look awfully cheesy, thinks Paul, taking her hand and leading her away. They hear the engine of the lifeboat start again, but they do not look back. A man is dead, thinks Madge. Dead. And we have *seen* it. No wonder I feel cold. But I couldn't eat, I really couldn't.

'I'm jolly hungry,' says Paul. 'Aren't you?'

'No,' says Madge. 'I feel funny inside, like seasick.'

'A bite to cheer you, the coxswain said,' says Paul. 'Give it a try.'

And the awful thing is, thinks Madge, a little later, licking the butter from hot toast off her fingers, and listening to Paul telling Gran all about it, and to Gran saying, 'Dear, oh dear,' that it *has* cheered me. There must be something wrong with me. I must really be vulgar and shallow like Jenny Martin said I was.

'I think I'll go and get the paint now,' says Paul, getting up.

'But there wasn't any the right—' Madge begins.

'There was lots saved for the Frenchman, and he won't want it now,' says Paul. 'See you later.'

* * *

'How dreadful for you,' says Ralph. 'It must have blighted your morning. And a sunny one too. It seems this summer will never end.'

'Oh, but the weather has gone different. There is a haze in the air, and the leaves are all golden on the trees now. What shall I read today?'

'It's an Alice day, today. Do you remember, we had left her in the shady wood, where things had no names?'

'Oh, yes,' says Madge, opening the book at her mark, and reading on. *Just then a Fawn came wandering by; it looked at Alice with its gentle large eyes, but didn't seem at all frightened. 'Here then! Here then!' Alice said, as she held out her hand and tried to stroke it; but it only started back a little, and then stood looking at her again.*

'What do you call yourself?' the Fawn said at last. Such a soft sweet voice it had!

'I wish I knew!' thought poor Alice. She answered rather sadly, 'Nothing, just now.'

'Think again,' it said: 'that won't do.'

Alice thought, but nothing came of it. 'Please would you tell me what YOU *call yourself?' she said timidly. 'I think that might help a little.'*

'I'll tell you, if you come a little further on,' the Fawn said. 'I can't remember HERE.*'*

So they walked on together through the wood, Alice with her arms clasped lovingly round the soft neck of the Fawn, till they came out into another open field, and here the Fawn gave a sudden bound into

*the air, and shook itself free from Alice's arm. 'I'm a
Fawn!' it cried out in a voice of delight. 'And dear me!
you're a human child!' A sudden look of alarm came
into its beautiful brown eyes, and in another moment
it had darted away at full speed . . .*

From where she is sitting, Madge can see Paul, on
the beach, below her, naked to the waist, bending
over the boat, with a brush loaded blue-green; she can
see the tiny splash of colour on the brush; she can see
the spreading brilliance on the old worn sides of the
boat. I am happy, she thinks. I am here, with Ralph. My
voice solaces him. But I, I can see Paul, and blue-green,
and sea, and the lighthouse, far away.

'Madge,' says Ralph, in the pause her dreaming has
made, in the book, 'you have been reading to me all
this time, and I don't know what you look like. I should
like to know, before you go away tomorrow. Will you
let me?'

'How could you know that?' says Madge, surprised.
'Will I let you what?'

'Let me touch you.'

'Yes,' she says, putting down the book, and going
towards him. She is not quite sure what he wants.
Reaching out in front of him, he gropes for her. Then,
finding her hands, he pulls her down towards him, till
she kneels on the grass in front of his chair, between his
knees. He tilts her chin, upturning her face towards him,
and covers her over with both his hands outspread. His
fingertips press gently on her temples, run along the line
of her eyebrows, across the lids of her eyes, weighing
them down, and lingering at the outer corners. His
cobweb touch weaves over her, finding the shape of
her cheekbone, and the turn of her jawbone, tracing
down to her chin, running to and fro across her lips,
and then he seems to have done, and holds her still,
hands cupped round her chin.

'Well?' she says, starting to laugh with a smile, and
at once his fingers catch the lips and swelling cheek

muscles of her smile and hold it frozen, dying away under his hands.

'You are younger than I supposed,' he says, a little sadly. 'Far younger.'

'I feel quite grown-up to me,' she says. He lets his hands fall, to her shoulders, and then to his knees. He has done with her. But carried away by the abandoned and generous feeling that lending him her face has aroused in her, Madge puts her arms round his neck, and kisses him swiftly as she rises and moves away.

'Madge. Dear girl,' he says, half-deploring, half-amused. 'Back to work. I want more of the horrible book now,' and Madge pulls a face at the front cover of *Seven Types of Ambiguity* and reads on steadily, raising her eyes at the end of each paragraph to watch the spread of colour over the boat, down below, beyond the gulls' cries, and the blackberry tangles on the cliff. The book drones on and on.

Coming home towards lunch, through the trees ablaze with fiery gold, rustling her feet through the leaf-fall, Madge thinks One More Day. Only one more day, and the thought of it hits her, the moment has come, which always comes at Goldengrove, when you must remember that you are only here on holiday, briefly, by permission. The going-home journey lurches into Madge's mind: the train chuffing round under the cliff, under the trees she walks through now, along the rocky coast. The sea-shallows, all green, and blotched with purple where the rocks run under water, and Godrevy, queen of the distance, still in view, and then another long golden beach with surf breaking, breaking white, and then, beyond a second headland, the great expanse of Porthkidney sands, wide and pale, with great lines of long surf rolling onto it. And then the train turns inland under Lelant church on the height, and there is a marshy estuary, and mud, and derelict buildings, and the landscape all chewed and uglified with the overgrown heaps from the tin mining. But beyond St Erth, looking back full of regret and feeling the uprooting in your heart, you catch just for one moment, one glimpse, through the gap where the river goes out to sea, far off, the shape of the town, and the colour of it, and then it has gone. And worse than ever this time, because what will he do without me? thinks Madge. He will walk round in his dark, and do without voices, and do without books, and never be able to work or think again. And for the first time in her life, she thinks all for herself, and unprompted by anyone, how cruel life is. Poor Ralph; even Mr Rochester got his sight back when he had someone to love and look after him properly, and Ralph has no-one. Swimming in sadness, she goes in to her lunch.

Across her plate is a letter from home, addressed in her mother's carefully elaborate hand. All through lunch the letter lurks by her side-plate, lying in wait for her afternoon.

'Don't come yet, Madge,' says Paul, bolting his rice-pudding, with a streak of paint on his cheek, and lots under his fingernails. 'Give me an hour, and then come and see it as a surprise.'

So Madge takes her letter and goes off walking to read it. Something warns her to take it somewhere special, as though to disinfect it, to overpower it with the feel of some good place. So she goes along the cliff path to the Huer's house, where she hasn't been yet this year. It is a little white-washed shelter, high among the trees on the cliff face, overlooking the bay. And here, long ago, the Huer sat, ready to make a hue-and-cry after pilchards, when he saw them in the bay. He made tick-tack signals with green branches in his hands, and the fishermen ran to their black-tarred boats, that were drawn up at the back of all the beaches, and rowed away after the millions of silver fishes.

'But they don't come no more,' Jeremy said, 'no man knows whyfore.' And, 'Jeremy, *how* can a man on the cliff see pilchards?' Paul asked, last year, or the year before. 'Do they swim near the top?'

'They make an oily mark,' said Jeremy. 'See this water here, wind-rough? Well, the pilchards are swimming eight, maybe ten feet down, in their 'undreds and thousands, and the pull of them makes the water sudden smooth.'

Madge sits down on the Huer's bench, and looks for oily marks for a long time before she opens her letter.

Dear Madge, it goes,

Your Grandmother has telephoned me in some distress and told me that she thinks you must now be told the whole truth about your father. I had hoped to keep it from you a little while yet, but it seems that something you have been saying to her about Paul has made your Grandmother believe that it is urgent. I have always told you that your father was missing in the war, and so he was in a way. He is missing as far as you or I are concerned because during the war he decided he could not stay with me any longer, but that he wanted to marry someone else. Please believe me that although he thought this was my fault, I did not, and we are not the first or only people to find ourselves in this sort of mess. Usually when such a thing happens the children of the marriage stay with their mother, but your father absolutely would not agree to part with his son, even though Paul was little more than a baby at the time. He felt very strongly that he wanted to bring up his son himself, and he made me believe that if I opposed him in this he would ask the court to let him take you too, and that they might agree. Of course, he had a home to offer, and a new mother waiting in the wings, and I had nothing. Because I was afraid of losing both of you, I let him take Paul without a fight. The two of us agreed not to subject ourselves to more pain and upset by allowing visits to either child. Especially once you had a loving step-father I thought it would upset you less not to know anything about it. So you see, Madge dear, it is natural for you to love Paul, indeed it is your duty, for he is your brother. But he can never be anything else to you. I hope, as I have always hoped for him, that he is well and happy, and that you are both enjoying your stay with your Grandmother. We will meet the 3.30 into Paddington on Saturday.

Your loving Mother

Looking up, Madge sees the bay, briefly, wind-streaked rough and smooth, as though the shoals had come back, and she was the first to see them. A little knot of pain and anger lies within her like a stone. Then suddenly tears spout from her eyes, floods of them, and everything goes blurry. 'Oh damn!' she says, rubbing them fiercely away. 'Why do I always do that!' and why, she thinks, couldn't Mummy leave me alone, at least while I'm here? Lying to me like that, lying to me night and day, for years and years, without so much as a flicker in her china-blue eyes, and then suddenly not being able to wait, blurting out suddenly like milk spilling, and hiding behind Gran and hiding behind writing letters! It isn't till the day after tomorrow I go home, and she has stolen my day here away from me, and I hate her! But no raging against her mother can stop the thought *He wanted Paul, and he didn't want me.*

'Well, I won't care,' she tells herself defiantly. 'Other people do want me.' She gets up, and goes back towards Goldengrove, leaving the letter to blow away, and catch on a thorn, and wave there like a flag.

Gran is sitting on the terrace, dozing, under her rug, and she has forgotten to drink her cup of tea. The lemon slice floats around in it, going brown unregarded.

'Hullo, dearie,' she says, waking up when Madge sits down at her feet.

'Oh, Gran, I don't want to go home,' says Madge. 'Couldn't I stay here?'

'You're not going yet, child,' says Gran. 'There's tomorrow. Still tomorrow.'

'Oh, but tomorrow's not enough, Gran. I'm not just saying it; I'm asking with all my heart. Please, Gran, I really need to stay.'

'There, there, dearie. There's no use fretting at what must be. You can come back next year, as usual.' And, how violent people are, before they're old, she thinks to herself. That sly, selfish woman has managed to tell her at last, then, and the letter has upset the child . . . Well, what could be expected, after all, what did they imagine would come of it? Perhaps I should not have said anything . . . not meddled with it at all . . . but it had to come sooner or later, had to come out, sooner or later had to be told . . . there is no escape from the truth. And now she troubles me with all this not wanting to go . . . I daresay things aren't what they ought to be at home, for her. I never approved of all that; I think I remember I never liked her mother at all much. But how the child takes on! 'Try not to take life so hard, dearie,' she says to Madge. 'You must take things as they come.'

And lose them as they go, I suppose, thinks Madge bitterly. And she wanders away under the tall trees, where the strawberries have been, and where now there is a russet carpet to kick through, and a view through the thinning mosaic curtains of shades of gold, to blue beyond, to sea and sky. At the end of the little wood where the land plunges downwards, and she can look through the last trees out to sea, Madge sits.

Well, who does want me? she thinks. They want me, in a distant way, at school, where the teachers like me, and like the things I say, and Jenny Martin does too, most of the time. But not really at home any more. I feel as if I were always trying to squeeze into a place too small for me; I feel that all the time at home. I am always a burden to them, especially to him. I cannot do anything they find pleasant and useful. Only one person has ever found me useful, is that why I love him so? What I really want is to stay with him. I could keep his house orderly, and take him for walks, and talk to him, and read, and write down his books for him. How happy he would be! I would need nothing else. Shutting her eyes she sees the dedication page of his great book: *To Margaret, without whose unfailing help this book could never have been written.* Grander still, she dreams, a book of his famous letters, his famous words, edited by herself, with a brief biographical note, written by herself. And she can't avoid thinking how much easier that would be than passing her own exams, and doing something of her own. And, she thinks, I could look at the sea every day. And it can't be quite time to go and look at Paul's boat yet; I'll go and ask Ralph about it now.

The roses round his cottage door are ragged; a wind-scatter of leaves litters the lawn. She walks through the unlatched door, and finds him sitting alone by the window, fingering his book in braille.

'Hullo?' he says, surprised.

'I've come to tell you that I'm not going home, Ralph,' she says. 'So I shall be able to read to you more than once more, after all. I shall read to you every day.'

'What's happened?' he asks. 'Are you staying on with your grandmother?'

'No,' says Madge. 'I can't make Gran see that I have to stay. So if I'm not going away, I will have to stay here, with you.'

'And I'll wrap you in a blanket at night, and put you in the attic room, and you will come creeping down, I suppose, and read to me when no-one's about,' he says, smiling gently. 'What a splendid idea, Madge. What a shame we can't really.'

'But I mean it, Ralph! Why can't we really?'

'Oh, you know we can't, dear girl. You can't be serious.'

'But I am, I am. How will you manage without me? What will you do? I can't bear to think of you, alone in silence and dark, so I think I had better not leave you.'

'Oh my God,' he says flatly. Then after a pause, 'I shall manage, Madge, as I managed before you came. I shall pay someone to read to me.'

'How horrible!' cries Madge. 'You know that wouldn't be the same! Why shouldn't I stay with you?'

'What would people think? What would they say?'

'You sound like my mother! I can't believe you give a damn about that. I don't.'

'Well then, in the second place,' he says, speaking quietly, in a grey kind of voice, 'because you wouldn't really stay. You'd quickly get tired of it, and go. Why should I expose myself to that?'

'If you let me stay, I will stay,' says Madge simply. 'I will stay for ever.'

'Madge, do you remember reading Milton to me? Milton went blind. He had daughters, and they had to read his books for him, day after day. And they hated him for it. It is a well-known thing that they hated him for it.'

'I couldn't hate you,' Madge declares, unshakeably. 'Not if there were twenty horrible books to be got through every week.'

'Who in hell do you think you are!' he cries, jumping up, and beginning to pace the room. He stumbles on a table, and then, groping, goes and leans against the window as though he were looking out. 'Listen, Madge. I had a wife once. She was a good and generous person. When I went blind she left me. If she couldn't stand it,

104

what makes you think you could? I know she wouldn't have gone if she could have helped it . . . it must be unendurable . . . I often wonder how much of what I am is blindness, and how much is me . . . And you would lighten my darkness, would you? Just some sweet shallow child could walk in here, and do what she could not do? Do you think I could believe that?'

'I would love you,' says Madge miserably, uncomprehending. 'I would read to you. I would tell you what the weather looks like every day. Wouldn't that help?'

'Oh my God,' he says again, clenching his fists. 'Life is very hard on me. I am so lonely. And I allow myself a little pleasure, just a little pleasure in a few hours of human company, and now look what happens! Listen, Madge, you have misread me. You have been very kind, though God knows, I warned you against it. And I have liked having you here, but there was nothing personal in it. Not *you*, you understand, but just your eyes and voice. I am sorry about this, but learn from it not to be so trusting, and some day you may even look back and thank me for it. You see, Madge, nobody can be trusted. People only love, or sacrifice themselves, to serve some need of their own. When my wife left me I came to see that it is wrong to expect anything from anybody. The best of us cannot be trusted with another's happiness.'

Madge hears him out and says nothing. She stares at his hollow face, with emptiness where eyes should be, and pain-lines at the corners of mouth and eyes.

'Madge, dear,' he says after a while, 'you are wrong to trust me. I am not going to trust you.'

'Oh, Ralph,' she says dismayed. 'Something much worse than going blind has happened to you!'

'What could be worse?' he says, morosely.

'Something worse *has*! You are all full of locked doors marked *No Kindness* and *Reading Voices Only* and not letting people help, not believing they will!'

'Madge, some wounds cannot be healed, some things are beyond helping, and cannot be put right. That's just how it is.'

'So even if I loved you, that wouldn't help?'

'I have liked your company, Madge. You have a lovely voice. But even if you loved me, I wouldn't trust you, or wish to rely on you.'

'That's it – that's what's worse – feeling like that is worse than darkness!'

'Oh that, Madge,' he says, shrugging his shoulders. 'That happens to everyone. That's called growing up.'

'It won't happen to me,' says Madge.

*　　*　　*

It won't happen to me, she weeps, going back through the trees towards the house. She throws herself down, and lies in the leaves weeping, till she feels sick, and dizzy with the force of her sobs. Then she remembers that she was supposed to be going to meet Paul on the beach, and she gets up, and staggers towards the cliff path. Coming this way to the gate, through the thickest part of the wood where rhododendron and escallonia grow rampant under the high branches and bamboo plants make little clumps of jungle, she passes the wooden hut where the boat is laid up in winter, and, with the instinct of a sick animal going to ground, she opens the door, and goes in, to cry in it. In the dry dusty gloom, however, her tears dry up, and she sits, staring aimlessly, sore-eyed. And, a broken heart really does *hurt*! she thinks, astonished, for really I am in pain, in bodily pain under my breastbone, and I always thought it was only a figure of speech. And it's a dreadful oppressive sort of pain, much worse than toothache, because where is the medicine for it, and how could it be healed? It is like that awful lurching sickness that comes when you realize you are actually hurt badly; like the moment you find that your leg is not sprained but broken, or see that the cut is deep and will need stitches. Not me, but Paul. Not me, but my lovely voice.

Vaguely her idle eyes notice that she is staring at something like a huge umbrella – a pole with cloth rolled round two-thirds of its length. She doesn't know what it is. She doesn't care what anything is. But at last she puts out a hand, and pulls at it. A triangle of faded brown-red cloth starts to unwind from the pole. It is the mast and sail from the little boat. Funny, she thinks, I didn't know it had a sail, and yet I do know, exactly. She tries to lift it, expecting it to be very heavy, but it isn't much heavier than an oar, and she drags it easily enough away from its cobwebby corner, and over towards the light. It takes several tries to pick it up ready to carry, for the way to do it is to get it onto her shoulder, nicely balanced, and it is thicker and heavier at the bottom end, so most of the length has to be in front of her, with her hand on it steadying it. It won't happen to me, Madge tells herself, starting carefully down the cliff path with her burden.

Paul has long since gone home, given her up. A pale afternoon silvers the silken sea. A quiet tide tosses and whispers on the sand. Smooth gentle waves roll in a great curve onto the beaches, like liquid emerald flowing, like liquid sapphire. Madge puts down the mast beside the boat and rests from carrying it. The ache that isn't after all a figure of speech is still with her. In a while she gets up, and tries to fit the mast into the boat. You have to slide it into the socket with the mast held at a slant that exactly matches the tilt of the boat, and it takes her several tries. When it is in she sees a little peg dangling, fixed to the foot of the mast on a frayed loop of rope, and she sees it is meant to go through both socket and mast, for a hole is drilled for it. She turns the mast in the socket till the peg will go through. Then she walks round and round the boat, with the sheet in her hand, unwinding the sail. Then she pushes and heaves the boat to move it down to the water. Paul's blue-green tacky paint comes off on her hands. But although it seems, since the storm freed it, to be riding high and easy on the slope of the sand, the boat is hard to move. Madge has to squat down with her back to the stern, and lean her full weight on it, pushing with her feet, before it shifts. But once it has started to move she can keep it moving, leaning her shoulder against it, down to the water's edge. And there the waves lift it, and the tilt suddenly straightens, and the mast swings upright, with the sail flapping on it. Giving one more thrust to the stern Madge wades after it, up to her waist in the cool water, and clambers over the side. She catches the sheet at the corner of the sail, and sits holding it, and the sail billows and pulls, and the boat moves out quite quickly on the calm water. A sudden joy sweeps away the pain that has oppressed her. I am going back, thinks Madge. I will go to Godrevy, I will see the garden on the rock, and the great light shining out . . .

She shivers in her wet clothes, in the cold open air. A light gust of sea-breeze tugs the sail, and it tears into ribbons, the rotten fabric splitting without a sound. The rags of sail flutter and pull, and the boat moves more slowly now, feeling heavy and sluggish in the water. And it's more than wet socks and sandals Madge suddenly feels round her ankles; the boat is half full of the sea. Suddenly panic-struck, looking round at the dark shore far behind her, Madge leans abruptly forwards, to reach the empty paint tin, and bail with it, and feels her weight take her feet right through the sodden rotten wood of the bottom of the boat. It won't, she tells herself, sinking. It won't happen . . .

*   *   *

'I suppose she's still waiting for me on the beach,' says Paul, when Madge isn't there for tea. 'I'll go and look for her.'

He sees first that the boat has gone, and then he sees Madge, lying huddled and wet on the shining sand, where the Frenchman lay that morning. He walks steadily and slowly towards her, and looks down at her pallid face, pillowed on the beach, and her sand-laden, seaweed hair. Her left arm lies along her body, with paint on the upturned palm, all that is left to show for the boat. 'Bloody girls!' says Paul. *Bloody girls!* I spend hours and hours on that boat, nearly all my time here, and she hardly helped at all, and it was lovely, the best thing to play in I have ever had, and all she can think to do with it is *this*! 'Get up, Madge!' he says savagely, nudging her with his foot. 'Oh please, do get up!' Madge opens her eyes, and with a slight convulsion vomits sea-water. She groans, and sits up, and vomits again.

'What the hell did you do that for?' says Paul, staring at her coldly.

'I wanted to drown, I think,' says Madge, emptying water out of her shoe. 'Or – I remember now – I wanted to sail to Godrevy.'

'Sail?' says Paul, 'You found a sail for her? Well if that's the mast, sticking just out of the water out there, you didn't go nearly far out enough. That water's too shallow to drown in, especially since you can swim perfectly well, Madge, you know you can. Get up and come home; you look cold.'

'Don't be angry, Paul. Paul, I'm sorry about the boat.'

'I am angry,' he says. 'I can't not be it. And it's not the boat it's about, it's you.'

Half-way up the cliff path he says, 'Here, Madge, put my sweater on.' She is shivering, and seems hardly able to walk. He pulls one of her arms across his shoulders, winds his free arm round her waist, and brings her on. Her trembling shakes him. Why this? Why this?

he thinks. Oh, Madge, you should have stayed and played with me. I love you better than anyone.

Then he has pulled her through the door, and she stands leaning on him, dripping water on the tiled hall floor, and he calls loudly for Gran and Amy.

'It was an accident,' he tells them later, when Madge is safely in bed. 'The bottom of the boat was rotten. I knew that. But she went down when I wasn't there, and tried to sail it . . . it was an accident.'

'Everything in life is that,' says Gran. And I remember the last time that boat was used, she thinks, when Madge's father took her, and she was a very small child then, and sailed all the way to . . .

'She *said* she was going to Godrevy,' Paul chimed in, 'though she knows you forbade us to launch the boat.'

'To Godrevy,' says Gran, in an exasperated voice. 'Oh, Paul, she needs her father. She needs your father. Say what they like, they were needed where they were.'

'So she *is* my sister,' says Paul. 'I always thought so. But we're not supposed to know about it, are we?'

Gran shakes her head. She is rocking fiercely in her old chair to comfort herself. 'Storms, storms,' she says, 'they touch me no longer. I am home and dry. But my heart bleeds for those who are out in them still!'

'The wind has dropped now, Gran, and the night is calm,' says Paul. 'Never fear, Gran.'

'I have no fear for you, Paul dear,' she says. 'None for you.'

*   *   *

All ready to go, Paul stands beside his bulging holdall in the hall, and restively lets Amy brush his fair, sunbleached head. Mr Arthur stands waiting with the car outside the door.

'Goodbye, dearie, come again soon,' says Gran, kissing him. 'Don't worry. It's only a chill, and she'll be over it in no time.'

110

'Wish I had caught one too!' he said, smiling ruefully.
' 'Bye, Gran.'

Going slowly – she always goes slowly nowadays –
upstairs to her room, Gran watches. She can see below
her, beside the beach, the little railway lines running
along to the station. As she watches, Paul comes onto
the platform, waves, and climbs into the train. It gathers
breath, and chuffs along, sending smoke balls up over
the garden as it goes. Gran goes along then to the spare
room, where Madge lies in bed, weeping. 'What's the
matter?' Gran asks, sitting in the chair beside the bed.

'All the golden leaves are blowing down,' says Madge,
looking at the branches outside the window.

'They are lovely while they last,' says Gran, 'aren't
they?'

In a little while the doctor comes. He arrives looking
cheerful, saying, 'Well, well, you've grown a good
deal since the year you had measles here, and even
more since mumps!' But he soon looks grave. 'There's
a feverish chill, and a rheum in the lungs,' he tells
Gran, 'as you usually find with people who've been
in the water. There's also the shock to her system
– nervous shock, you know. And the fever may
get worse before it's better. We must watch her
carefully and keep her quiet.'

'Shall I send for her mother?' Gran asks, in Madge's
hearing, on the landing, beyond the door ajar.

'Well now,' says the doctor carefully, 'above all she
needs peace; no excitements, no upsets. You must
judge for yourself.'

When the fever gets worse Madge's mother does
come, briefly, down on the overnight sleeper to
Penzance, and back on the afternoon train, and Madge
tossing and talking to herself hardly remembers at
all; only when she wakes up suddenly cool and
peaceful, and feeling very weak, there are flowers
and grapes in the room, and a huge box of chocolates,

111

though they turn out to be all plain chocolate, and Madge likes only milk ones. Pity Paul's not here, she thinks, and gives them to Amy.

The evenings draw in. Amy lights fires behind the mica windows of the stove in the bedroom. The harbour lights, the squat one halfway along Smeaton's Quay, and the tall one at the end of it, and the brilliant green flare on the end of the little pier, all light up earlier and earlier each day. And like a low-hovering golden star, Godrevy answers them. The weather is soft; watery, washed with pale colours. Every few days the doctor comes with his gold watch chain looped across in front of him, and sees Madge, and takes her pulse, and at last lets her get out of bed, though not into the open air.

Down in the warm kitchen Amy sits with Walt, wearing her diamond engagement ring, looking at America on a map. 'You should have heard her when she was feverish,' she tells him, 'talking to herself, rambling on about the lumber room, and shut doors, and reading to that Professor. I don't know what hasn't been going on there. Educated, posh people that ought to know better so stupid and cruel you'd not believe it.'

Day follows day. Madge looks out of windows, and reads. Her teachers send her bundles of books from the school library, and brisk sympathetic letters. She seems very limp and uninterested. She looks pale. The doctor tells Gran that depression following a shock to the system is common and never permanent; Gran frets at Madge's small appetite, at her pale cheeks, and gets Jeremy to send mackerel for breakfast. The year drifts into winter. An icy pallor hangs in bleached distances over the sea. Nothing happens. Madge gazes out of windows.

Then at last something happens. Paul comes. He rings on the door a little after the three o'clock train has puffed in, and comes in, still unwinding his scarf, to say, 'Hullo, Madge! I came to see you.'

Madge seems not to have enough energy to be surprised, but she is pleased. The first smile, the first real smile Gran has seen in a long while, spreads over her face.

'Hullo, Paul,' she says. He has come straight from school, and looks oddly adult and smart in his school shirt and tie. 'Gran says you're allowed to go out today, if you want to,' he says. 'Will you come to the beach with me, Madge?'

'Oh, yes!' she says, jumping up, and clearly they have it all planned, for here is Amy, smiling, coming with her coat held out for her, and Gran with her scarf and gloves. So the two of them go down through the rose garden, where a few frozen roses, unopened, forlornly survive, and out of the back gate, brushing past the hedge of escallonia that even in this chill moist weather gives a trace of its hot spicy summer smell. Down through the tangle of brambles beside the path, hand in hand, to the lonely sands, with their scatter of weed and shell, and a winter glaze on the water, and a winter harshness in the voice of the waves. Once there Paul runs and shouts, and finds a stone to throw into the sea, and Madge smiling, hands in pockets, walks after him.

He looks round at her, and sees overhead the cottage on the cliff. 'Has that Professor guy been to see you?' he asks.

'Once or twice. A bit embarrassing really. He's gone back to London now.'

'Does he write?'

'No, he just sent me a book with this in,' and she brings from her pocket a crumpled printed slip of paper, decorated with printer's flowers, and bearing the words *With the Author's compliments*.

'Ugh!' says Paul, 'I always did think he was a creep!'

'Yes, didn't you!' she says, smiling again, wanly.

'Did they tell you,' he asks, looking at his feet, and kicking the sand, 'that I'm really your brother?'

'Yes.'

'I think I always knew, really, but you didn't seem to. Are you glad, Madge?'

'It's too late, Paul,' she says, gazing out to sea. 'It was cruel of them not to tell us all that long time when I really needed you, when I wanted a brother so badly . . . but now it's too late. It just made me feel as if I had lost you, too.'

'Oh, come off it, Madge,' he protests. 'It got me here, for a start. I said, "If she's my sister I'm seeing her whenever I like, and starting now, I'm going to go down and see her, because she's ill." And they just looked helplessly at each other, and said yes. So here I am.'

'I'm glad you're here.'

'What happens when you're better? Will you be somewhere I can come and see you?'

'Yes, they're sending me back to school. Mother wanted to send me to some place in Switzerland, but Higgy made her change her mind.'

'Who's Higgy?'

'Miss Higgins, the headmistress. She said it would be a criminal waste of talent if I didn't go on.'

'Well, you are rather brainy, I suppose, for a girl. That's good, then.'

'I'm sorry, Paul,' she says, 'I haven't been out for so long, I'm getting cold already.'

'The trot up the cliff will warm you,' he says, taking her arm.

At the turn of the path they stop, and look out for a moment over beach and harbour and town, over the serenely restless sea, tossing and dreaming eternally in the great bight of the bay.

'I don't see what you meant just now, when you said it was too late, Madge, honest I don't,' says Paul.

'Lucky you, Paul!' She turns her back on the wide view and walks slowly on. Behind her in the early lilac dusk the yellow light of Godrevy winks on. 'Ralph said some things couldn't be mended, some things were too late to put right. And I just thought that sounded sick and wicked, I didn't understand what he meant at all. But now I see.'

Unleaving

The house is full of voices, full of movements. Whichever room one is in, one can hear in other rooms the sounds of talk and coming and going. The windows are open to the sea, to the murmuring wash of the waves, and the salt tangy air. The front door stands wide, admitting a quadrilateral of sunlight onto the carpet, and small Beth, her fair head blazing white with day, runs in, and out again, seeing and not seeing the meticulously illuminated Turkey pattern, the grandfather clock counting its way towards four, and Gran making her way downstairs for tea, holding the banister rail all the way, patient at her own slowness. Reaching the foot of the stairs, she straightens her cardigan, and advances with careful steadiness towards the living-room door, hand outstretched for the brass doorknob. The hand has crooked finger joints and three rings, and a fretwork of blue veins beneath the brown freckles.

*   *   *

There had been a journey. A night journey, in a train with prickly plush on the headrests that had indented Madge's leaning cheek, a train with sweating windows obscuring the only thing to be seen – the occasional light nearer or farther away in the passing featureless dark. Madge was in uniform, and her nightclothes were in a sports bag, for the trunks were all locked away in the

119

school attic; there had only just been time to catch the night train when the telegram arrived.

So she has reached the change point – St Erth for St Ives – in a leached and pallor-struck darkness, with an hour to wait for the first train on the branch line. The darkness slowly leaks away, and instead there comes a grainy greyness, like an old photograph, that makes you frown when you look, in which you can see some distance, but nothing clearly, and more of the gleam on the polished railway line than of anything else. Madge is entirely alone on the platform. The train arrives, and is empty. She gets into it alone, and it leaves. Into the rising morning light.

There is colour in the land by the time it reaches Lelant. Watery pale colour, suffused with gold. Pale sands, pale sea, so glazed and shining with sloping light that it looks silken grey; under Carrack Gladden, and not a single footprint on the wide, wide open sands, only the white waves moving. The train runs into the station, up to the buffers, that final full stop. Madge struggles with the door, opens it, gets out. There is nobody waiting for the train; it will stand for an hour before it returns.

Madge has been all night without sleep; she is light-headed. She feels as insubstantial as the town, mistily present, hovering vaguely in the gentle dawn. The sea in the harbour is shallow, creeping softly, with little waves breaking at the last moment, in small hushed splashings, as though not to wake, as though to come tiptoe up to the leaning boats, and quiet dew-sleeked quays. What do I feel? Madge thinks. Do I feel anything? I have come, that is all.

From the station to the beach, and her footprints on it first, lonely, winding along the waves' edge. She takes off her shoes. She comes up the path, through the back gate, into the garden – a bird is singing – and walks across the grass barefoot. There is a gossamer web laden with shining dew strung between the handles of the french windows. To enter she must break it. She stands still. And turning, looks out to sea. The dawn has triumphed. The sun has risen out of the blurry wisps of restraining cloud; the sea is blue, blue, and breaks loudly white, and Godrevy has come out of the misty margin of the sky, and stands on the horizon, black rock, white lighthouse, the endless burst of surf at the foot of the rock frozen by distance.

The house is utterly silent. The shutters are up, refusing the dawn. Madge looks at the spider seal upon the door. When Paul is here there is sometimes a little ribbon of paper from the edge of a sheet of stamps glued across a door to telltale it has been opened, and Amy, Gran's pretty maid, grumbles, scratching the scraps off the paint with her varnished fingernail. Madge has so acute a sensation that she is not there – that, ghostlike, she must enter without trace – that the sparkling trap on the door handle deters her. She reaches in her coat pocket for her door key – she has had a key to Goldengrove some three years now – and walks around the house to the front door, away from the sea, and lets herself in.

The house is silent within, and dark. Madge puts down her shoes and her bag, and hangs up her coat. Her naked feet, dew-wet, leave ghost footprints on the polished floor. She turns the cool brass doorknob, and goes into the darkened room beyond the living-room door.

*   *   *

Tea is set on a white cloth. Lavish tea. Round it sit Gran and her summer houseful – her daughter, Harriet, suntanned and sun drowsy, and Tom, her son-in-law, full of holiday cheerfulness, and their three children: Peter, and Sarah, and Beth. And how old are they now? Gran wonders. I always need reminding. Peter is eight, by now, 'so Sarah is six, and as clever as clever,' she says, smiling at Sarah.

'Yes. Sarah thinks poems are *true*,' says small Beth, the youngest, and the deep one.

'Here, child,' says Gran to her upturned freckled face, under a bush of bleached pale hair. 'Have *cream* on it.'

'I've already got jam,' says Beth, thoughtfully. 'Quite a lot.'

'Have cream as well,' says Gran, extending towards the scone on the flowered plate a thickly laden spoon. 'You'll like it with jam, I daresay.'

'I like it here!' says Beth. 'I like your house, Gran.' And all the adults laugh.

*   *   *

That house was always a good place. Mr Fielding wanted it, wanted it for himself and his sons, and is appalled when he learns how his mother has left it. 'It's quite inappropriate,' he tells the lawyer. 'Not right at all. I had always assumed it would be mine and Paul's. She can't have thought what she was doing.'

'This will was not made recently,' says the lawyer. 'It was made the day after the settlement of your divorce, which gave custody of the son to you, and the daughter to your wife. Your mother had plenty of time to reconsider it had she wished.'

'But . . . it is most distressing. There ought to be something I can do.'

'Take advice if you wish, sir,' says the lawyer, shaking his head. 'But merely to leave property to a grand-daughter instead of to a son is hardly grounds . . .'

And Madge, to whom her father's distress is shocking and distasteful, says, 'I don't want it. Let him have it.'

'I advise you to say nothing of that kind, till *you* have taken advice, Miss Fielding,' says the lawyer quietly.

'Then let Paul have it,' says Madge. 'If it's mine, surely I could give it to Paul.'

'Thank you, Madge, but I'd rather share it than have it,' says Paul.

'Quite so,' says the lawyer, looking with ill-concealed chill at their father. 'Surely some arrangement could be found . . .'

'And what of money to maintain it?' Mr Fielding demands. He gestures towards Madge. 'Her mother hasn't anything, and she gets nothing from me; and a place like this . . .'

'There is some money with the house,' says the lawyer. 'Enough to maintain it if Miss Fielding wishes to keep rather than to sell it.'

'And a residue to me, I suppose?'

'A substantial one. Perhaps you do not realize the extent of your mother's estate? Shall I read the rest of the will?'

* * *

Gran sits like a queen among the teacups, pouring the pale amber liquid from a pot into the little fluted flowery cups, and naming her family one by one as she passes the cups among them. The cream and jam have produced a brief deep silence among the children, their fingers sticky in spite of licking and surreptitious wiping on their shorts.

'Can we go back to the beach?' they are asking in a moment or two. 'Oh, can we? Oh, please!'

'You've been there all day,' says Harriet. 'And all the grownups are tired of being there with you.'

'*I'll* take them this time,' says Gran, getting up from her chair, both hands down on the chair arms to raise herself.

'Oh, no, Ma-in-law,' says Tom. 'Not you. I'll go.'

'Oh, Gran, yes, Gran, oh, *Gran's* coming!' the children cry.

'I can manage,' says Gran. 'I had a rest this afternoon. I can get down the path if I take my time, you know. I'll be sensible and take them to the big beach instead of our own little one, and then perhaps, Tom love, you'll bring the car down to fetch me back by suppertime. It's the climb up, you know . . . but I can manage *down*.'

And off she goes, through the french windows, with the children all around her, tugging her skirt and hands, shouting and leaping, through the garden, through the gate, down the path to the beach, to the sea. The oldest child, solemn Peter, is carting Gran's chair and her knitting. Their voices, as they descend the cliff path, fade; and left behind in the peace among the crumbs and jam and unwashed teacups – someone has licked the cream spoon cloudy clean – the grownups smile and sigh.

I should come down more often! Gran thinks, as the beach opens wide, opens great space around her, and the waves run vaulting towards her, and climb on each other's back, and leapfrog over the rocks in bursts of pearly foam, and her eyes travel out to sea, far away, beyond Godrevy, beyond the lighthouse on its dark cleft rock. She stumbles ankle-deep in slithering silken sand, and the wind runs fingers through her grey silk blouse, and bellies her cardigan behind her, and ruffles her hair; and, suddenly skittish, she skips and runs a few steps among her pack of hallooing and circling children, wheeling and crying around her like gulls, though Peter now solemnly tries to make the deck chair stay up, and curses mildly but passionately as he nips his fingers.

Soon she is sitting down, and fumbling in her bag, not for her knitting, but for some sweets. 'Don't tell,' she says to them, as she hands out forbidden goodies. 'Don't tell, and wash your teeth well tonight.'

'It's treasure,' says Sarah. 'Treasure. I'll bury mine. Deep and secret.'

'Why?' asks small Beth.

'I'm a pirate.'

'So am I!'

'Let's bury it all.'

Gran closes her eyes, which are watering in all that wind. Their voices come to her.

'Bury it all in the ground forever.'

'Food for worms!'

'That's not chocolate, silly' – Peter's voice – 'that's dead people!'

'Ugh!'

'Better be food for worms than have worms for food.'

'Oh, I don't know, though. You could always sick up worms for food, but once you're food for worms that's irrevocable.'

'What does irrevocable mean, Peter?'

'It means you can't take it back. It's forever.'

'Well, my chocolate is pirate gold, and worms don't eat that.'

'You'd better *tell* them it's gold, you know, Sarah, because it does look and smell awfully like chocolate, and they might make a terrible mistake.'

'I'll come and bury you in a minute!'

'*Oliver Cromwell is buried and dead*,' sings Peter, in a thin high voice, digging with his wooden spade. '*Heigh, ho, buried and dead!*'

Gran sits, eyes closed, looking out to sea.

* * *

There had been a funeral. A walking funeral, for it was a local custom to have it so. Six men wearing black standing at the door of Goldengrove, the minister with his black book open in his hands, and a crowd of folk of all kinds.

'*Whether we live, we live unto the Lord*,' says the minister, as the six bring the coffin out to him, the sun bright for a moment on the brass handles, and then muffled again in clouds. The wind lifts off the ring of

125

lilies and tosses it to the ground. Someone replaces it. *'Or whether we die, we die unto the Lord; whether we live, therefore, or die, we are the Lord's.'*

The coffin begins to move up the drive onto the road. Mr Fielding goes behind it, and his second wife beside him. And Madge and Paul, in new black clothes, come next. All the way down Tregenna Hill people join them. Anyone who had sold Gran tea or apples leaves the shop to walk. Down the turns of the steep road, and the coffin sloping on the shoulders of the bearers as they pick their way carefully over the cobbles, shiny with moisture from the rain that stopped only an hour since. Where the road turns sharply above Pedn Olva Point, the minister halts, perhaps to give a respite to the bearers. The harbour lies in view below them.

'Therefore shall they receive the crown of royal dignity, and the diadem of beauty from the Lord's hand . . .' Madge, standing miserably in the drab crowd, lets her eyes travel down to the harbour full of grey, troubled water, and the deserted quays against which exploding towers of foam mount and fall. A black dog rushes to and fro, barking wildly at the leaping spray.

'In the eyes of the foolish they seemed to have died,
And their departure was accounted to be their hurt,
And their journeying away from us to be their ruin;
But they are in peace. . .'

Suddenly an explosion cuts through the minister's voice, a bang like a gunshot. The maroon leaves an arc of fire in the sky for a short second, launches a brief green star in the daylight sky. Smoke billows thickly around the doors of the lifeboat shed, and a red pennant glides up to the masthead on its roof. The coffin-bearers shift uneasily. The crowd of mourners look at them;

a second maroon finds them all silent, waiting, even the prayer suspended. The second summons cannot be ignored. The bearers put up their hands to the coffin, raise it from their shoulders, and lower it to the ground. One of them – Jeremy the fisherman – looks around with a brief glance to the minister, before all six break into a run, and clatter away down the street. The coffin lies on the sleek cobbles, with its flower wreath askew.

'Really!' mutters Mr Fielding, distressed, nearly uttering his outrage. But the minister is not disconcerted.

'Well, my good people,' he says. 'You see how it is. Now who will come forward to help bring our sister on her way to her last rest?' There is a moment of confusion. A little group of men measure up to each other to match the height of their shoulders, and one brother borrows another's dark coat, and struggles into it. Gently the coffin is lifted again. The minister resumes his reading. *'For even if in the sight of men they be punished, their hope is full of immortality . . .'* but all the mourners' eyes are on the harbour below them. The lifeboat in its trolley is being trundled out. It fills the waterside street, looms high above the group of men beside it. At a sinister slow speed it is towed along the quay, the spraybursts clawing at its tall sides as it goes. The faint sound of the coxswain's distant shouting punctuates the minister's voice. But the cortège is moving on now, past the viewpoint, and down the narrow street. They begin to sing, a river of voices, flowing:

'There is a land of pure delight,
Where saints immortal reign,
Infinite day excludes the night,
And pleasures banish pain . . .'

Down they go to the foot of the hill, past the parish

church, and along Fore Street towards the chapel, singing:

> *'There everlasting spring abides*
> *And never withering flowers . . .'*

while the wind, ripping through the narrow passages and courts between Fore Street and the harbour, ruffles and tears at the pages of the hymn books, and blows the sound of voices through the town in broken gusts:

> *'Death like a narrow sea divides*
> *This heavenly land from ours . . .'*

and at the end of Fore Street, where the path of the mourners comes out upon the quay, all eyes are for the water, and the lifeboat can be seen, just rounding the end of Smeaton's Quay, and meeting, bows under, the white rage of the storm. It looks small, small, now it is in the water, and tossed like a cork float on the contemptuous strength of the sea. In a moment it is out of sight.

> *'But timorous mortals start and shrink,*
> *To cross this narrow sea . . .*
> *And linger shivering on the brink*
> *And fear to launch away . . .'*

Madge sings too. And could it be true, she thinks, could it possibly be only a journey to some other place? Of course not, not possibly. And yet, she asks herself, remembering the other morning, when she came up to the house alone, entered alone, very early, where is Gran now?

> *'Could we but climb where Moses stood,'*

the swelling voices assert all around her,

*   *   *

'And view the landscape o'er,
Not Jordan's stream, nor Death's cold flood
Should fright us from the shore!'

The coffin is taken into the chapel, and prayed over. The congregation spills over into the street; some people whom Madge hardly knows are crying. ('Your mother had many friends among us,' the minister has said to Mr Fielding, whose eyes are dry.)

Madge hardly hears the prayers. The close atmosphere of the little chapel oppresses her, makes her feel faint. In a while Paul takes her arm and leads her out. She sits down on the step and gasps the cold air like someone saved from drowning.

'Are you all right, Madge?' asks Paul, anxiously. She nods. A little group of women, detached from the others waiting in the street, stand down on the shore where they can watch for the lifeboat. In the full harbour the moored boats heave and toss on their ropes, and the waves break loudly through the sound of singing from within.

In a while the coffin is carried out again, and the procession moves on, over the shoulder of the hill, through narrow streets of fishermen's cottages, and out onto the farther shore, where the green burying ground slopes down to the Atlantic surf. There is a great amphitheatre of grassy hill, curving around from The Island with its little chapel atop it, to the dark rocks of Clodgy Point. A moon of golden sand lies between, at the foot of the slope. And onto this shore the great surf rolls and roars. Half a mile deep, the breaking waves come on, in a fury of whiteness, and, beyond, the sea stretches leaden-grey, ruffled and troubled as far as the eye can see, with the sky pressing low, rain-threatening, above it. The force of the wind strikes them, and the vastness of the sound of the surf. Not only the soft plosive ejaculations of the breaking waves, but beneath that, continuous, like a great engine, like a wild beast, a deep unceasing roar, the grinding of the sea bed – water on rock, element against element to eternity.

And the mourners pick their way down the path, between the gravestones – church to the left, chapel to the right – towards the twin chapels of rest, nestling close together, but still two, one for each kind. Safely sorted out, the dead lie waiting for a judgement, which can hardly, thinks Madge, make *that* distinction between them. She is expected, she discovers, to stand close by the earthy rim of the grave, to see the coffin into the ground; *'earth to earth, ashes to ashes, dust to dust; in sure and certain hope of the Resurrection . . .'*

Now it is nearly over. The crowd begins to sing again, in loud unison, pitting their voices into the teeth of the wind.

> *'Ah lovely appearance of death,*
> *What sight upon earth is so fair!*
> *Not all the gay pageants that breathe*
> *Can with a dead body compare . . .'*

There is a sudden tremor through the crowd. And they all look out to sea, to see the lifeboat, barely visible in the storm-tossed water, making its way back, and just coming into view around Clodgy Point, dipping in and out of sight behind walls of grey salt water, but sending up high and clear the green flare turning white that means 'All saved.' Its mission is safely accomplished, and all is well. The singers do not hesitate or falter, but relief and joy sound in their voices triumphant as they steadily sing on:

> *'With solemn delight I survey*
> *The corpse when the spirit is fled*
> *In love with the beautiful clay*
> *And longing to lie in its stead.'*

It is suddenly all too much for Madge, who runs away, down the green slope, dodging between the granite crosses and the coffin-shaped marble memorials, to leap over the wall at the foot of the churchyard, race across the Zennor road, and jump down onto the sands, to run along the seething margin of the sea. Faintly the singing pursues her:

'*In love with the beautiful clay*
And longing to lie in its stead!'

but she runs, fiercely, till the surf blots out all other sound, and leaping from rock to rock at the end of the sands, she climbs the Island to the top. Watching the bursts of foam at its jagged foot, with spiralling flights of nameless feeling she stands there, wind-lashed, and, soon, drenched in rain and spray, till she has seen the lifeboat safely in.

*   *   *

'I've come to take you home, Ma-in-law,' says Tom. Gran starts a little as she hears him, for she was far away.

'Come on, kids!' he bellows, and, gathering up chair, knitting, and old lady, he Pied Pipers with her along the beach, while a litter of children trails and scampers behind them. In a while the bath at Goldengrove will have a long shoal of sand lying in the bottom of it, and Harriet's goodnight story will be stopped less than halfway through, its audience all asleep.

There have been other deaths, other rescues. Only last year, Gran tells her family over the dinner table, with an avalanche of wax cascading down the red candle in its silver candlestick, the lifeboat was called out in the depth of darkness, and the wind blowing fit to lift the tiles off the roof at Goldengrove. 'When I hear the maroon,' says Gran, 'I can't sleep again till I know they are safe back in. That time they were gone a long while; in the morning I could see the lifeboat station doors still standing wide – you can see from here if you look, from the bedroom window. I went down after breakfast to ask, you know, and I met Mrs Nance, the coxswain's wife, on the quay, waiting around, poor soul, and not looking as though she'd slept a wink all night, and the sea still making an uproar. When they came, almost midday – that's sixteen hours they had been out – they had four living and two dead aboard. Terrible. A terrible thing.'

'You shouldn't be troubled by it, Mother,' says Harriet. 'You surely need your sleep. You have been very ill and it isn't as if you could *do* anything.'

'Well, no, Hal love. You're quite right, I daresay, but I can't help the way I'm made. Then perhaps you're not so right. One can't do anything; is that a reason not to feel anything?'

'Well, most people manage it, Ma-in-law,' says Tom, grinning at her.

'When I was a girl I knew a boatman quite well,' says Gran, 'who was lost at sea in a lifeboat accident. And you know, that man feared drowning, feared it greatly. I remember once he told me that he regretted having learned to swim. Most fishermen don't, he said, and it was better not, that drowning if it comes may be quick and easy. And you know, I so *admire* that; out they go, only when the weather has defeated some other souls, and, going, they risk for themselves what they save others from. So brave – like loving – and they make so little of it, take it so for granted.'

There is a brief pause, then Harriet, changing the subject, says, 'I meant to tell you, by the way, that twice this week I've seen someone hanging about the gate, looking into the garden.'

'Oh? That sounds sinister, Hal. What sort of someone?'

'Not to worry, Mother; he wasn't wearing a dirty

raincoat; he was a very respectable-looking, upright, elderly gent.'

'Grey-haired and with an ebony cane?' says Tom. 'I saw him too. He really must be lurking about.'

'Well, next time anyone sees him,' says Gran, 'ask him in for tea, and we can find out *why* he's lurking.'

'Don't be ridiculous, Mother,' says Harriet. 'You can't ask a total stranger in for tea. He might be a burglar.'

'That's just what she would do, though,' says Tom, vastly amused. 'She'd ask a burglar to take tea, and interview him on why he was doing it. Can't you just see it?'

'*Would* I?' says Gran, delighted. 'Well, perhaps I would. So next time anyone sees the burglar, just invite him in, and we'll see what I'll do.'

'You're incorrigible, Mother,' says Harriet. 'And, no, dear, you can't have coffee, you know it keeps you awake.'

'What with coffee and lifeboats, it's amazing you sleep at all,' says Tom, still smiling.

'As far as *coffee* goes,' says Gran thoughtfully, 'it was Oxford that ruined my character. Definitely. It's a very immoral place. I'll have a little brandy, then, please, since *you* are all drinking; why should I be left out? The lifeboats, I suppose, are from further back still.'

'I really believe, Ma-in-law,' says Tom, 'that nobody gets as skinless as you except by being born that way.'

'Oh, no,' says Gran. 'We're all born fairly coarse and cheerful, *I* think; it's life that flays us.'

'Coarse and cheerful certainly would describe our lot,' says Harriet.

A thin, high-pitched wail sounds eerily from the landing. 'Sarah dreaming again,' says Gran. 'I'm on my way up. I'll see to her and forego my brandy. You two enjoy your coffee in peace.'

*　　*　　*

One would not think of Oxford as a place where characters are ruined, to judge by the earnestness with which Miss Higgins wants her pupils to go there. Madge only expresses a little uncertainty about it, and she is summoned to the headmistress's study, ostensibly to talk about entrance exams, and which colleges Madge is to try for.

'Correct me if I'm wrong, Margaret,' Miss Higgins says, 'but do you not own a house now, a house by the sea? In Cornwall, I seem to remember?'

'Yes,' says Madge. 'Goldengrove. I inherited it.'

'I will tell you why I ask. I have a friend who needs a house to rent for this summer. Is it a large house?'

'Yes. But I don't let it,' Madge says.

'He is a university professor, Margaret, from Oxford. An old friend of mine. He wants to take a reading party of undergraduates. I thought an acquaintance with some studious people might be of use to you, my dear. Will you be there yourself, do you think?'

'No,' says Madge. 'When it was Gran's we went there a lot; but now it's mine we can't. It's all shut up and there's nobody to run it, and my mother won't let me be down there by myself.'

'Cornwall is very pleasant. Doesn't your mother sometimes go with you?'

'You know how my family quarrelled,' says Madge. 'It's my father's mother's house. My mother won't set foot in it. She wants me to sell it – "cash it in," as she calls it.'

'Well, how would it be if Mr Jones and his wife opened it up and ran it for their students, and paid you rent for it, and you went down there too? Might not that work out rather well? I will speak to your mother, if I may.'

*   *   *

So Goldengrove is unlocked and opened up for Mrs

Jones, who walks around it, liking it, with lists in her hands, and asks Madge before she opens the linen cupboard for sheets, or uses the china. Madge helps all she can, but cannot imagine the house as full of people as Mrs Jones intends, and is awestruck by the college servant in his shirtsleeves, unpacking books, and is overwhelmed by suddenly missing Gran, and Gran's way in this house, and Gran's small kindnesses. And though she isn't anywhere, Madge mourns (for where could she possibly be?), here above all is where she isn't. Here reminds me. Madge goes down to Laity's on the quay to buy coffee in incredible quantities, and on her return takes refuge in the attic sunroom, lying on the wide cushioned window seat, her nose pressed against the window, watching the cars drive up to the front door, and the strangers arrive.

There are, of course, a lot of young men. They arrive in twos and threes, carrying holdalls and bulging sports bags. Madge loses count – six? eight? Here are two more – a short stocky dark-haired lad, and a very good-looking tall fair one. That must be eight of them. Now here is a taxi from the station and three small children, and a grown-up man in a shirt and flannels. Mrs Jones is emerging through the front door to kiss first him, and then them; that must be Mr Jones and three Jones children. Madge can see little more than the tops of their heads from up here. It strikes her suddenly that perhaps she ought to be downstairs to welcome them. After all, this is her house. Even though she isn't in charge . . . She jumps up, and starts down the stairs, two at a time.

Swinging herself rapidly around the banister post on the landing, she collides with someone coming up – the dark boy, with the fair one. She almost knocks him over.

'Hello!' he says, smiling. There is a pause. She waits for them to make way for her, but they hesitate.

'I'm Madge Fielding,' she says.

135

'Oh,' says the dark boy blankly. 'Oh – er, I'm Matthew Brown, and this is Andrew Henderson.'

'How do you do?' says Andrew Henderson.

'Yes,' says Madge. 'Well, I was going downstairs. . .'

'Of course,' says Andrew Henderson, standing aside.

Another car draws up as Madge reaches the entrance hall. She watches a thin, very tired-looking woman in a suede coat get out of it, followed by a striking man with dark hair, grey at the temples, and then by a small thickset child with a shock of red hair. They seem, Madge thinks, rather old to have such a young child. They come leading it by the hand.

'This is Professor and Mrs Tregeagle,' says Mrs Jones at the front door, offering a welcoming cheek to the other woman.

'You must be Madge Fielding,' says Mrs Tregeagle. 'This is Molly. Say hello, Molly.'

Madge stoops towards the child, hands held out, and smiling. 'Hello, Molly,' she says.

The child looks up. Its face is very ruddy, with almond-shaped pale blue eyes, and hardly any lashes. It smiles, and as it does so the smile fills with spittle, which overflows and oozes down its chin. The eyes swim inward into a squint.

Madge sickens for an instant, then realizes, then covers up and steadies her smile. Forcing herself, she bends and picks up the child, staggered at its solidity and weight.

'Would you like to look at the view?' she asks it. 'You can see the sea from the other side of the house.'

'See, see,' says the child. And then, as Madge moves out into the drive to carry it around through the garden, she sees someone watching her. A boy has got out of the car on the other side, a grown boy, Madge's own age, or a little older. He is lean and dark, with a long nose and full lips. He must be the Tregeagles' son, with his father's face, and his mother's curls, but what Madge notices first is the stare he is giving her – looking at her, she thinks, astonished, with an expression full of anger – but the moment she catches his eye he turns away, and stalks into the house. Flinching, she takes the child onto the lawn, and plays with her there, with elaborate kindness. The child is pleased. It plays a lumpish dance with Madge, and chuckles a lot. Together they pick a bunch of flowers from the untidy borders, and go in to find a jam jar for them.

'Where will you want to sleep, Madge?' asks Mrs Jones, meeting them in the hall. 'How good of you to cope with Molly.'

'There's an attic I like a lot,' says Madge. 'I'll have that, I think.'

'Attics, too? How many? Could I put some of the young men up there? Oh, I'll come and see in a minute when I've just seen to this.' And she pins up on a board in the hall a typed list of *House Rules* which begins *Breakfast, seven to eight. Silence for individual study will be maintained throughout the house till one o'clock.*

Upstairs, Madge unpacks her own books. 'Looks as though I'll have time for these after all,' she thinks. And Mrs Jones finds what used to be Amy's room, next to Madge's sloping attic with its view to the sea, towards Godrevy, and decides to put Patrick Tregeagle there.

*   *   *

Toiling up the stairs to the very top, taking her time, taking time to draw her breath, Gran reaches at last Sarah's bedside in the little whitewashed room with its sloping ceiling.

'What's the matter, Sarah?' she asks. 'Did we hear you call out?'

'I had a bad dream. Gone now.'

'Sure, are you? Tell me, if telling helps,' says Gran, sitting heavily on the bed, and taking the child's damp hand.

137

'I was falling, forever and ever,' says Sarah, shuddering. 'But I'm all right now, Gran.'

*   *   *

A dream of falling. Patrick. Madge is moving around her attic, sitting in the window, looking out to sea, to the lighthouse. A storm wind is blowing, although the day is bright. The water is opaque and sullen, the surface dark like hammered metal, though between the cloud shadows on the bay the sun green-glosses the top inch or two, and the waves break white all over it like huge snowflakes, and glaciers of foam fill the rock crevices of Porthminster Point, and avalanche over and over the black rock crags below her.

Madge thinks about the boy with angry eyes whom she can hear moving about in the next room. He can't be much older than me, she thinks, and he looks interesting, and if he weren't angry it would be a good thing to gang up with him, to have some friend and ally among all these strangers – why ever did I say they could come? – till Paul gets here next week. Perhaps if I show him the way out to the roof valleys he'd like that.

She knocks on the attic door. He does not answer properly, just grunts. Madge marches in, before her courage fails her.

'I've come to show you this,' she says, and opens a little door in the wooden panelled wall under the slope of the eaves, which gives into the dusty space over the joists, facing a dirty window. Madge stoops through the door, pushes the window open, and wriggles out. The roof is made of slate hills and valleys, all zigzag up and down, with lead gutters in the bottoms of all the dips. For a moment or two Madge is alone, walking unsteadily in the narrow gutter, and then the dark boy comes too. They lean against a slope of slate and look at the sky. 'I want to see over,' he says in a while.

'You can climb up and sit astride the ridge if you're

very careful,' says Madge. He begins a scramble up. But when he reaches the top the wind buffets him, rolls him nearly over, whips his hair into his eyes, and tugs at his shirt, filling it like a white sail.

'Help!' he cries, and hastily dismounts the ridge, and slides down into the sheltered lee of the roof valley where he lies askew, legs up one slope, back leaning on the other, and begins to laugh.

'Are you going to show the Jones kids this?' he asks.

'Oh, no!' says Madge. 'And don't you dare. This is a secret, Paul's and mine. It's only you I told.'

There is another pause. The sun has warmed the tiles out of the wind to almost tropical heat. They lie snug like lizards.

'Who's Paul?' he asks in a while.

'My brother. He's coming next week.'

'So why are you here? I'm here because I always have to come, wherever they go for their beastly vacation parties, Mother and Father, I mean.'

'This is my house,' says Madge.

'Wow! You don't care much about cracked slates, for a landlady.'

'Well, I'm not into that yet. Perhaps I'll have to. What a horrid thought. Hey, if you're always on these reading parties, you can tell me what it's going to be like.'

'Bloody boring. Very quiet mornings, when you get skinned for making a noise, while they all read, and they won't let me play; then brisk walks and debates in the afternoon, and then they read papers to each other some evenings. I go out if it's not raining, and lie as low as I can if it is.'

'What did you mean, they won't let you play? Aren't you a bit old . . .'

'The piano.'

'Oh,' says Madge, blushing, but Patrick is smiling.

'Come to the beach,' says Madge.

'The one I saw from up there?'

'No, that's one of the big ones. We have a small one all our own. Well, you can't own a beach, really, but there's one you can only get down to from the bottom of our garden. I'll show you.'

So down. Through the window, squeezing, Madge first, across the dusty patch of joist and plaster, and through the door to Patrick's room, with its huge dormer window facing over dark wind-tossed trees to the south. 'What was this room for?' asks Patrick. 'It's a sunroom; Gran had a couch here to lie on and catch the winter sun,' says Madge, hurtling down the pokey panelled stairs to the landing with bedroom doors, down the main stairs, racing through the hall and the porch with its mosaic tiled floor – 'Who was W.H.B.?' says Patrick, looking at the monogram in the lozenge in the middle of the tiled design – around the house at a run, leaping down the steep descent of the terraced garden, out of the back gate to the cliff path, where the view arrests them for a moment – beach, town, harbour, quay, rock, sea, the green hill of the Island rising behind the harbour, and beyond it, right over it, far, far, the immense wide deep blue sea, across the skyline to the lighthouse – but only a moment, then down the stony zigzag path, running, Patrick ahead now, swinging around the turns and corners in the hairpin path, over the railway bridge, and then sharp right, off the sedate and ordinary path, past PRIVATE LAND, the way nearly overgrown from either side by nettles and wild flowers, out onto the point, and down, down, to the golden shore, on which the loud waves roll, leaping in great toppling glassy walls, one behind another, hissing and jumping, exploding in soft furies of foam, casting scallops of spume-webbed water over the shining wet slopes of sand, and pulling back in looped ropes of froth-edged, puckering shallows, over which the next wave breaks and sweeps, and the two of them run, swerving up and down the slopes of sand, flirting with the water, down as it retreats, and, Help!

racing away as it gathers strength to fling its pawing edge after them, engulfing their running feet. Wet to the knees and laughing, they slow up, walk on.

'This is a northeasterly,' Madge says to Patrick. 'It turns the town inside out; this is usually the sheltered shore, and the far one the wild one.'

A great wave breaks, and charges up the beach in bolsters of thick foam so that they skip hastily out of its way; and as it retreats it leaves a little brown bottle at Madge's feet. She picks it up. The sea comes back again, pawing the sand, reaching for her.

'No message,' says Madge, looking at the bottle. She hurls it high and far, as hard as she can, out into the staircase of rising breaking water, and they walk on.

'What will they be like, all those clever people?' Madge wonders aloud.

'They're not so clever, really. Only about *the subject*. About people, they seem rather stupid to me, usually,' says Patrick.

'I knew a professor once,' says Madge. 'He was blind.'

'Quite.'

'No, but he was *really*,' says Madge, protesting. 'Is your professor father very famous? Might I have heard of him?'

'Shouldn't think so.'

'Only I thought I'd heard your name before, somewhere.'

They have walked some fifty yards farther when the waves, breaking in front of them, roll the brown bottle up the beach at dizzy speed, and deposit it again at Madge's feet.

'Heavens!' says Madge, picking it up. 'It wants me to have it!' But once it is in her hand the sea churns and rages at her, pours into her shoes, and worries around her ankles. She stands there, looking at the bottle, and then at the sea, unsure.

'What if it had a message in it now?' says Patrick.

Madge shudders at the thought. 'I'll throw it back,' she says, 'but if it comes again we'll *know* the sea means me to have it.'

The bottle leaves her hand in flight, and describes a long arc out into the turmoil of the surf. They walk on, right to the end of the little beach, and turn back, retracing their steps. Madge thinks about the bottle. It will not come back again; the sea has a direction; they were walking with it, now they are going against it. But she has forgotten the eddying backwash where the surf is thrown back off the rock point. In a short while they can see the bottle again, bobbing and rolling in the edge of the boiling surf a little way ahead of them – hurtling inland on a burst of breaking wave, and then dancing out again in the backwash. In silence they stand and watch it. To and fro it goes. Madge does not wade after it, but merely waits, and by and by the bottle is laid on a stretch of glossy, momentarily dry sand within reach. She stoops, and possesses it. It lies cold in her hand while she looks with astonishment at the cavortings of the sea. And the sea tosses in the wide bay, girds the lighthouse with a changeless brief wreath of white, and towers and falls before her with the same mock ferocity as before.

'I knew at once you were an unusual person,' says Patrick, behind her. 'Or nearly at once, because Molly liked you. I've forgiven you that first moment, you know, because she liked you later.'

Turning to look at him, Madge finds his eyes intensely meeting hers. They are as brown as the bottle in her hand.

'What an odd thing to say,' she says. 'You are a strange one, Patrick Tregeagle.'

'What about you, then?' he says. 'What about a person who gets presents from the sea?'

'Hey, look!' says Madge, laughing, holding her bottle high. 'The sea gave me a present! It really did!'

'Oh, I'll beware of you!' says Patrick.

*   *   *

It's a Cornish name, Madge thinks, still wondering later
in the day where she had heard it before. And that
thought reminds her. She goes into the little room, the
'front parlour' that served as a library. The two dons
have assembled all the students there, and they are in
deep discussion. Unabashed, Madge starts to search
for a book. It takes her a while to find it; Gran's
books have all been moved into one corner. Instead,
there are volumes bound in heavy fake leather, with a
college crest on the spines, and unfamiliar titles. What
strange things philosophy books are called! *Leviathan;
A Critique of Pure Reason; Action, Emotion, and Will;
A Discourse on Method*. Method for doing what? And
why isn't there one called *Thinking*? And here is
one called *The Blue and Brown Books*. It is just
one book, bound in the same deep green as all the
others. Madge moves along the shelves, looking for
Cornish Folklore, and as she does, gradually begins
to listen to the conversation in the room.

'. . . a whole constellation of topics to bring to your
attention, concerning the soul, the connection between
soul and body, and, reluctantly, since it has occupied
the minds of so many philosophers, immortality . . .'

'Pre-existence, surely, is of equal importance . . .' It
is the fair-haired Andrew Henderson speaking up.

'It can't be of equal importance, can it?' says Madge,
amused. 'Because it's too late to do anything about it,
whereas if we're immortal we shall have to prepare to
meet our doom.'

Nobody answers her; nobody even looks at her. There
is a pause. Then Professor Tregeagle says, 'Yes, Andrew,
that seems a logical pair. As I said, we have to probe
a constellation of inter-related topics . . .' And as
if repeating himself reminds him that he has been
interrupted, he frowns for a moment.

Madge finds *Cornish Folklore* and flees the room.

143

'You're just not used to it, that's all,' says Patrick, when she tells him about it. He has found the piano at the far end of the dining room, and is trying it out. 'Nobody interrupts them. I wouldn't; neither would either of their wives. Listening with due humility is allowed – contributing is not.' He strikes four solemn chords in sequence.

Matthew Brown arrives, seemingly looking for Madge. He pushes back the dark tuft of hair that falls over his forehead, ineffectively, and grins at Madge.

'Don't take offence, will you?' he says. 'None was meant.'

'Oh,' says Madge. 'Was what I said very stupid?'

'Not stupid – just not philosophical.'

'Non-philosophical remarks, for the enlightenment of our young friend,' says Patrick, from the piano, 'are the class of all remarks made by non-philosophers. Or, in plain English, if you are not studying philosophy what you say doesn't count.'

'What if what you say is so reasonable that it jolly well does count?' asks Madge.

'It *can't* count,' says Patrick. 'If you aren't a philosopher you are always offside.'

'Take no notice, Miss Fielding,' says Matthew. 'Professor Tregeagle is a brilliant man. If he doesn't always notice social niceties . . .'

'This is Patrick Tregeagle,' says Madge hastily, through another set of mocking heavy chords from the piano.

'Oh,' says Matthew, 'I *see*. Well, whoever he is, his father is brilliant, and I admire him.'

'And rude with it, whenever his mind is elsewhere,' says Patrick. Matthew shrugs. 'I tried,' his eyes signal to Madge, and off he goes. Madge takes her book upstairs.

She finds it at once – here it is – TREGEAGLE. There are dozens of stories about him. Alive he was the wickedest man in Cornwall; dead he is a wild and evil spirit. His is the voice that howls in the storm over

144

the moorland heights, and keeps the villagers awake. To master him he must be bound to some hopeless task – to emptying Dozmary Pool with a cockleshell drilled with a hole; to weaving ropes of sand along the restless tides' edge. Well, if he was a man once, I suppose he can have descendants, thinks Madge. I wonder if Patrick knows about it? He won't find out from me, that I do know. And till supper she reads in the book the stories her Gran used to read to her, years back – tales of the Knockers in the mines, and the Spriggans in the heather, and the sad Lady with the Lantern, crossing the churchyard wall, and looking all night among the wave-washed rocks for her shipwrecked child.

*   *   *

The train from St Erth is a sleek diesel slug, two carriages long, rattling under the drop below the garden, snaking around into the station among the parked cars. Harriet is holding Beth up to the window in Gran's bedroom to see the train come. There is too much to look at, sea and beach and town and harbour and hill, and the child has to be talked to attention.

'Cousin Emily is coming to see us,' Harriet says. 'You remember her. You liked her last summer.'

'See the boat,' says Beth, pointing out to sea.

'Look, here comes the train,' says Harriet. 'With Emily on it. You remember Em.'

'That big girl with a hole in her trousers,' says Beth.

Below them, Em jumps out of the train, dragging a battered canvas satchel, wearing torn blue jeans, her long hair swinging to her waist. A dark sweater is tied around her waist, sleeves knotted against her navel, the rest hanging like a tabard over her backside.

'There she is!' cries Harriet.

'Oh, good, good. So she caught the train,' says Gran from her afternoon lie-down on the bed behind them. 'One never knows with Em.'

'Em! Em!' shrieks Beth. 'She's going to the beach. Isn't she going to come and say hello?'

'Along the beach is the quickest way here from the station,' says Gran. Em weaves a path along the edge of the waves towards them. 'There seems to be somebody with her,' says Harriet. For a lean black-clad figure has detached itself from the crowd disembarking from the train, and is following Em along the beach, two steps behind her. Em finds something in the sea wrack at the waves' edge, and shows it to her companion, her outstretched arm linking the two tiny figures in Harriet's telescopic view.

'No message,' says Em, and throws the bottle back. The two figures run diagonally across the sand, and jump the little stream and come nearer, but out of sight, up the zigzag path to the house.

'Did you invite some friend to come with her?' says Harriet.

'No, dear, but . . .'

'We haven't a room ready. Where can we put another person?'

'They can share, or something, Hal.'

'It seems to be a boy, Mother,' says Harriet.

'Where has Em gone?' demands Beth. 'Isn't she saying hello?'

'He'll have to go in the attic, then,' says Gran. 'There's room. There's always room here.'

'This is Jim,' says Em, putting her scruffy bag down in the hall. Jim is wearing jeans and a black sweater. His hair is long, hanging in a tousled mass to his shoulders. He is tall and thin, and were it not for the owl-like gold-rimmed spectacles he wears would look like a walk-on part in a cowboy film.

'Hi,' he says, shaking hands with Gran, and smiling down at her from head and shoulders above her.

'This is Jim, Aunt,' says Em to Harriet.

'Yes,' says Harriet. 'We weren't expecting anyone with you, Emily.'

146

'There's room . . .' says Gran. 'Let me look at you, Em love. Have you grown at all? Grown different, I see. I don't know about taller.'

'Don't worry about me,' says Jim. 'I've got a sleeping bag. I'll kip down anywhere.'

'We can clear one of the attics,' says Harriet. 'It's just that we weren't expecting you.'

'Now, don't *fuss*, Hal dear,' says Gran. 'I expect you two would like a cup of tea after your long journey?'

'Yes, if it's going,' says Jim. 'Look, what about that summerhouse thing on the garden wall at the foot of the garden? That looks great; can I sleep there?'

'Heavens!' says Harriet. 'Won't it be damp and cold?'

'It'll be fine,' says Jim. He smiles at Harriet. 'And I won't be in the way there. OK?'

'Well, if you're sure you'll be all right . . .' says Harriet, dubiously.

The tea is served on the terrace, on little cane tables among the deck chairs. The adults sip it, and pass the biscuits. Neither Em nor Jim comes to drink tea. But the garden below the terrace is riotous. Em and Sarah and Beth are in flight round and round the house, through the shrubs, along the paths, bent double at a run, fleeing and hiding, and Jim and Peter are roaring after them, howling and leaping in ambush, and the children become hysterical with excitement, their screams and laughter becoming indistinguishable. When the noise finally persuades Tom to rise from his chair to see what is going on, there is a heaving mass of bodies, all flailing arms and legs, on the lawn, from which he presently makes out that everybody is sitting on Jim. 'Ugh! Arrgh! Mercy!' cries Jim.

'Seems an amiable brute, anyway,' says Tom.

'I rather think,' says Gran, 'that Jim is the one her father approves of.'

'He looks like a navvy, or a plumber's mate,' grumbles Harriet. 'And obviously lives like a tramp. Fancy wanting to sleep in the belvedere.'

'He may *look* like a tramp,' says Gran, smiling mischievously, 'but I think he's an undergraduate.'

'People get degrees in plumbing, these days, I expect,' says Tom.

'Yes, dear, but not at Balliol,' says Gran. And it must be middle age that makes people so sticky, she thinks smugly, for *old* age leaves *me* all right. It has escaped her notice entirely that if an attic had needed clearing out this hot afternoon, it would have been Harriet who would have had to do it.

Em appears on the terrace like a pantomime entrance, leaping the lavender hedge, and landing neatly between two chairs. 'Can we take this mob down to the beach till supper?' she asks.

'Oh, do. Certainly,' says Harriet, relenting a little.

'I don't think I'd have spent hours playing with kids when *I* was an undergraduate,' says Tom.

*   *   *

On the beach, time drifts, suspended in the heat. The undergraduates are all up in the house, reading of the last days of Socrates. Down on the sands of Porthminster beach—'The children prefer it, and you can get ice cream,' Mrs Jones has said in response to Madge's offer to show her the special one – are Mrs Jones and Mrs Tregeagle, sitting side by side in deck chairs for which by and by the chair man will come and take their sixpences, with a huge striped beach bag between them, full of towels, and coffee in a thermos, and buns, and lavender oil to repel insects – I'm not surprised it does that, thinks Madge, sniffing – and paperback Agatha Christies, and Mrs Jones's knitting, and wooden spoons for the children to use as spades. 'Safer and cheaper,' Mrs Jones says. The youngest of the three Jones children is digging a castle nearby. Molly, too, is digging with a spoon, though to no purpose, achieving neither mound nor pit in the patient silting surface of the warm dry sand.

Patrick lies face down, stretched out on his bathing towel, propping arms on his elbows, and chin in his hands. Beads of salt water gleam on his back, drying off in the sun. He looks vaguely out to sea. And Madge sits beside him in a white dress, under a huge straw hat, with a book on her knee. The page glares dazzling white at her, unreadably bright, and she is sleepy with sun and lunch. They had been talking earlier; now they are silent.

The sea is smooth and tranquil. The waves are so small and late they hardly look real. Rising from the sun-shot shallows like little jade lions, they arch green, glossy backs, come rearing and pawing a little way, and break foaming, tossing their suddenly tawny manes. Behind them in the glass-clear green water lie shimmering golden nets of floating light. In the distance Godrevy light, haze-softened, looks like a stick of blackboard chalk against the sky, and the sea lies quiet all the way there, like the waters of some limitless lake.

Molly finds a shell, a crab's claw, and shows it to her mother, tugging her skirt. Mrs Tregeagle shoos her gently. 'Go and play with the others, Molly,' she says. Patrick stiffens, and turns his head to watch. Molly staggers towards the little Jones boy, playing nearest. His castle has battlements now, and windows made of pressed-on mussel shells. He stands up as she comes, and gets between her and it, arms stretched wide to stop her. 'You walk on my castle and I'll hit you!' he says. 'You *get*, or you'll be sorry.'

Molly trots down the beach towards the others. They are whirling at the run around the scribbled paths they have drawn. Molly begins to run, too, treading on all the lines, and blurring them. She laughs her low-pitched chuckle. Soon she is circling alone; the others have withdrawn without a word spoken, have left their spiralling mazes to her trampling naked feet,

149

and migrated yards along the beach to the edge of the stream. It is a little stream of fresh water, disgorged onto the sand by a rusty pipe through a grille; where it falls it has cut a whirlpool that bubbles thick with sand. Overflowing from that, it runs down into the sea, making channels and shallows and meanders, cutting little gorges and rapids like a geography lesson. The two Jones girls begin to dam its flow. Molly wheels drunkenly on, alone. Soon she sits down alone, and looks at the sea.

The two women are talking about college houses. One will be available when old Grimbly retires; there will be a shuffle and change about.

'I'd like the one in Walton Street,' says Mrs Jones. 'But we'll never get it. Not unless Hugh is made Dean. But the college doesn't really appreciate him. Perhaps if he became Dean, though, we could do better than Walton Street.'

'We couldn't have Walton Street. We need a garden. And a fence. A high one. Molly can climb these days.' And here is Molly again, returning to tug at her mother's skirts.

'Oh, do go and play!' says Mrs Tregeagle, sharply. Molly starts off towards the stream. And Patrick lies still tense, watching, with Madge beside him. He is watching so intently that Madge, still serene and sleepy, and lulled by looking into vast lovely distances, watches too. They see Molly's dumpy figure in the distance, reaching the dam-builders. They see the two girls, bent over their labours and digging frantically, straighten for a moment as she comes, and face her. Then she turns around, and comes away, retreating.

Patrick gets up, and strides down the beach towards her. He takes her hand, and leads her back to them. And Madge jumps up too, and follows, sure he is making a mistake, and yet not quite wanting to call out to him, not wanting to speak, just to catch his eye, and glance, 'Be careful; are you sure?'

A big pool of water is building up behind the sand dam. It brims it, sneaks around the ends till choked off with another pile of sand. It licks at and topples the crests of the sandy battlements. Patrick leads Molly by the hand right up to the bank of the pool. 'Surely she could help?' he asks, and so catches, full-face, the expression of revulsion which crosses the pretty, knowing countenance of Prudence Jones, flecked with sandy splashes from her struggle with the pent-up stream. Her sister avoids looking; simply flushes and turns away. They all stand frozen for a moment; and the meek and tiny stream has built up enough ferocity at its confinement to overbrim the barrier, and scour through it with joyous speed. The defeated engineers gaze at Patrick with sullen reproach. He turns on his heel, and marches back to the deck chairs, still leading Molly by the hand.

'*Don't* send her to play with them, Mother!' he says.

'Why ever not?' says Mrs Tregeagle in a pained voice, and Mrs Jones says at the same time, 'Oh, no! Were they unkind?' And Patrick says, choking and furious, 'You know why!' and suddenly races away from them down the beach, plunging into the sea, and swimming, head down, arms flailing, boring his way out far, beyond the diving raft, and on and on, as though to reach the horizon.

He leaves trouble behind him. Mrs Jones stands up and yells, calling her offending offspring to her.

'Why won't you play with Molly?' she demands, as they come within earshot of a normal voice.

'It's not *that*, Mummy,' says Prudence, aggrieved. 'She really ought not to come there, that's all. That whirlpool is awfully deep, and it sucks down. It's dangerous.'

'Oh,' says Mrs Jones, disconcerted.

'You really ought to stop her coming after us,' says Prudence gleefully, as they start back to their abandoned project.

'Come and play with me, Molly,' says Madge.

It seems to get hotter and hotter. The sea looks almost oily in the glare. Molly wants to pick up shells, and hand them to Madge, and take them back again, over and over, grunting a bit, and digging her soles in the sand. She will not play burying feet, or making castles, or any variation Madge contrives. Mildly amused at first, and then gradually stupefied with boredom, Madge sits, taking shells, and giving them back again. After some long while Patrick comes striding up the beach, leaving a trail of disclets of wet sand from his dripping body, and comes past without a word, stooping to pick up his towel without stopping, and races towards the path for home.

And in a while longer, Molly, handing her shells over ever more slowly, falls asleep, and Mrs Tregeagle moves her deck chair to cast some shadow on her sleeping child, and Mrs Jones gathers up her three, and begins a lucky-dip plunge into the beach bag to hand out tea. The sand on her fingers sticks to Madge's sugar bun, and grinds against her teeth. She isn't hungry. She slips away and goes in search of Patrick.

The house is quiet and cool. Madge brings sand with her on her feet and clothes; it is alien here, out of its element, suddenly gritty and uncomfortable. The fresh open-air salt smell of it mingles oddly with the smell of polish and warm dust, and the hot open-window scent of drifting heat off the garden, that fills the indoors. Madge climbs to Patrick's room, and taps on his door. He does not answer. She waits. After a while he pads softly barefoot across the room and opens the door.

'Are you all right?' Madge asks, feeling foolish, not knowing quite what to say.

'What will become of her?' Patrick says.

'Or of you,' says Madge, 'if you are going to feel like that about it.'

'It doesn't matter about me!' says Patrick in his choking voice. And then, 'O God!' and he plunges down the stairs out of sight, still barefoot, and disappears into the garden.

Hours later, when dinner is laid, and he still has not returned, Madge finds him in the summerhouse, sitting in a ruined chair, gazing at Godrevy, far out, and coaxes him to come in.

*   *   *

Propped into an angle of the hillside, with a cushion for her back, Gran feels for a moment like a parcel – put down and not forgotten, to be picked up later with relief that no harm has come. In front of her the grass slopes easily to an edge, and disappears. And the party has scattered, diverging like ships on different errands. Only the voices, unrelated, climb back to her: the cries of children discovering small wonders. Until a face appears over the little rise to her right, then shoulders, arms, bare midriff, shorts, bare legs. Sarah, a scurry of flashing legs, rushing towards her, as if she had no time at all – not a moment to spare. It is age that has no time, thinks Gran, and age that takes it, all the same.

What brings her? A crisis? An accident? A small foot too near the perilous high edge – leaning over, looking down? Of course not.

'Can I have a biscuit to be going on with?' Sarah calls. 'The ones in silver paper.'

Gran draws the hamper towards her. Harriet probably wouldn't allow it, with proper teatime so near, she thinks, but Harriet is some little way off, and the endless conspiracy between young and old is in force. She gropes in the basket, hands out a biscuit. 'Here,' and, silently, she pushes another one after it.

'Oh, *thanks*, Gran!' says Sarah, but the words are left behind, thrown over her shoulder, for she has run away from them. Gran smiles, remembering in her legs the feel of scurry. And in a moment Sarah is back, to add her afterthought: 'Can I have one for Peter as well?

153

Can I have two for him? Or shall we have one and a half each?'

'What about Beth?' Gran says. 'Take two for her.' And really, she thinks, I like it here. Hot grass, high above the sea, and a fine prospect all around, back across the bay, or out to sea. I like it in spite . . . The cliffs are a grand sight, one would have to admit, although so far to fall. And who could not like the little wet clouds of froth, floating salt-spray spume, like cuckoo-spit flying, blown from so far below on the smart offshore breeze? She sees her son-in-law stand on the brink to take a photograph, and smiles. It will be like a poster for a railway holiday, she thinks, all bright blue and dark rock, and melodramatic, with precipice and wave. He could get a postcard; the focus would be sharper and all for sixpence. Now if he faced about . . . but her mind refuses to turn, refuses with eye or mind's eye to contemplate the lighthouse from here, from this different angle, and eerily near. Though she knows how it lies, dark against the sun on its sloping island in a sea that glitters with floating but unextinguished stars of light; how it looms, peering over the top of the cliff with its one Cyclop's eye. She deliberately fixes her eyes on the smooth grass, the clumps of thrift, and the little gold bird's-foot trefoil at her feet, and deliberately drowses away in the heat, like some sailor, giving Godrevy a wide berth, sailing by.

*   *   *

If Miss Higgins thinks highly of the company of intellectual people, Madge reflects, then surely she, Madge, is supposed to find glory in it. Glory of some kind . . . inspiration? . . . insight? Or is she perhaps to learn from them, share their perception, gain understanding? But perhaps Miss Higgins herself has never been on a reading party. For the reading party does not seem very inspiring to Madge. Only one of the eight young men seems what Madge imagines an intellectual to be, when off duty. He is given to striding up and down, talking to himself under his breath when not actually reading. But the others are more interested in climbing. The porch is cluttered with their gear – coils of rope, and little pickaxes, and rows of pins in canvas belts, and heavy boots with studded soles. They talk eagerly about this face and that face, and use words Madge doesn't know. They are all rather sun-tanned and beefy, and always very brisk and cheerful; except for the mutterer, who is called Jake, and for Matthew Brown, whose opinion of rock-climbing is given in three words: 'Not for me.'

And so all morning the house is breathless with their need for silence; Patrick runs his fingers silently over the keys of the piano, and looks at the clock; Madge reads the volumes of Yeats and D. H. Lawrence that Miss Higgins recommended, and learns the splendid bits of poems by heart. The younger children are on the beach, whether they will or no – not that they show the least sign of tiring of it.

At lunch there is cheerful talk to listen to, but it is all about who is walking where and who is climbing what. Andrew Henderson, Madge notices, will never make up a group, always goes off by himself, even if he is climbing very near some of the others.

'Why don't you go with the others, Andrew?' she asks him once, meeting him in the garden.

'I prefer to climb alone,' he says.

'Isn't it scary, all alone?'

'Oh, no,' he says. 'One can concentrate better. One has only oneself to worry about.'

'Oh.'

'It's not only that; you can stop when you feel like it. Nobody looking to think you are being a bit cautious, or that they could manage that, even if you can't. You don't have to push your luck.'

Madge finds all this very interesting, but it isn't exactly intellectual.

The nearest distance to the intellect Madge can come is sitting listening to them talking in the evening. They occupy the comfortable end of the living room, and read and discuss around the hearth. And Madge does not understand the discussions at all, and yet in an odd way is absorbed by them. They seem to soar at once into a realm so abstract that it *has* to be both beautiful and profound, Madge thinks, rather as one thinks that the stratosphere has to be clean. The altocirrus clouds shine above us, and we see their shapes, she thinks, but we do not feel the wind that moves them. I can see the *shape* of this talk — a ferocious capacity for doubt, a search for precision as heroic and unnecessary as all the rock-climbing, a surgical capacity for laying bare the bones of things. Bones are narrow, hard, and dry. And, God! how fuzzy I am. It has never occurred to me to doubt that the I that thinks is the I that am, for instance. And bemused, she begins to pick up and dip into the books that lie around the house, looking for a foothold, for a little light. *An Essay Concerning Human Understanding* she finds, and opening at random, reads:

OF THE REALITY OF KNOWLEDGE: *I doubt not but my reader, by this time, may be apt to think that I have been all this while only building a castle in the air, and be ready to say to me: to what purpose all this stir? Knowledge, say you, is only the perception of the agreement or disagreement of our own ideas; but who knows what those ideas may be? Is there anything so extravagant as the imaginations of men's brains? Where is the head that hath no chimeras in it? It is no matter how things are; so a man observe but the agreement of his own ideas, and talk conformably, it is all truth, all certainty. Such castles in the air will be as strongholds of truth as the demonstrations of Euclid. That a Harpy is not a Centaur is by this*

*way as certain knowledge, and as much a truth, as
that a square is not a circle.*

Madge reads. Why does this make me remember the
attic? she wonders. What am I seeing? She is seeing Paul, in her mind's eye, sitting beside her on the
bed in the attic room, very small and neatly made, in
grey-and-white-striped pyjamas, and a book, someone
reading from a book:

> *They told me you had been to her,*
> *And mentioned me to him:*
> *She gave me a good character,*
> *But said I could not swim. . .*

and you think, Madge realizes, light suddenly dawning,
you *keep* thinking, that if you concentrate only a little
bit harder, only a little bit longer, or hear it once
through again, you will understand it; but however
long you try the moment eludes you. I remember now,
Gran, reading *Alice* to us when we were small, and how
Paul lit up and laughed. And yet, of course, it isn't quite
the same, not really, for soon one realized the trick,
knew that there wasn't anything there to get a grip on
. . . but with this stuff . . . She closes the book and turns
it to read the spine. *John Locke*: I've heard of him. So I
suppose if I *do* try harder . . . I must improve my mind,
it clearly isn't good enough. I must make myself good.
But not yet; not now; right now I shall go for a walk.

*   *   *

The reading party are all spread out on rugs and warm
stones on the top of Zennor Hill, by Zennor Quoit.
The young men have walked here, all the way along
the cliff path, but the dons and wives and children
have come by car, carting food and rugs and thermos
flasks. The hilltop is laden with geological debris: grey
stones stacked up like toppling piles of oat cakes, or

157

littered everywhere in lichen-splotched lumps. One of these piles is the Quoit – made on purpose, and with a hollow chamber inside, to be a burying place – but no-one seems quite sure which. The eroding wind has played such improbable tricks here that it is hard to argue that this or that could have been made only by human hands; for human hands, when they made one of these stone stacks, whichever one, were content to ape the brutish untidyness of the geological process. The stones are all grown round by gorse and heather and upland grasses, and humming with insects. The Jones children are playing hide-and-seek in among the outcrops; Molly is still steadily eating. Mrs Jones and Mrs Tregeagle lie stretched in the sun. Madge and Patrick lie face down on a tall flat rock, looking down on everyone. They are overlooking the edge of the world.

West of them, shadowy against the light, are the last heights before Land's End; between lie a few farms, a scatter of patchwork fields, bathed in soft heat-haze sunlight, with a cloud shadow crossing here and there. And the land plateau ends, abruptly, and beyond are the plains of the sea. Raising one shoulder into view is the dark rocky bulk of Gurnard's Head. No more of the cliff can be seen, nor the remorseless, pawing, sapping assault of the sea on the foot of the landwall; only a tranquil blue shimmer melting into the sky. Midway to the floating edge of the land lies Zennor, its church tower squared clearly with sun and shade, its few houses clustered around it, and a ribbon of road winding by.

Whatever Patrick may find to hold his attention in all this, it is the conversation below that engages Madge. They are talking about innate ideas. At first she is adrift, through not knowing properly what 'innate' means. But gradually her limping understanding picks up a thread or two. They are saying – or are they only saying that other men have thought it? – that there might be inward knowledge, inhering in the soul. Perhaps before anything is learned by us, there were things we knew, that all men know. Are there some truths so crystalline that they compel the assent of any human soul? Or does the soul bring into the shades of life some small reflected fragments of the bright light of some other place, trailing a few clouds of glory, though it be only to know that a thing cannot both be and not be at the same time?

The young man with the cropped red hair thinks that it is not any particular proposition, or set of propositions, of which there might be innate knowledge, but it might be rather a knowledge of the laws underlying propositions, a sort of subconscious early-warning system for detecting invalidity. Madge imagines that; one might know, not exactly where the wood will split, but that there is a grain in the universe, and which way it runs. And, ah, she thinks, how marvellous such knowledge would be – *I want it!* How does one get it?

They are saying, now, that if God, then the innate could be his mark upon the soul, the potter's fingerprint. Is there perhaps innate knowledge of God?

'But could innate knowledge then be lost?' asks Matthew Brown, in his flat northern accent. For no knowledge of God has ever appeared to *him*. There is something wrong with this remark, for it does not impress the others as clever, as it does Madge. They find it both expected, she sees, coming from him, and unsubtle.

'Were we to *accept* that there is innate knowledge,' says Mr Jones, 'we should have to tackle Locke's refutation.'

'Which is,' says Professor Tregeagle, 'that no idea alleged to be innate, even the simplest, does in fact command universal assent.' Behind him the bobbing golden heads of the children dip and bounce between the sunlit stones. 'For it is evident that children and

159

idiots have not the least apprehension or thought of them.'

Madge stares at Molly, whose coarse features and sluggish understanding are thus enough to strip the soul of God's fingerprints, extinguish the undeniable truth, and send us into the world naked with all to learn. Molly has gathered a handful of stones, and is putting them at random on top of the nearest boulder.

'I'm off. Coming?' says Patrick, on his feet abruptly beside Madge.

They pelt down the long slope, and trot along the road to the village. Zennor Church is quiet and cool inside. Madge finds the Merrymaid carved on a pew end, and tells Patrick the tale she heard long ago from Jeremy. 'Don't you go singing so sweetly out by The Stones, young Madge,' Jeremy had said to her, grinning. 'Or the Merrymaid'll come and get you to sing below the waves.'

'He was called Matthew Trewhella, the boy the merfolk stole,' Madge tells Patrick. 'They could hear his voice, from where they swam, when he sang on Sundays, in Zennor Church. And it seemed mortal hard to them that earth folk should sing so sweetly, and all of them be dumb. And for years after they took him, folk could hear his voice in Pendour Cove, as he sang to her who took him.' And what would it sound like, she wondered, a song from beneath the mute and roaring water? Just a note or two, pure and simple, she thinks, something very plain, like a scrap of knowledge, coming with a new soul from some clearer atmosphere above.

'Look at this, Madge,' Patrick is saying. There is a gravestone with a curious figure on it. *Of pagan appearance*, says the guide leaflet in Patrick's hand. *Possibly holding a serpent swallowing its tail – a symbol of eternity*.

And nearby another stone declares:

Hope, despair, false joy and trouble,

160

Are those four winds which daily toss this bubble.
His breath's a vapour, and his life's a span,
'Tis glorious misery to be born a man.

'I don't see what's misery about it,' says Madge. And,
'I don't see what's glorious about it,' says Patrick in the
same breath.

*   *   *

The heat is tremendous. There is no wind, and scarcely
even a movement on the air. The garden is suffocating
with sweetness as the fragrant oils of leaf and flower
exude an odour which hangs over the wilting plants. The
beach is like a desert, blinding, and too hot to walk on
with bare feet, and even the sea has been stupefied into
a glassy swoon, with languid waves rising wearily and
sighing on the shore. The children are indoors, upstairs,
drowsing naked on top of the bedcovers, in rooms with
the curtains drawn, the attempt at a morning on the
beach having sapped and defeated them. Downstairs
the adults sprawl and sip tea. Tom is reading the *St Ives
Times* – last week's copy, but he hasn't noticed that.
     'God, how frightful!' he says suddenly.
     'What?' asks Harriet, looking up from writing her
postcards.
     'Some child went missing from a picnic party on
Zennor Hill,' he says. 'They think it fell down a
mineshaft. Just listen to this: *The whole area is pitted
with disused shafts. During the nineteenth century
there were regulations that on abandoned mines all
shafts should be made secure. In many cases a
round collar of stonewalling was built, in others a
simple fence, or timber platform placed over the
mouth of the shaft had to suffice. During the passage
of time some of these constructions have required
replacement, but this has not always been done.
Overgrown with brambles and hidden from sight,*

161

*the occasional shaft remains – and the long drop
into total darkness below. If this is what has befallen
the missing child, there is little chance of finding
or recovering the body . . .'*

'How horrible!' says Harriet. Tom turns a page, and
reads on.

*   *   *

On Zennor Hill the reading party's picnic is being
gathered up to carry home.

'I can't think why the loaves and fishes redounds
such credit on the Messiah,' says Mrs Jones. 'There
always *is* far more left over after a meal than the
meal itself consisted of. Now a picnic with *fewer* than
seven baskets to pick up afterwards would be a much
nicer miracle.' Patrick and Madge can be seen below,
climbing back to join them on the hilltop.

It is suddenly realized that Molly is nowhere to be
seen.

They call, and begin to look for her, casually at
first, then gradually more and more urgently, farther
and farther afield. Andrew Henderson suddenly takes
command, divides the terrain roughly between this line
of sight and that, and divides also the members of the
party, giving each a sector to pace over. A grim self-
possession descends on everyone, as the task begins.
The blithe unawareness of Patrick, still some distance
off and perfectly at ease, infuriates his mother, who
screams frantically at him, trying to pitch her terror
across half a mile of sunlit gorse and stone.

'Listen, everyone!' calls Andrew, self-appointed cap-
tain, standing on a stone, and cupping his hands
round his mouth. 'Take *care!* There are some disused
mineshafts on this hill that may not be fenced!' It is
as if he sees the shadow of his warning only after
it is spoken. He goes pale. The long drop into total
darkness gapes in everyone's mind. 'I don't want to

have to climb down one of those for *anybody*,' he mutters.

But soon, before Patrick and Madge have approached far enough to distinguish the cries of Mrs Tregeagle, there is a shout nearby. Someone has found Molly asleep between one warm rock slab and another, and Professor Tregeagle is running, stooping, picking her up in his arms, and carrying her towards her mother. Molly wakes at his unfamiliar clasp, and tries to give him the ghost of a flower which her strong grasp has taken, root and all, together with a random handful of grasses and prickles that were growing by.

'Present,' she says, smiling. 'Present.'

At once a sense of foolishness sweeps over everyone. How melodramatic they have all been! They remember that things hardly ever really *happen*; misfortune is almost always just shadow-boxing. Or at any rate, that things hardly ever happen to oneself, or anyone one knows. And cool sensible young Andrew, who kept his head with Mrs Tregeagle going frantic at his side, and knew how to arrange a proper search, unfairly feels most foolish of all.

'What's up?' says Patrick, arriving.

'Nothing,' says Mrs Tregeagle, hugging Molly. 'Nothing. False alarm.'

'Is that for me, Molly?' asks Patrick, taking the crumpled flower.

'*Nobody* has eyes in the back of their heads. Nobody could watch all the time,' murmurs Professor Tregeagle, taking his wife's hand. 'But it would help,' he goes on loudly, 'if Patrick pulled his weight, instead of going off like that. Does it always have to be your mother, Patrick, who keeps an eye on your sister?'

Only Madge sees the set of Patrick's face. He offers no reply.

*   *   *

163

Someone is playing the piano in the drawing-room. It is an elaborate, extraordinarily precise and patterned sound. It draws Madge from the garden, through the french windows, to sit in the window seat at the quiet end of the room, and listen. The two armchairs either side of the bowl of dried flowers in the empty hearth are occupied by Professor Tregeagle and Mr Jones. It is the muttering Jake who is playing. His music is very domineering, despite its tact. It marches in on you, and orders your soul, undertakes a metaphysical spring-cleaning, in which every disordered overemphasis is set to rights. It does not deny emotion, but it gives every shade of feeling only its true weight exactly, and no more. Madge surrenders to it, and savours a mathematical tranquillity.

After a while Jake stops, and closes the varnished lid upon the keys.

'Won't you go on?' asks Professor Tregeagle. 'I, for my sins, have a son who not only prefers piano-playing to thought, but also Chopin to Bach.'

'I have a letter to write before dinner, sir,' says the young man, retreating.

'They're a very tame lot, really,' says Mr Jones, sighing. 'Not a patch on last year's.' They seem not to have noticed Madge, who is put thus in the position of eavesdropper. But it's my house, she thinks rebelliously, and stays where she is, knees tucked up to her chin, sitting on the chintz cushion between the window curtains.

'Perhaps we could strike a spark or two with a Pop subject. An "if God" debate. The argument from design. That's quite fun to shoot holes in.'

'Have we the patience for it?'

'Well, some bit of old-fashioned metaphysics to jolly them up . . .'

'God, it's hot,' says Professor Tregeagle. 'You know, Hugh, quite a lot of the time I wish she were dead. All the time. It seems the only way out for any of us. Have you *seen* an adult mongol? Or the kind of home we could put her in when she gets too much for us?'

'My dear Gilbert, I'm sorry. I didn't realize how this afternoon's brouhaha had upset you. Let me pour you a whisky, and leave the debating topic to me. I'll think of something. Tell me – isn't she unlikely to reach adult life?'

'Maybe. They often are sickly. One almost wants it. And yet, for all that, when I thought something *had* happened to her . . .'

'Of course, of course. Drink up, Gilbert, you need it.'

* * *

Madge, withdrawing, wanders in the heavy warmth of the evening down the sloping garden with its spectacular view of sand and town and sea. She finds Patrick sitting in the hot shade of the summerhouse with Molly, trotting about grunting to herself, and dark-haired Matthew.

'We were wondering if we'd go and swim this evening,' says Patrick.

'Or at crack of dawn tomorrow,' says Matthew. 'Will you come too?'

'Oh, yes, if you go tomorrow. But tonight I think I'll listen to the philosophy debate. It's going to be "if God? or the argument from design."'

'Please yourself,' says Patrick. '*I'm* not going to sit there listening to them in their cultured precise tones discussing obscenities!'

'God is hardly an obscenity,' says Matthew, smiling.

'No?' says Patrick. 'If the universe is designed, then God; if God, then the universe is designed. If God, then things are *deliberate*. Someone looked at my mother, and decided to inflict Molly upon her. Someone made Molly . . .'

'Me,' says Molly. 'Me.'

'. . . purposely with no capacity for growth and little for happiness, and chose us for her kin. There are, of course – I don't lose all sense of proportion – a thousand worse outrages occurring every day. How about senility, for instance? Now *there's* a funny practical joke to play upon a feeling creature! If God, he's a bloody bastard!'

'Patrick, no!' murmurs Madge, horrified.

'Ah, but there's the world to come,' says Matthew brightly. 'Our sense of injustice is caused by our partial knowledge. But in the light of eternity, justice will be done; rewards in the hereafter await those who suffer now.'

'And God is the great accountant, keeping the books? What kind of person could accept a credit in the hereafter in exchange for the suffering of some poor inoffensive creature now? And what are we to make of God's conduct which apparently consists of torturing people, and then paying them a reward providing their submission was abject? We know what to think of that, if it is perpetrated by a human being!'

'One could hardly give the God of the Bible much of a testimonial for good character, I agree,' says Matthew. 'But you'll have to admit the old boy can design tremendous sets.' His eye travels over the shining bay below the summerhouse windows, over the green and gold farther shore of sand-towan and pasture, and the white lighthouse on its black rock. 'He's quite a conjuror; he does lay on a marvellous spectacle.'

'And who are we to argue, you are about to say,' says Patrick, sarcastically, 'since we were not there when the foundations were laid, and all the stars of morning sang together. The argument from authority is a rotten argument, no matter who pushes it.'

'Well,' says Matthew, 'where *were* you, Patrick my friend, when he shut up the sea with doors, when he made a cloud the garment thereof and wrapped it in a mist as in swaddling bands? Or when he said, "Hitherto shalt thou come, and no further, and here shalt thou break thy swelling waves"? Have the gates of death been opened unto thee, and hast thou seen the darksome doors? Hast thou considered the breadth of the earth? Tell me, if thou knowest all things.'

'But, Matthew,' says Madge, outraged. 'You don't believe all that; I heard you the other day saying you didn't believe in God!'

'No, I don't,' says Matthew. 'Though that isn't what you heard me say. Of course I don't. Like Patrick, I'd rather have random chance any day. But that's philosophy. It's like chess, Madge. If he plays the black pieces, I'll play the white.'

Mrs Jones suddenly appears in the summerhouse door. 'I've come to find you for dinner,' she says. 'You didn't hear the bell down here.' As Patrick, picking up Molly, and carrying her, goes up the garden with Matthew, she says to Madge lightly, 'Did I hear you lot talking philosophy too?'

'I don't *think* it was philosophy,' says Madge. 'It was important, and it wasn't cool.'

'Goodness!' says Mrs Jones, suppressing a grin, and thinking: Just wait till I tell that to Hugh!

*   *   *

'Off you go, Emily love,' says Gran. 'Now there's a quiet moment, with the children all asleep. Jim will sit beside me and tell me all about himself.' Emily saunters a little way, and sits on the lawn making daisy chains. Gran begins upon Jim. Shamelessly curious, she extracts from him the names and ages of his two brothers, a description of his father, another of his mother, and a third of his house, before she gets around to asking what he is studying.

P.P.E.? Does he like it? Do you need a grasp of maths to do the economics? What does he make of philosophy?

. . . Emily, overhearing all she can, is half amused, half embarrassed.

'Yes, it is interesting, of course,' Gran is saying. 'It is fine as long as you don't take it seriously. Ethics particularly. Never take them seriously.'

'That's wild advice, from a respectable . . .' Jim stops.

'From a respectable old lady to a nice young man,' Gran finishes for him. 'Don't take ethics seriously. Sounds bad, doesn't it?' She chuckles to herself. 'Now Lawrence, D. H. Lawrence, was very against having sex in the head, you know; it's the wrong place for it. I'm just as against having morality in the head. Tell me now, what do they think of Wittgenstein these days? Is he still Moses from the mountain? And what exactly does this Chomsky man mean by his something grammar?'

Jim's expositions go on so long that Emily, festooned with yards of daisy chain, gets tired of waiting, and eventually comes bounding up, saying, 'Fancy you knowing anything about philosophy, Aunt!'

'Cheeky monkey!' says Gran, shaking her fist at Em. 'Why shouldn't I?'

*   *   *

Madge sits, alone, at her high window, watching the long ebb of the evening across the bay. She is thinking about Patrick. He is very puzzling, she tells herself, and then corrects the thought – (I must try not to be so foggy!) – what I mean is, I puzzle myself about him. He is like the sun coming out – he sharpens the edges of things, heightens the contrasts, light and dark. And I don't see why. Or do I mean I don't see how? I see some things it *isn't*. It isn't that he is handsome, for a start. Andrew Henderson is far better looking, with his fair hair, and wide forehead, and wide-set blue eyes. But Andrew is always somehow chill; one can like to look at him without liking him at all, as though he were a statue, or a picture of someone one doesn't know. He doesn't concern me at all. Looking at him is like seeing the departure time of a first-class train that I'm never going to take anywhere. It tells me something I have no use for. But Patrick . . .

Patrick, she admits reluctantly, is almost ugly. Too long a nose; cheeks too lean; eyes set too deep. But at least I want to know . . . He has weather in his face, endless changes. Like the sea below, he changes abruptly, varying wildly from one mood to another, and at worst ferocious, frightening. And I mind about it. Why should I care? Because I don't like him – she sees how true it is as she thinks it – I really don't like him much! He's too churned up; he makes too much fuss; he matters too much to himself. No, that's not quite it – everything matters too much to him. But then everything includes me – I feel I matter too. He pays such searchlight attention to one. He makes me feel what I say matters – the exact shades of meaning, the exact way I feel. Oh, dear, this doesn't look good, does it? It looks as if vanity is behind it, that's all. No, blast it, that's not it. After all, Matthew likes me too, and I hardly think about him at all. When Matthew is cheerful – well, Matthew always is cheerful; but when Patrick is, one is as pleased as at a fair-weather picnic, knowing how easily it might have been different . . .

Darkness has engulfed the bay. There are stars to see, and the flash of Godrevy. Madge has fallen asleep where she sits, with the mystery of Patrick still unsolved. When a banging door wakes her, she rolls into bed still in her dressing gown, and drowsily resumes her drift of thought. I can call him to mind so precisely when he isn't there, she muses; his long narrow hands, pale-palmed and sun-tanned on the backs, and the fingernails cut off very square and short – for playing the piano, I suppose. I can imagine him into a chair, and see exactly the angle he would sit at, and the set

169

of his leaning head . . . and, damn Patrick, I shall go off by myself tomorrow . . .

*   *   *

It is still hot. Madge is stretched out like a cat, on a warm corner of sand in the lee of a baking rock which keeps off the light breath of air from the sea. She swelters contentedly. The sound of the sea caresses her drowsing mind, pierced by gulls, crossed by the *chuff chuff* of a train arriving from St Erth. A golden brilliance transfuses her closed lids, and fills her eyes.

A shadow falls across her. She stirs; it remains. She opens her eyes, shading them with her hand, and blinks up frowning at the young man standing over her. He is a black outline, aureoled in light. His gold hair blazes. He swings a rucksack off his back onto the sand beside her, and smiles. 'Hullo, Sis,' he says.

'Paul!' she cries, joyfully, struggling up to sit beside him, and lay a hot sunburned arm around his shoulders, over his damp shirt. 'I'm so glad to see you! At last!'

'What do you mean, at last? I'm early.'

'Yes, yes you are. Come and swim.'

'Finding your clever crowd too much for you, are you, and wanting your own mugwump brother?'

'Well, they are a bit . . .'

'A bit what?' He is laughing at her.

'A bit . . . Oh, you'll see. Come and swim!'

'I'm straight off the train . . .'

'Your trunks must be in your bag, and I've got a towel. I'll buy you an ice cream while you change.'

The ocean may look hot; it looks, Paul says, like green chartreuse at the edges, it is so clear, and the shallows so lightened by the golden sandy floor beneath, and full of the endless web of floating wavering light. And it is sticky with salt, but it is always cool, even on the slope of the burning

170

beach, and beyond knee-deep it is cold, sharply cold. It is, after all, the ocean, continuous from here to America, from here to the poles. It has its style to keep.

Hours later they trail up the path to the house, barefoot, swinging Paul's rucksack between them, and stop at the turn of the path to look at the view. They stand waist-deep in weeds and wild flowers just under the summerhouse, on the garden wall of Goldengrove, and through its open window they can hear voices: Patrick's, and Molly's.

'Here's a sweet for you, Moll,' he is saying. 'But first you must say something. Say for me, Cogito. Co-gi-to. Now you say it.'

'Coggletoe,' says Molly.

'Co-gi-to.'

'Cogito,' says Molly. Madge is obscurely uneasy. She calls to Patrick. 'Hello! What are you doing?'

Patrick's head appears in the open window. 'This is Paul,' says Madge. 'He's my brother.'

'I can see that,' says Patrick, in a less than friendly tone. 'Hello.'

'Hello,' says Paul.

'Whatever were you doing with Molly?'

'My father is under the impression that two-syllable words are her limit,' he says. 'I'm trying to teach her a word with three.'

'But she *likes* words with three,' says Madge. 'She was saying petrol-pump and butter-knife the other day, over and over. Try her on one of those.'

'Petrol-pump,' says Molly, from behind Patrick.

'Say Cogito,' he says, reaching in his pocket for another sweet and turning his back on his audience.

'Cogito. Sweetie?'

'Cogito ergo. Then sweetie.'

'Why can't he try petrol-pump?' mutters Madge.

'*Cogito ergo sum*. It's a Latin tag. It means: *I think, therefore I am*,' says Paul.

171

'Oh, *really!*' says Madge, in disgust.

'Cogito sweetie,' says Molly cheerfully. It is obvious Patrick is in for a long session. Madge and Paul leave him, and go up through the house to the attics, where Paul is to have the room he always had, because Madge has saved it for him. The lunch bell goes in the depths of the house below.

'Oh, damn that!' says Paul. 'If they're all like that utter nutter in the summerhouse, I can do without meeting them all at once. Let's go down to the town, and buy a sandwich, and look for Jeremy to say hello. Have you looked him up yet this time, Madge?'

'No,' says Madge. 'I haven't yet. I've been a bit tied up with . . . the utter nutter!' She suddenly laughs.

'Come on,' says Paul. 'Come out!'

*   *   *

Through Downalong, the district by the Island, through the maze of narrow streets and little cottages with steps up to the high front doors and pilchard cellars below them, past cottages set around little courts, they skip and laugh, looking for Jeremy. They find him at last, sitting in the sun in the lodge on the quay, by the sailors' chapel.

'Sold your boat?' says Paul, horrified at what he hears. 'Sold it? What are you doing now?'

'Well, there wadn't much in it, not now, you know, young Paul. A few trippers to take around the bay, or off to Seal Island. A string of mackerel to sell now and then. But not real work for a man. Mind you, 'tis our own fault. St Ives folk so dead set against Sunday fishing, so all the East Coast boats brought their catches in to Newlyn. Trade's all gone there now, save for a bit at Hayle. I bought a little charabanc, that's what. I take people over to Land's End, or Kynance, or wherever. I'm doing all right. Tell you what, I'll take you anytime – we'll traipse off just like old times.'

'You know, Jeremy,' says Madge, sighing, 'you never took me to Godrevy, and now it's too late.'

'Oh, I dunno about too late, then, girl,' he says, smiling at her, his bronzed face crinkling deeply into a weatherworn pattern of smile and frown. 'It's seldom that. Someone'll lend me a boat for that.'

Paul and Madge wander all afternoon, from beach to beach, climbing the rocks, picking thrift at the edge of the grassy cliffs, talking. It is late when they climb back to the house, but, still reluctant to go in, they pass it, and go round as far as the Huer's House, where, long since, men watched for pilchards in the bay. Madge gazes at the endless show put on by the Almighty: the movement of clouds and waves in the soft evening light, the moon-shaped coves of sand, the black rocks, and white spume breaking on them, the panoramic sweep of the ceaselessly changing sea, a paper moon in a still-daylight sky. They sit there till the light goes off the waters below, and the golden eye of Godrevy begins its night-long winking to the count of ten. Then they come back through the shadowy bushes, and in through the gate to the garden. Through the open window of the house, music is pouring; the piano is storming through an outburst of passionate notes, raw feeling naked in the sound, like blood from a wound. The others have gone in to dinner, and Patrick is playing, alone, in a darkened room.

*   *   *

All afternoon the heat has thickened. The blazing sunlight has gone, and a low, grey sky like a thick blanket suffocates the day. Everyone is sticky and cross and damp. Even Jim is sitting down, sharing the general lassitude. It sounds at first as if a light breath of wind is rustling the dry leaves – and then it begins to patter and drum; rain is falling, a heavy downrush of liquid darts under which the leaves tremble and bend; the

173

earth dimples, the pavement makes tiny fountains. The adults leap up and run to close windows all over the house. Glazed with sliding streaks, the windows blur the leaves beyond, and distill a fresh green shimmer cleansed of distinct form. Gran, too, rises and goes, though slowly, to close the window of the living room, and shut out the wet that is spotting the cushions and beading the painted sill.

So she is the first to see the children, her grandchildren, Peter and Sarah, and small Beth, dancing naked in the cool rain, their tender bodies shining wet with the falling drops, throwing their arms up, tilting their faces to the sky, eyes closed, mouths open, their bare feet drumming the soft wet grass, making a trodden ring among the daisies. They sway in sensuous abandonment under the rain god's soft palpation. Their golden heads are sleeked and darkened by the silver torrents, and become heavy, and shed bright droplets like the green leaves around them, the trees above them, and the grass beneath.

Gran leaves the window unclosed. The adults gather behind her in the room full of stillness and stale heat, looking with a kind of awe. When Harriet speaks she does not say, 'They will catch cold,' but, softly, 'They are not of our tribe.' And Em and her Jim, who feel almost always the youngest, the strongest, closest to the rising sap, are upstaged entirely, and for a moment feel the sober steadiness of age.

But Gran looks and smiles, holding the window catch and never dreaming of shutting the window. And in her mind the rain is an element of eternity, showing in its brilliant light-catching instant of fall the eternal aspect of the momentary now. Just let it catch the light in such a way, and the whole world shows this double aspect, an immortal brevity, an infinite particularity. It was Traherne – (will I never outlive quoting, and telling myself where the quotation comes from?) – who saw the orient and immortal wheat, which knew no seed

174

and yet no harvest time. And boys and girls playing like moving jewels. '*I know not that they were born, or shall die,*' she murmurs. Coolness flows around her into the room, the rain softens, falters and stammers and dies away, leaving a pattering of laggard droplets sliding from sloping leaves and high branches, and falling late and reluctantly from the constellation of others on the diamonded leaf-webs of the trees. Gliding on leaf and petal, the drops collide and fuse into shining pools in the throats of flowers. The children circle slowly to a halt and sigh, begin to shiver, and hug their bare ribs with their thin glossy arms, and run indoors. The spell-bound adults move back from the window. And the warm wet ground of the garden gives off a smell of earth, a smell of the leaf mold of summers and summers back, and of green growth now.

There are wet Man Friday tracks all over the polished floor in the hall, and the towels are mud-streaked, and full of blades of grass. Small Beth is worried about what the grown-ups will say, and sits on the bathroom floor picking grass off Gran's towel for ages after the others have gone to play upstairs. Harriet finds her later, sleeping in the towel, curled up on the bathmat, the grass still sticking firmly to both towel and child.

*　　*　　*

'Not today, then, Madge girl,' says Jeremy. He is sitting on the quay in the warm sun, with his shuttle in his hand, mending nets among the other fishermen. Madge has brought Patrick, too, for after all, it would be nicer if he and Paul would get on.

'Is it too rough?' asks Paul, looking at the sea. It is sportive today, leaping about, tossing and choppy, and the crests of the waves are wind-sharpened before they break, to a ripple-flaked edge like a flint blade from the museum. The sun strikes through the dark water and gives it a translucent blue-green glaze. Yet the weather is hot, and the wind on their faces light. 'Surely the boats go out in worse weather far than this?'

'No,' says Jeremy. 'T'idn't too rough.' He knots off his work, and nods to the net's owner before drawing them away out of earshot. 'T'idn't rough,' he says. 'But we can see Ghost Island. The fish'll wait till tomorrow.'

'It wasn't fishing we wanted,' Patrick ventures, smiling hopefully at Jeremy. 'It was a trip to Godrevy.'

'I've even bought some fresh baked heavy-cake to give to the lighthouse men,' says Madge.

'Bless you, there's nobody on it now,' says Jeremy, shaking his head at the bag of sugar-coated raisin buns Madge holds out to show him. 'The light went automatic years back. You'll have to eat your heavy-cake yourself, that's what.'

'Oh,' says Madge, sadly.

'What did you mean about the island, Jeremy?' asks Paul, and it's all right for him, thinks Madge crossly; he's been to Godrevy. Jeremy took him once when I wasn't there.

'You go up the hill, and look seaward, and you'll see 'un,' says Jeremy. 'Now if a poor seaman lands on a ghost island, it fades away with him on it, and he's never seen again.'

'And is that why you won't go out today? Really, Jeremy?' Madge is entranced.

'Now does that seem like a rum idea to you, young Madge, or to your friend here?' Jeremy is smiling. 'I'm glad to be off the sea. She's a fickle hoor, that's what. Any man going on her in small craft know that. Know that mortal well. I've had a good run, never lost a boat, never been in the water head under. Time I came ashore, afore my luck changes. And when it comes to a little trip to oblige an old friend, well, I'm not running in the teeth of any rum ideas about luck; I'm not aiming to. Now t'idn't just me, see. None of the other men are out today. Boats all in harbour. Or young Tom Parsons – Josh's boy, you know. Last Good Friday he goes off with the other boys sailing model boats on Stannack Pond; and his won't sink, see. His dad knocked two or three holes in 'un, but the bugger stayed afloat. So they 'aven't bin out this season at all. Not once. You know whyfore? Because they used to reckon if the wicked old lady took your model she'd leave the real boat alone; that's why. T'idn't only me, Madge my love.'

'Of course not, Jeremy. Another day will do,' says Madge.

'Tell you what, though. I've got an errand to do over to Zennor this morning. You walk up over and meet me there, and I'll take you for a drive-around. Land's End maybe, and Sennen. What do you say to that?'

'Great,' says Paul. 'Thanks. We'd like that. Hey, Jeremy, though, your name's still up in the lifeboat shed, on the crew list, isn't it?'

'That's different,' says Jeremy sharply. 'Got to go then, haven't I?'

Leaving him, they climb the slopes of the green hill that is called the Island, slipping on the glossy grass, and stopping to feed each other with handfuls of hot currant-stuffed heavy-cake, and finally they reach the little chapel on top of it, and sit in a row of three, Madge in the middle, on the little wall that runs around it.

And they can see Ghost Island, quite clearly, out to sea, very far away, northeasterly, beyond Godrevy: a steep-sided lilac shadow, just perceptible in the misty shining distances between sea and sky.

'*I* think,' says Paul in a while, 'that's Lundy Island.'

'Can't be, can it?' says Patrick. 'The curvature of the earth would stop one seeing so far, no matter how clear the day.'

Paul gets out his compass, and takes a bearing. 'I'll look on a map when we get home, but I bet it is,' he says. 'What else could it be?'

'Well, it *could* be Ghost Island, lying in wait for poor seamen to land on it, all ready to spirit them away,' says Patrick. 'I can't see that that's any more unlikely than suddenly being able to see around the curve of the earth.'

'You *are* a nutter!' Paul complains. 'You're as bad as Madge!'

'Well, I don't mind being that,' says Patrick, smiling.

*   *   *

Through the churchyard, above the roaring beach. In the tall dewy grass the gravestones stand knee-deep, declaring the names of the bodies, the faith of the souls. *She is not dead, but sleeping*, says this slab. *In sure and certain hope of the resurrection*, says another. *He has kept the best wine until now*, says THOMAS WEDGE, *1881 to 1925. An unknown sailor, drowned on these shores* R.I.P., says a granite slab. For Gran there is only *And* MARY *his wife*, under the dates of long-forgotten Grandfather. But this place is radiant with the bright light of the shore, and loud with the sound of waves.

And beyond, across the road, out onto the grassy clifftops around the tall brink of the black rough broken cliffs, goes the path to Zennor. It curves around, skirting the wide sands to Clodgy Point, all littered with rough chunks of stone, untidy with the detritus of ages. Here they climb a rock and sit, looking across to the Island from its unfamiliar western side, and, sideways, across the great surf rolling in. Between them and the Island the whole depth of the bay is white with breaking water. Roaring, the curling frothy crests sweep across to the sands, combing out behind them long tresses of undulant smooth white, their soft violence making an endless dim uproar on the shore. Beyond the Island, Godrevy rock seems to have moved inshore, and to lie close to the headland on the far side of the bay; beyond that, farther and yet farther headlands fade eastward in shades of haze indigo, lilac, and violet. At their feet, fountains of foam rise and fall, leaping into view up the cliff face and falling in shining showers of white beads back again.

'Why is it called heavy-cake,' asks Patrick through the last crumbling sweet mouthful, 'when it's quite light?'

'Ah. They upcountry folk don't know much, do they, Madge girl?' says Paul. Patrick puts up fists to him, and they shadow-box.

'*Because*,' says Madge, 'it used to have pilchards in it. Like mince pies used to have meat, actual meat.'

'What do you mean, "because"?' demands Patrick. 'To say "because" in a well-formed formula, you have to assign a reason for something. What kind of reason are pilchards?'

'Well . . .'

'Of course, they could have been *weighty* pilchards, I suppose – vast heavy creatures like small silver whales!'

'Fool!' says Madge, giggling. 'You caught pilchards by having a "hevva" – a kind of hue and cry after them – called from the clifftop by special lookout men, and they directed the boats rowing in the bay below them to put a big net all around the shoal. First a hevva; then cooking heavy-cakes.'

'Do you think they had currants in them as well as pilchards?' asks Paul. 'Because I don't know if I *could* have eaten that . . .'

'Don't know that I like pilchards *much* even without currants,' says Patrick.

'Well, Cornishmen like them. Gran's maid, Amy, said her mother used to cook them in a pie for all her brothers, with the heads all sticking up through the pie crust,' Madge tells him. 'And do you know what they called that?'

'Tell me. I'm no good at guessing,' says Patrick.

'Starry-gazy pie!' cry the other two in unison, laughing.

They walk on. Town and bay now lie all behind

them, and they clamber on the rocky clifftop, looking down spout holes through which the wild sea cannons upwards and dews them with light drifts of spray. It is salt on their lips. Madge finds a spectacular crag to sit on, while the boys scramble off somewhere. The sun warms her back, and on her face the spray drifts, floating landward across the grassy brow of the rock walls, and shot with brief faint rainbows where it catches the sun. She watches, dream-bound and rapt. Suddenly something falls across her head, and casts a shadow web across her view of spray; she starts, and finds herself tangled in a length of torn fishing net which Patrick has found and, creeping up behind her, has thrown over her, and is holding down.

'Caught you!' he says.

'Oh, I say!' cries Paul, from a rock nearby. 'You ought to throw the tiddlers back, you know. It's not sporting to keep them!'

'Grr! Agh!' yells Madge in mock fury, writhing about in the net.

'Ah, but I don't fish for sport, you see,' says Patrick. 'I fish for survival. And I've got her tangled.'

'Well, you'll have to untangle her just for now, if we're getting to Zennor in time,' says Paul. 'Come on.'

And Madge really is caught up in the net, her struggles having thrust legs and arms through the rents in the mesh, so that it does take Patrick's help to disengage her.

'I'll let you go, Merrymaid,' he says. 'But you'll promise me not to jump back into the sea.'

'I'll promise that,' she says, smiling. 'But I'll not make any other promises, mind. I'm not good for fishes with gold in their bellies, or three wishes, or magical calm in terrible storms. I've nothing of that sort to give.'

'Haven't you, though?' says Patrick, as Madge runs after Paul.

It is too hot to run far. Between the outcrops of rock the grass on the clifftop is bright, rippling with a wind-silken sheen in the sea breeze. And it is patched yellow with bird's-foot trefoil and clumped with tufts of sea pink. And high. It has a hilltop wide-open feeling, and the view is of the glittering and dark-blue sea, and it feels wider and nearer than on a beach, in spite of the beach's fuss and fury of rolling surf. The land here does not slope, or crumble away, or give the sea space and licence to come in and out, but stands out boldly into deep water, and offers an unyielding confrontation to the endless turmoil below.

*   *   *

Jeremy is parked beside the church. His bus is hot with standing in the sunlight, but when they get moving the flow of air through the wound-down windows soothes the stickiness of their skin. Madge puts her arm out, and claws a handful of onrushing air, and holds it pressed on her palm. Her hair blows wildly. The road winds and ribbons around the hillsides, under the barren tops with their heather and gorse and stones. Westward and westward they go, past the tall engine houses of abandoned mines, with their towering chimneys, their squalid grandeur, outlines black against the sun, gaping windows, sloping roofless eaves. The road leaves the coast, turns right, and at last runs out to the very end of the land. With everything behind them, they get out of the bus. There is an asphalt carpark, and an ugly hotel. There is a kiosk selling postcards and lumps of polished serpentine made into vulgar souvenirs, and ice creams. A strong wind blows off the sea. Climbing over the carpark wall, the four of them walk the brink path, looking westward. They can see the land ending with craggy magnificence. A huge humped rocky height, nearly as tall as the land itself, stands islanded in the sea below; across the

181

silver-streaked, twinkling plains of the sea are more rocks, and a lighthouse standing on them.

'There's men still on that one, Madge,' says Jeremy. 'You were crestfallen that Godrevy's gone automatic, I saw that. Well, cast your mind out yonder. There's the Longships light; that's got men on. And look southward now. No, that way. Can you see that tower light, standing right up out of the sea, like it was set on nothing? Got it? It's far, mind; hard to make it out. That's the Wolf Rock. There's men on that one, too. Waves break right over that one, when it cuts up rough. Think on it.'

'You know, I think I'd like to be a lighthouse keeper,' says Patrick.

'Terrible life, that is,' says Jeremy, bringing out his tobacco tin, and beginning to roll himself a ragged cigarette.

'Wouldn't you be afraid of being lonely?' asks Madge.

'Yes,' says Patrick, looking steadily out towards the distant lighthouse tower. 'I'm afraid of that more than anything else in the whole world, really.'

'Seems a bit perverse to be a lighthouse keeper, then, doesn't it?' says Paul.

'Well . . . but it would have a meaning,' says Patrick, quietly. 'One would endure it, that thing one feared most, not just because life is bloody, but because one chose to. And it has a reason. One would keep a light that other men find their way by.'

'Has a reason, that's for sure,' says Jeremy. 'This is a hard coast for seafarers. Can't think how many ships would come to grief without the lights. And even with them, mind, things happen. Now, when I was a boy, I remember seeing a steamer wrecked on those skerries out there, right beside the light. Wrecked on a clear night, that one was, just a matter of yards from the light. Never did account for that. I've seen some terrible wrecks.One morn when I was a boy there were two of them, sitting side by side on Porthminster sands, right up beside the railway station. Rum sight: torn sails flapping, and the hulls just stranded, sitting there – two on 'em.'

'What's the worst you've seen?' asks Paul.

'Ah,' says Jeremy. 'In '39 the lifeboat went out in weather so bad she capsized just as she rounded the end of the quay. She righted herself, and went over again in the next wave. And then again. After the third time there was only one man left aboard her. That was the worst I've seen, young Paul. Now we must be going back along, for I've this and that to see to at home.'

'Why are you afraid of being alone?' Madge asks Patrick, in the windy back seat of Jeremy's bus.

'I know what it's like, that's why,' says Patrick.

'You've got your family . . .'

'We're not allowed feelings in my family,' says Patrick. 'Only thoughts. So if one has any feelings, one has them alone. That's partly why my father can't do with Molly. She has feelings all right – simple ones. But she'll never have anything he would call a thought.'

Madge instinctively puts out a hand to him, meaning to touch him lightly. But he interrupts the gesture by un- expectedly taking her hand and holding it tightly in his. It seems to fit very well. She glances at him, mildly as- tonished, wondering what he means. Then, 'You know, Patrick,' she says, 'you have very complicated eyes.'

'I have *what* eyes?'

'Complicated,' she says, beginning to laugh. 'They are a sort of green colour, with a darker rim, and then golden amber in the middle. Everybody else makes do with just one colour.' But she knows the darkness in Patrick's eyes has nothing to do with the colour. Up in the front seat Paul is talking fishing with Jeremy. Madge begins to sing softly to herself a snatch of song from among the many that drift through her mind:

'*A ship there is, and she sails the sea,*
She's loaded deep, as deep can be . . .'

183

* * *

'Now don't you go singing as we go by Zennor,' says Jeremy, 'or the merfolk'll come and take you down among the dead men.'

'I don't think you believe half the rot you talk, Jeremy,' says Paul. 'You can stop playing the crusty old local with us.'

Jeremy roars with laughter. The bus comes along the back of Porthmeor beach, threads its way through Downlong, and stops on the harbourside.

* * *

There is a tranquil deep evening on the town, quiet and without a wind. The tide is out, leaving the harbor half full of still, dark water, in which the lights around the harbourside hang glittering, drawn down into shimmering columns. Bright sapphire shining banners waver below the blue navigation light on the pier; amber stalactites suspended in the cavernous depths of azure water descend below the light on Smeaton's Quay. The sands show just perceptible at the whispering water's edge; a gull still screams overhead. Only if you know exactly where the land lies across the bay can you believe that you can still see the shadow shape of it in the dusk, or make out the white tower of Godrevy where the light shines on and off.

From the quiet dusk on the brow of the hill, over the unlit shrubs and bushes one can see the harbor lying like a scatter of jewels on purple velvet. Gran is outside, standing on the lawn, listening to the distant sound of the waves. She sees a dim glow in the summerhouse, and notices the window open. She goes to shut it. The summerhouse door is ajar. It creaks softly open to admit her. The summerhouse smell reaches her – deck-chair canvas, and grass mowings, and dusty confined air

184

baked dry under the slate roof in the hot sun. In the middle of the floor a candle burns, held in the neck of a wine bottle, which is submerged under a web of wax like a rock under the edge of a wave. Beside it lies Jim in his sleeping bag, and with him lies Emily, face down, her hair spread out across his pale naked chest. He is sleeping with his arms around her in total stillness. The candle flame burns tall and steady, perfectly vertical.

Gran stops. She looks at them long and shamelessly before turning away and, going out, gently putting the door nearly to behind her. She goes back to standing on the lawn, looking at the view.

Would her father mind? she asks herself. Ought I to do anything about it? And she knows at once, without more than a moment's consideration, that Emily's father would mind. That straightness and simplicity, that perfect candour which he had as a boy has gradually hardened into a habit of thinking and feeling the ordinary things; his frankness has become conventionality. But she knows, also, that he would not expect her to do anything about it; he knows her better than that. He would know she would no more move to change it than to alter the fall of the light, or re-orchestrate birdsong. One should just be pleased, if one can, by events. Gran is pleased. Perhaps, it occurs to her as she goes in, Emily knows me as well as her father does. And not for the first time, Gran feels deeply pleased at herself. She goes slowly, smiling, along the terrace through the open garden door, and asks her son-in-law to put some Tchaikovsky on the gramophone.

'Oh, I meant to tell you,' he says, getting up. 'We met the burglar on our expedition to Land's End today. And we did invite him to tea. He's a Canadian, over here visiting the scenes of his youth. He'll come tomorrow at four.'

'Oh good. How exciting. I'll look forward to that.'

'Does it have to be Tchaikovsky?' he asks, getting

out a record. 'You are a sentimental old thing, aren't you?'

'Yes, dear, aren't I?' she says, still pleased and smiling.

*　　*　　*

For the last weekend of the reading party a large outing is planned. Not Zennor Hill again; and not Trencrom Hill, for that has been climbed by most of the young men on one afternoon or another during the fortnight. Somewhere farther off: Godrevy Point. Everyone would like to see the lighthouse closer to. There is an animated discussion on how to get there, for the two family cars will not hold everyone, and it is some nine miles around the rim of the bay. Mr Jones proposes to hire a car from the garage up the road, and Andrew, it seems, can drive a party in that. Madge and Paul think of the bicycles they used to ride, and go looking in the shed for them. There are four bicycles in the shed, all rusted solid, and with flat tires.

'We can fix these,' says Paul cheerfully. 'Ours and one for Patrick. Who shall we offer the other one to? Are any of these weirdies good fun?'

'Matthew is the nicest. He doesn't believe in God,' says Madge.

'Christ! Don't you know anything less dramatic about him?' says Paul.

'He comes from Darlington.'

'I sometimes wonder about you, Sis,' says Paul. 'Let's go and offer them, then. We'll need help fixing them all.'

Matthew turns out to be very handy at bike-fixing, Patrick to be useless. He can, however, find punctures by holding the inner tubes under water in a bucket, so he is left doing that, while Madge applies glue to the rubber patches, and the other two wield spanners and oilcans.

'It's going to be heavy going, riding these uphill,' says Matthew.

'We could put them in the guard's van on the train to St Erth, and ride from there,' says Madge.

The adults are pleased to hear about the bicycles. 'It's remarkably kind of you,' says Professor Tregeagle to Matthew, 'not to mind being separated from the main party.'

Matthew pulls a wry face at the professor's departing back. 'The main party *is* where we are, so there!' he says, and Patrick laughs.

That night there is a knock on Madge's door. She is propped up on one elbow, reading *Sons and Lovers*, with a secret treat beside her – a huge box of chocolate creams. Thinking it will be Paul, she says, 'Come in.'

Patrick comes in. He is in a dark-red dressing gown, and holding a half-empty bottle of amber liquid in one hand, and his toothmug in the other. 'This stuff is supposed to be good,' he says to Madge, conspiratorially. 'Why should they have it all? Where's your toothmug?'

'Over there,' says Madge, pulling the sheet up over her nightgown to her chin. 'What is it, Patrick?'

'Whisky.'

'I don't know if I like that,' she says. 'I've never tried.'

'You are about to find out. It says *Glenfiddich Pure Malt* on the label.'

'Coo-er. I'm impressed. Or, I daresay I would be if I knew what it meant. Shouldn't we invite Paul?'

'I have. He's fast asleep, flat out. He invited me to go away and leave him be – with considerable emphasis. And everyone else is in bed one whole floor down. No-one will suspect our midnight orgy!'

'Is whisky enough to make an orgy by itself?' asks Madge, relinquishing the sheet, and relying on her nightgown. 'Maybe,' says Patrick, pouring it out. 'Traditionally it goes with cigarettes and wild wild women, to drive one insane.'

'Would chocolate creams do instead of cigarettes?' Madge wonders. 'Do they go with whisky?'

'One more thing we are about to find out.'

'I don't know that I can be a wild wild woman, though,' says Madge. 'Quiet and thoughtful and muddled is more like me.'

'You seem rather crystal and clear-cut to me,' says Patrick, looking at her assessingly. 'But in any case, that is Madge-before-booze. Madge-after-booze may turn out wild. Drink up and see.'

Madge swigs back a large gulp of the liquid in her glass, and is left gasping with a burning tongue and throat, and tears in her eyes.

'One is supposed to sip it judiciously,' says Patrick, looking coolly at her distress.

'*Now* you tell me, you brute – you positively *hairy* brute!' she says, for his dressing gown displays a triangle of dark hair on his chest, and his wrists, emerging from the cuffs, are decorated likewise with dark brown, growing sideways around their slender shape.

'I'll be beast to your beauty,' he says, sipping his mug. 'Hey, this is good. Try tasting it slowly.'

'It does have a nice taste,' Madge says thoughtfully when she has tried again. 'It tastes like cornfields look, only very pure and clean,' she says. 'If only the taste weren't so *ferocious*.'

'Him firewater plenty hot.'

'Try cooling it with one of these,' Madge says, offering her box of chocolate creams.

'I thought you were too good to be true. And I now know that chocolate is your secret vice,' says Patrick, taking two.

'It does work, rather well,' says Madge in a while, having experimented with alternate mouthfuls of chocolate and whisky.

'You don't think it muddies the pure essence of each?'

'Oh, pooh.'

'An adult, I suspect, would be appalled at the thought of eating chocolate with whisky.'

'Patrick, what's it going to be like, being an adult? Doesn't it scare you a bit?'

'Well, yes, in a way. But what scares you about it?'

'They seem so different from us; and I don't seem to change much. Can I really be going to be like them? And when will I start to get that way? And shall I find it bearable?'

'What's wrong with just being Madge?' he asks, smiling.

'But I've never known a real adult who was a bit like me. And how shall we manage to care about the things they care about, and carry their responsibilities?'

'I don't know, I honestly don't,' he says gloomily. Then: 'I think, you know, they have secret consolation.'

'How do you mean?'

'The lucky ones have love for someone. And it makes a private world nobody else can see at all. Then they're all right.'

'How do you know?' she asks.

'Well, I don't, in a way. I'm guessing. But take my mother, for example. Her life really is all ground down under caring for Molly. But my father loves her as a carefree pretty person. He gives her clothes and perfumes and bits of jewellery. He makes her a kind of secret self, to be for him, at least – whatever she may have to be for anybody else. I think it will be all right being an adult if we have found someone to love us – and pretty awful otherwise.'

'We couldn't just keep the way we are, being ourselves, for ourselves, and not worrying too much?' says Madge, sipping the whisky again.

'Well, I don't *see* why not, but I think not, somehow,' says Patrick. 'I don't know any adult person who seems to manage that. Do you?'

'No,' says Madge, after thinking a while. 'We had

189

a history mistress two years ago who fell in love. It made her much nicer to us. She told us a bit about how marvellous he was; and then on prize day he came to the school, and he was awful! Just awful. Positively *fat!* But they kind of shone at each other. So perhaps you're right about a secret world. But then, on the other hand, Patrick, you're making me think about Marie, who was the elder sister of Jenny, my school friend. Marie was at college, and engaged to this student, and he kept buying her books about her subject, and wanting to take her to see cathedrals and Roman ruins, and she would pull wry faces at Jenny behind his back. Jenny was very worried about it. So perhaps it isn't any good having a secret self for someone if it isn't the self one wants to be.'

'Well, no,' says Patrick. 'I should think not. Have some more whisky. And how does one know who one wants to be? I feel all shapeless most of the time. Positively amoeboid.'

'So I suppose,' says Madge, sipping more whisky, 'that real happiness is having one's favourite self, the person one most likes to be, loved by someone. That's quite a thought, Patrick.'

'And that's not all, either. Because I don't think it's one's *favourite* self exactly – I mean, not necessarily the person one flatters oneself one is, like I fancy myself as a great pianist – I think it's the nearest self – the one one truly is. And I don't think being loved by just anyone will do it either; I think it has to be a special person.'

'It seems a lot to ask,' says Madge. 'Is it all right to finish the bottle?' for Patrick is filling his mug again.

'It isn't finished yet, there's some left. And, well, I think it *is* a lot to ask. I expect it doesn't happen very often. After all, people don't seem all that happy, by and large, do they?'

'I suppose not. Have another chocolate. You know, that's a very different kind of happiness from the sort we've had up to now, isn't it?'

'What *have* you had up to now, do you think? Just put it simply.'

Madge grins. 'Well, it's mostly been being in special places, for me, I think. Places are so detailed and actual; and they last so long. You know they were before and will be after. I'm happy, *looking*, mostly. This is a crummy way to talk, you know, Patrick. Do you think it's the whisky?'

'No,' says Patrick. 'Not really. I think it's the way we are. I've only known you a couple of weeks, and there isn't anything I wouldn't talk to you about.'

'I'd tell you anything, too,' says Madge. 'And I can't think why!'

'There's all this energy sparking off between us, and it doesn't know where to go yet.'

'I suppose *this* couldn't be what it's like to . . .' says Madge, wide-eyed.

'I don't think so. It isn't what I expect. I feel all tugged about, and tossed up and down. It isn't at all pleasant – it's like changing gear all the time in a car with no synchromesh.'

'Well, I'll have to take your word for *that!*' says Madge, laughing. 'But it does feel a bit jerky. I think if it went on for long it would be more like being seasick than anything else!'

'Thanks!' says Patrick. He is sitting on the floor at the foot of her bed, resting his chin on the bedclothes, and smiling at her. They begin to laugh, helplessly.

'So I'm like seasickness, am I?' he says after a while, giggling.

'Well, you said I wasn't at all pleasant, blast you!' says Madge, leaning back on her pillow, choking back giggles. 'Oh, Patrick, it *is* the whisky! I've got such a funny feeling in my head, like an eightsome reel going on all by itself, and my tummy feels all warm!'

'Well, if it is, then we'll be different in the morning,' says Patrick. He gets to his feet, and picks up the bottle and his mug, very slowly, and with elaborate

191

care, as though the floor had become a tightrope under his feet. 'Good night,' he says, smiling. He has a very sudden smile. It creases his lean cheeks, and around his eyes deeply, and he looks years older, and much more carefree, while it lasts. He shakes Madge's foot gently where it bulges through the bedclothes, and makes carefully for the door.

'Good night, sleep well,' says Madge. 'Good night, sweet prince.'

'Typical. That's a bloody quotation,' says Patrick, closing her door.

*　　*　　*

Godrevy morning breaks fine and bright, with a brisk wind blowing, and the wave crests just touched with white across the bay. The bicycle party leaves straight after lunch, shaking free of the bustle of preparations in the kitchen, the piles of rugs and baskets in the porch, and escaping gladly from the fuss.

Beyond Hayle the road rolls up and down, going along the shore, but out of sight and sound of the sea, for the sand dunes lie between. They are grassy and smooth, and shaped as a child might draw a hill, humpy and round, and over them is blue sky with clouds and larksong. The road rolls enough for the rises to be hard work, the dips to be joyous freewheeling. They come to Gwithian, sheltering among its trees, little church, stone cottages, and rooks' nests – so inland a place you could never believe the sea was nearby; and the tall towans keep it from the wind.

On the road beyond Gwithian they are overtaken by the first car from the house – the one driven by Andrew – just before the little bridge descends the slope and crosses the Red River.

'My God, what makes it that colour?' asks Matthew, looking startled at the crimson cloudy waters of the little stream.

'Spoil from the tin mines,' says Paul.

'It seems odd it should sound the same as clear water when it looks like that,' says Patrick.

'Yes,' says Madge, pleased. 'It does, rather.' But she is eager to go on, to see the lighthouse. And across the stream the road turns suddenly seaward, becoming a rough track that climbs around the hill so steeply that they walk, and push – Matthew unasked pushing Madge's bike as well as his own – until it turns on the height above the beach, and shows them, in a great sweep, the shore: rocks, sand, huge waves, and Godrevy island ringed in white water, just offshore. It stands alone, a short way into the immense vastness of the sea under the sky, that huge theatre on which the light exults, sweeping great streaks of silver across the ocean distances, gleaming on the lovely glassy curves of the rising waves, blinding white on the breaking crests as they avalanche in walls of white foam racing shoreward, transfusing the drift of smoke, as they break, and the spindrift blows off them on the wind. The lighthouse tower is painted white, hexagonal, one of its three visible sides lit brightly, and two in light shadow, softened by reflected brightness from the dancing sea.

Throwing down the bikes, they run along the grassy tops above the rocky beach, and up the path that mounts and mounts the steep promontory, and swings around it till it brings them high up on the outermost corner, overlooking the island, and the light. They can see down into the ring of stone wall around the tower, and onto the grey sloping roofs of its cottages, and outbuildings, and the parched tawny grass where once the garden was.

'When we were children,' Madge says wistfully, 'there were men on the rock, and they kept a garden. Paul saw it once.'

'Only a little thrift, and some wallflowers,' says Paul. 'Look, Patrick, at that pole sticking up. That's the breeches buoy they used to get in and out of the relief boat. Still want to be a lighthouse keeper?'

'Glory!' says Matthew. 'Whatever for?'

'What do you mean, what for? You know what lighthouses are for!' says Patrick, grinning.

They fall silent, gazing at the sea, the rock, the island below them, and the tall tower rising firm and white to its bright, caged glass eye. The waves play around the rock, filling the foreground with endless movement, with random bursts of white, and the more distant ocean juggles with falling light, keeping a million sequins of sunshine rocking and gleaming and shining back. The four figures seated on the brink of the land hear the cars behind them come near and stop, hear faint voices. Paul gets up and goes to beg a drink for thirsty cyclists who cannot wait till the rugs are spread and the hampers opened.

He comes back with four bottles of fizzy pop and four bent straws. The bottles spew out half their contents on being opened, expressing their disgust at the warm, shaken ride in the car. Patrick, having seen Paul's drink half lost, manages to get his bottle into his mouth a split second after flipping the cap off it, and it fills him with froth, and leaves him gasping for air, and hiccupping helplessly.

A gang of gulls comes wheeling by, screaming overhead.

'Just listen to that vulgar screeching,' says Patrick. 'And the sky was a nice district before that fishwife crowd moved in!'

'When was that, then?' says Matthew darkly.

'Hark at you!' says Madge. 'What could be more vulgar than burping away like you!' Patrick grins, and burps.

'We're not very refined,' says Paul solemnly. 'Not as elevated as the rest. You really ought to go back there, you know, Matthew, and listen to that philosophy. They're at it already. And that's what you're here for,

194

you lazy dog, not lying about, slumming it with us dummies.' He dodges Matthew's mock blow.

'What are they on about, Paul, old son?' says Matthew, lying back comfortably on the grass, with his hands behind his head, and his eyes closed to the sun. 'And if it's anything critical, I'll leap up and rush back so as not to miss it.'

'Well, don't ask *me*,' says Paul. 'I'm just a peasant from a county grammar school; *I* don't understand it. Ask my clever sis. Or the Great Philosophy Professor's son, here. They might know.'

'Alas!' says Patrick. 'The Great Philosophy Professor, for all his art, cannot transmit his profound insight to his son. Small genetic accident prevents. He doesn't have any luck, genetically.'

'Ugh!' says Paul.

'*I'll* have to tell you what they're on about, then, won't I?' says Madge. 'Tell me what they were saying, Paul, and I'll expound it.'

'Means and ends. Justification of the one by the other,' says Paul.

'What sort of ends?' demands Madge. 'Bin ends? Bale ends? Loose ends? Journeys' ends?'

'You don't know what "ends" *means*!' cries Patrick, burping and laughing. 'An end, friends, is what we intend. We intend our ends.'

'Oh, I don't think so,' says Madge. 'Surely not. Wished upon us, more likely.'

'God, what womanish logic,' says Paul. '*I* will explain. When one has an end in view . . .' A gust of wind ruffles them as it leaps inland.

'Hold your skirt down, Madge,' says Patrick, 'or all this vulgar crowd will have an end in view.'

'Speaking personally,' says Madge, coolly, leaving her skirt to blow as it likes, 'I end in a set of toes. And I like them in view, I like to wiggle them.'

'Now if the class will come to attention, please,' says Matthew, 'I will expound means and ends, and thus prove that, knowing it all already, I have no need to go and listen to all that carefully chiselled rot, but can stay peacefully idle, lazing about here, putting all thought of it out of my mind.'

'Hear, hear!' says Paul.

'Here, here!' says Madge.

'An end,' says Matthew, 'is an intention. A thing aimed at. Thus you have an end in view – let us say, for example's sake, that you want to visit your aunt in Tooting. To achieve that end you take some means – a train, or a 57 bus, or a long walk. There.'

'But what,' asks Madge, baffled, 'seriously, Matthew, what is interesting about that?'

'Well, Madge, dear child, you know that you are not allowed, repeat, *not allowed* to have a wicked end. That is nasty and immoral and ruled out of court straight away. But what if you have a good end, and the only way of achieving it is to use wicked means? What then?'

'I should think,' says Madge, briskly, 'it would depend *how* good the end, and how *evil* the means.'

'Careful!' cries Matthew. 'That is common sense. Common sense will extinguish the discussion, and leave us all confusedly agreed. One must take it to the extreme. Suppose, for example, that your end is to save the lives of thousands. Would it be right to do it by killing one man?'

'Such a thing couldn't happen,' says Madge.

'I'm afraid it could,' says Matthew. 'In war, for example. With a hostage. Or with a prisoner who knows where the bomb has been put. Could one torture him?'

'No,' says Paul. 'Absolutely not.'

'So Paul believes in absolute moral values. There are things he would say one must not do, even to save the world. For him the ends do not justify the means. Quite a clear and respectable belief. We could prod him a bit, by thinking of more and more frightful

196

examples of tough situations, so that he will have to sit there consigning his fellow men to endless suffering in order to avoid telling a lie, say, or giving a prisoner a black eye; but if he's a Christian he will stick to his guns; I mean his absolutes. One may not do evil that good may come. That's Paul.'

'Well, what's wrong with that?' says Paul.

'Nothing. But it isn't the only opinion. One could go to the other extreme, and find someone who was completely utilitarian. Willing to achieve a good result by any means whatsoever. And while Paul won't torture the prisoner to save a thousand, this other chap will murder ten people if it will make eleven people happy. And then in between there's dear foggy Madge, who thinks it depends; she would do a little wrong, I expect, to do a lot of good, but she would keep a sense of proportion about it. If we asked her enough questions we could find out a lot about her sense of proportion; but once good ends justify just slightly suspect means, you are firmly on the utilitarian, which is to say the practical, which is to say the immoral side of the dispute.'

'I can't be expressing myself right,' says Madge. 'I don't at all think what you describe me as thinking. Happiness can't be what matters most, can it?'

'You mustn't take this personally,' says Matthew. 'You're just an example, for the sake of discussion. You can have a different set of opinions next time round if you like.'

'Good,' says Madge.

'What we need is an example. I take it we are all agreed that lying is wrong? Right? Well, then, there you are in your study, peacefully reading *Crime and Punishment*, and a fellow bursts in, crying "Hide me! Hide me!" and crams himself into your wardrobe. And a few moments later this madman bursts in after him, waving a butcher's cleaver, and yelling "Where is he? Where is he? Let me get at him, aarghh!" The question

197

is, do you say, "He's in the wardrobe," or do you prevaricate, like not answering at all, or standing across the wardrobe door or trying to take the cleaver away, or jumping out of the window, or do you lie like a gentleman, and say, "He ran out that way just before you came in"? And if the latter, you think the end justifies the means, and in a corner you would probably kill, maim, cheat, fornicate, etc., etc., as long as doing so would achieve some good end or other.'

'Don't be ridiculous, Matthew,' says Paul.

'I'm not being ridiculous; I'm telling you about means and ends.'

'Well, what about a serious example?' says Patrick. 'What about the doctor who came and cured Molly last year, when she was quietly dying in her sleep of some infection or other? What about that?'

'No, Patrick, don't!' said Madge.

'Why not?'

'I think,' says Madge, deeply agitated, 'you probably shouldn't do philosophy with serious examples!'

'One could only say,' pursues Matthew, 'that in that case the fellow had got his ends wrong. To-keep-alive-regardless not being a proper end.'

'Don't!' pleads Madge. 'Please stop!'

'If a person was in terrible agony, and you had the morphine bottle, you'd give an overdose, Madge, wouldn't you?' asks Patrick.

'Molly's not in terrible agony,' mutters Paul. 'She's bumming about picking flowers.'

'*Wouldn't* you, Madge?'

'How do I know what I'd do? I'd do what felt right. But I think . . . what I think is, one shouldn't . . . you see, I don't think one should *calculate*. I don't think one should do sums with good and evil, and what will happen if, and if not. I don't think one ever knows.'

'Sort of pacifist position,' says Matthew, cheerfully.

'I think one should watch; and be. Not always be tampering, doing things,' says Madge.

'As I say, quasi-pacifist position,' says Matthew.

'You have a sardonic attitude to the whole damn thing, don't you, Matthew?' says Paul. 'What the hell made you study philosophy?'

'Oh, I don't know. It has a sort of fascination about it, doesn't it, Patrick?'

'Yes it does. One can never decide whether it's the only subject that matters at all, or just a load of abstract crap that doesn't matter a pin. And it has to be one or the other.'

'I rather think,' says Matthew meditatively, rolling over to prop himself on one arm and look at the shining sea, 'that I read it because I like thinking. Like I like playing chess. But Patrick here didn't choose it; it's all around him, like the smell of fish if you live beside the quay. So what do you think, Patrick? Where do you stand among the means and ends?'

Patrick does not answer. He plucks a little stem of grass and looks closely at it.

'Is there *anything* we must not do, regardless of the consequences? Are there absolute moral values?' continues Matthew, exuberantly.

'I think to have absolutes is to blame God for the way things are,' says Patrick. 'And there is no God.'

'We'll have only ourselves to blame if we don't get any grub,' says Paul in a little while. 'Let's go and get that picnic.'

*   *   *

The picnic is not on the cliff's very top, but down the slope, a little way off the brink, to be out of the way of the wind coming over the edge from the sea. The grassy dip in which the party is sitting turns its back on the wide sea, and the lighthouse, therefore, and commands instead a view of the bay: of Hayle towans, the vast expanse of Porthkidney sands, waves and breakers, and the reaches of rusty-pink staining in

199

the sea where the Red River runs out. On the far side of the bay they can see the great bulk of Rosewall hill, and the harbour and town lie indistinguishable beneath it, contre-jour in the afternoon sun.

The picnic party has split into two groups: women and children in one, philosophers in the other, either by accident or by design. The philosophers are holding a colloquium, grouped around their food in various attitudes of formal informality, as though posing to be painted al fresco. Andrew, for example, lies stretched out, head propped on his right hand, at the feet of Professor Tregeagle, who sits rather upright in a folding chair. Beside them Mr Jones sits cross-legged on the rug.

Madge joins the two women, and for a while is happily busy buttering baps, and putting paste and cucumber in them, and handing them around, making sure Patrick gets what he likes, and Paul gets only crab paste, because he doesn't like sardine, and Matthew, whose likes are unknown, gets consulted each time. She makes little squares of cheese to feed Molly, and gives her sips of orange juice. In a while they need to carry plates piled high with buttered baps, across to the other group. Madge trots over and back again with more.

'The gist of the Platonic argument is,' Mr Jones is saying as she brings the first plate, 'that we can look at objects, and judge them to be more or less equal. Yet we can never have encountered two perfectly equal objects, in this world. But knowledge of equality is necessary to permit us to judge things to be more or less equal. Therefore we encountered equality in some previous existence, and have remembered it, though dimly. Our souls therefore existed before our birth, and if they did, may perfectly well survive our death. Plato teaches, remember, the incorporeal nature of the soul.'

'It is a strange belief,' says Jake, 'that a soul must be an incorporeal thinking substance — a ghost in the

200

machine – that consciousness cannot be an attribute of a wholly material being, when, as a matter of fact, every instance of consciousness we know of is, as a matter of fact, associated with a material being.'

'Presumably, it is the widespread acceptance of Christian doctrine that makes that commonplace,' says Andrew. 'For to believe that people are wholly material would be to believe that death was the end, as birth is the beginning.'

'Christian doctrine asserts, not the immortality of the soul, but the resurrection of the body,' says Matthew, arriving with two plates of buns, 'which is not at all the same thing.'

'So you mean to say that a Christian could believe, as I do, in a completely material view of persons; could think that "soul" is a word for certain functions of living material beings, and nothing else, and still believe in an afterlife, because the resurrected body will resemble the body before death in having the attributes called "soul"?' Andrew asks.

Fascinated, Madge lingers, listening, and not fetching more food. 'Why not?' says Matthew. 'We shall sit under the trees in Eden, and talk and eat, and hold hands with those we love, and pass me a ham bap, Jake, please.'

'But *who* will, Matthew?' asks Professor Tregeagle. 'The difficulty with this view is not that resurrection is impossible, for an omnipotent Deity could reassemble the elements of a body, and produce a perfect replica of any of us. But, however perfect, that replica would not be the same *me*, the same *you*. God could not make a replica of myself, actually myself, for the same reason he could not make a square circle.'

'Bother,' says Matthew. 'And yes. Why do I always play the religious pieces which always get fool's mate?'

'You're the only one of our number who can play them at all, Matthew,' says Mr Jones.

'But it seems obvious to me,' Matthew says, 'that

people are material objects, and I should have thought that the sight of one dead body would be enough to convince anyone of it, unless they were a mad mystic.'

But, no, thinks Madge, oh, no, it would not . . . there had been a journey, very early in the morning, bringing her up to the house with a telegram in her pocket, a bird singing in the still garden . . . 'Have you ever seen a dead body, Matthew?' she asks him in a whisper, and he shakes his head.

'It seems doubtful to me if any knowledge of the changes occurring to bodies, including death, can of itself demonstrate that there are no souls,' says Mr Jones. 'For there are some strong moves from religious pieces, Matthew — there's Bishop Butler's argument. Hold on while I get my notebook.'

While he tugs a battered exercise book out of his jacket pocket Madge skips away to bring baps, and cress, and tomatoes. When she returns, he is reading: '. . . *for we see by experience that men lose their limbs, their organs of sense, and even the greatest part of their bodies, and yet remain the same living agents* . . . Then he points out how small we were as children, different bodily, in fact . . . and then, *we have several times over lost a great part or perhaps the whole of our body according to certain common established laws of nature, yet we remain the same living agents. When we shall lose as great a part, or the whole, by another common established law of nature — death — why may we not also remain the same? We have passed undestroyed through those many and great revolutions of matter, so peculiarly appropriated to ourselves; why should we imagine death will be so fatal to us?'*

'Oh, but really!' exclaims Jake. The students clamour for a moment, all talking at once, while Madge, her attention fixed, fails to hand around the cress.

Paul and Patrick arrive, commissioned by Mrs Jones to bring the tea flasks and beakers, and pour for the thinkers.

'Well, what did Aristotle think?' asks Andrew. 'He must be free from Christian taint. Did he think death would be fatal to us?'

'It's far from simple, I fear,' says Professor Tregeagle. 'Aristotle defines "soul" as "substance-as-concept". The "what-it-is-to-be" of something. Matthew's soul is what it is to be Matthew, let us say. Not only living things have this sort of soul – being-an-axe is the soul of an axe. Could we imagine being-an-axe separated from the axe itself? This definition makes nonsense of the idea that soul could exist without body, and therefore of pre-existence, and survival after death. It involves a wholly materialist view of persons, and is quite clear. Unfortunately Aristotle felt obliged to make a most difficult reservation, one might almost call it a retraction, in favour of the intellect, his word "nous". Nous is not the same as soul, but is a faculty concerned with truth, which the philosopher takes to be one element in the human, and only in the human, soul. Now I, too, shall read from my notes, like my colleague.' He finds a small black leather book, puts on his spectacles, hastily bites a mouthful of sardine-filled roll, and reads, '*Love and hatred are not attributes of the intellect, but of the person who has it, in so far as he does. Hence when this person perishes he neither remembers nor loves, for these things never attached to the intellect, but to the whole which has perished; whereas the intellect is no doubt something more divine, and something more impassive.* Now what shall we say about that?'

'If I understood it correctly, sir,' says Jake after a pause, 'the intellectual faculty, though only possessed by human souls, is possessed *more* or *less* – yet one could hardly be more or less immortal, could one, according to how clever one is?'

'Aristotle does not teach personal, individual immortality; it is not in that context he must be understood,' says Professor Tregeagle. 'The interesting point is that for Aristotle there remained a division that had to be made between reality which could be attributed to material things, and realities which could not, and that, for him, that division lay not between living and non-living, nor between conscious and not-conscious, but between the intellectual and everything else.'

Round the rim of the grassy hollow in which they are sitting come the two younger Jones children, running. They stumble and laugh, their noise pouring obtrusively into the talk. Behind them comes Molly, chasing, trying hard to catch up, falling back, losing ground. And behind her comes Prudence Jones, walking knees splayed, flat-footed, deliberately aping a clumsy gait. She is dribbling, letting spittle run down her chin, and has her fingers in the corners of her eyes, pulling them upward and outward, dragging her face into a hideous likeness of Molly's. She cannot see where she is going, doing that, and so when Molly gives up suddenly, slithers down the bank, and sits down among the students on the rug, she staggers on, and comes face to face with Patrick, handing his father a mug of tea, and with Professor Tregeagle.

'Put in the balance against that, Wittgenstein's "*The human body is the perfect image of the human soul . . .*"' the professor is saying.

'Pru! Look out!' shrieks her brother, and she opens her eyes, tosses her head defiantly at her unwanted audience, and runs off before her father can catch her. Patrick and his father remain frozen, side by side. The tea in the beaker Patrick has given his father slops over a drop or two.

Molly, sitting on the rug, is picking stalks of cress, and putting them carefully between her toes. 'Coggle-toe. Petrol-pump,' she is saying. 'Butter-knife. Cogito.' She looks up at Patrick, and says sweetly and clearly, 'Cogito ergo sum.'

Everyone stares at her. And Patrick says to his father, speaking in a very soft voice, though Madge, a little distance off, can hear every word, 'Well, is that proof good, or isn't it? Because she can say it as well as anyone else!'

'Oh, my God!' says Professor Tregeagle, and with the words come sobs, uncontrollable for a moment, shaking his rib cage, while he struggles to choke them off, and falls silent, shamed.

'Come, Molly,' says Patrick, getting up, and taking her hand. 'Come walk. Find flowers.'

'Cogito ergo butter-knife,' she says, trotting off at his side.

Everyone is suddenly very interested in his share of food. They pass plates, and ask each other keenly if they have tried this yet, or that. They need more tea, and Madge, kneeling on the edge of the rug with the flasks, is busy pouring, and cannot, as her soul, if she has one, cries out to do, go after Patrick.

And minutes pass.

*   *   *

Coming up the slope towards the cliff edge, she meets the wind head-on; it has freshened and is ripping across the grass, tugging at plants and people, and blowing up from the seething water far below, chunks of dirty spindrift, like massive cuckoo spit. Madge cannot see Patrick. She calls, but the wind whips the words away in the wrong direction. The bright shining sea dazzles her beyond the grassy brink. She begins to run towards the point.

'What's up, then, Sis?' says Paul, catching up to her with easy strides.

'I don't know, quite,' she says, stopping. 'But I feel bad. I think we ought to find Patrick.'

'You're rather wrapped up in him, you know, Madge,' says Paul. 'Are you sure you want to be?'

'Oh, boo, Paul. No, I'm not. But I want to find him now.'

'I can see, sort of. He's never two moments the same; he thinks the way I swim. You like that. You don't like people to be open and simple, really. Only . . . only he has a sort of downturn to him, Madge.'

'Where has he got to, though?' says Madge. They follow the track along towards Godrevy Point, zigzagging around the bites in the cliff. At first they cannot see the lighthouse at all; it is hiding below the cliff. Then as they go towards it, it appears to rise out of the land, looming up over the grassy shoulder of the hill, eyeing the path; and then as they come nearer still, it recedes again, seems suddenly not near and rising up, but a little way off, standing offshore, with white horses ramping across the gap, and swinging around, breaking into the bay.

No Patrick, no Molly, to be seen.

They turn, and go back the other way.

*   *   *

The land rolls eastward from Godrevy Point. Little rises lift the path, like a boat going over waves, and finish in headlands; then the path descends and curves inland around a small bay. You can see very little over the edge; but from the headlands you can see the black angry broken chaos of the rocks where the sea has smashed and chewed inland, you can see the waves pawing and crashing to and fro beneath. You can see the precipitous side of the next bluff. The sea draws your eyes always outward, afar, to an empty horizon; but you need to look carefully where you put your feet on the rough footing of the path. Clumps of thrift and grass lean over and conceal the edge of the fall.

At the top of the second bluff going towards Navax Point, they suddenly see Patrick and Molly ahead of them. Molly is scampering around Patrick's tall lean form, bringing him flowers. He has a big straggly bunch in his left hand.

'Paa-trick!' Madge calls, through cupped hands, but he does not hear. And the wind presses so fiercely off the sea that they all lean outward, into it, as they walk, to keep their balance against its thrust. Now Patrick is in sight, Madge relaxes. They will catch up with him soon. He is climbing that massive rise ahead. It curves upward, like a whale's back, rusty brown rocky sides, green-patched like the sea-slimy seals that swim below. On the rock wall the grass hangs halfway down, a skirt of tattered salt-bleached growth; below that, the sea has undercut the rock face, and the bright light throws cavernous black shadows down to the tumult at the water's edge. A hole in the rock makes a shadow eye on the shark's-head outline of the foreland.

*   *   *

Up the path on the brink scramble Molly and Patrick. She is picking the thrift at the edge, brightly visible in her emerald-green dress. Patrick points; she leans out, stooping over the outermost clump of flowers; and behind them both Paul and Madge see Patrick's arm suddenly lifted, see him stretch out towards her as she falls.

Her stumpy little form shoots down the long slide of grass-clad rock, spreadeagles with sudden grace in the free air, and is gone. The overhang of the cliff prevents one from seeing down, and she has made no sound. Madge and Paul break into a run that brings them rapidly up towards Patrick. They cannot see down. Waves and sunlight and wind continue as remorseless as before.

It cannot have happened! says Madge's mind. Desperately it replays the sequence: Patrick points, Molly leans . . . it jerks through again and again.

As they reach Patrick's side the turn in the path has brought them back to face westward again; over the humped back of the cliff's edge rises Godrevy light —

207

just the top of it, looking over the crest of the land at them with its one dark Cyclops eye.

*   *   *

Running. Screaming. Paul and Madge, crying out to the adults. The grassy clifftop slides under Madge's feet, rising and falling below her, as though her legs were wooden, as though she floated, and the land raced by.

'There *are* some prohibitions evident even to children and idiots: thou shalt not . . .' the fragment reaches Madge before her shouts interrupt it. Then everyone is running. There is no trouble finding the particular point on the cliff's edge – Patrick is sitting there, eyes closed, shaking from top to toe, with his teeth rattling audibly together. You cannot see down. There is an overhang.

Matthew reacts first. He is the first to stop staring downward, and begin a run towards the cars. Madge watches him running away, like a figure in a film (this isn't happening, she is sure!). They hear the car clatter loudly, and fail to start. Once . . . twice . . . then it roars. Matthew drives it straight through the pole gate across the path, and wildly away in a cloud of sandy dust. People standing. One of the undergraduates proposes to climb down. 'I forbid you. I forbid that absolutely,' says Professor Tregeagle. The wind blows hard off the sea, and whips dry across their faces. The sun slides behind a patch of cloud. Far off, the sea shines silver; nearby, it has a dark gunmetal gleam. It heaves and swoops. A swell is rising. Beneath the next headland they can see the water furious, storming and lashing the land, breaking white, and sucking back again in a long fierce backwash from the teeth of the jagged rocks. But where they are, they cannot see down.

'It is impossible, quite impossible, that anyone could survive that long enough to feel a thing,' Professor Tregeagle is saying to his wife. He is holding her in

208

his arms. The sun shines briefly, but another cloud has come up from somewhere, and masks it again at once. Mrs Jones is gathering up her children, taking them away, protesting, loading a car with things. It is Madge who runs after her and stops her taking the rug. She brings the rug, shaken free of crumbs, and puts it round Patrick, across his shoulders and tucked in round his arms, where he is clinging to himself. He is still shaking.

There is nothing to be done. The group mutters, moves aimlessly, makes twitchy gestures towards each other, falls silent. A lark rises above them, squealing its sharp rejoicing.

Much later they hear a dim thud, like a cannonshot from across the bay. And then another. Relief floods through them. They can see the green stars of the maroons like Roman candles rise above the distant town. They cannot see down. Something will be done: someone has called out the lifeboat.

*   *   *

It looks very small in the water. It comes fast, turning back a deep scoop of surf from each side of its prow. It swings wide of Godrevy, very wide, and then makes a great loop to come in nearer to the tall shore. The group on the cliff can hear its engine throbbing as it sweeps along below them. Paul has taken off his sweater, and tied it by the sleeves to a piece of fencepost. He holds it high in the wind to pinpoint where they stand and lead the rescuers' eyes.

The men are visible in the boat's cockpit, in their bright yellow gear. One of them is scanning the foot of the cliff with binoculars. The boat turns, swings offshore, and beats back again. She keeps her distance from the cliff. And she comes by again at full speed, while the swell tosses her about. On the third passage along the shore someone points. The boat swings around again, and describes a tighter loop. And then she drops anchor.

At first to the impatient watchers they seem to be doing nothing. The boat rides the swell, up and down. Her engine still drones, although she isn't moving. The wind blows fragments of shout up to the clifftop.

'They're veering down,' says Paul, suddenly understanding.

'What? What are they doing?' asks Professor Tregeagle.

'They can't come in too close to a lee shore – with the wind blowing them landward,' says Paul. 'They have dropped anchor, and they are paying out the anchor cable, and easing her towards the rocks. Then when they can reach, they can haul the boat back again against wind and wave by winching the anchor cable in. It must be very tricky.'

'Will they reach?' asks the professor.

'They must be able to see something, or they wouldn't be trying so hard,' says Paul. 'But it must be bloody tricky.'

He is right, everyone can see. The boat tosses and yaws on the swell, more wildly as it is dragged nearer the cliffs. The clouds have crowded and massed above them. There is a grey evening light, and a steely sheen on the surface of the water below. The lifeboat draws slowly nearer and nearer in.

Patrick is still shaking, and still sits watching.

'Come and sit in one of the cars, Patrick,' says Madge. 'Don't watch.' He shakes his head, and stays where he is.

The boat is on the very edge of breaking water now; almost where the rocks chew up the sea in surf. A surge of backwash takes her hurtling out again; the engine goes into higher revs, fighting against it to keep her steady. She wings up and down on the humpback of the wave's last rise before it breaks.

Suddenly they see someone in the water. Shouts

rise to them, unintelligible. One of the crew has gone overboard on a line, and is swimming, pushing a life-ring ahead of him. Madge's eyes water in the lashing wind as she watches. It seems impossible to swim in that fury beneath; to pick one's way through breaker and undertow, between this black rock and that in the boiling surf. It is unbearable to watch, and impossible to turn away one's gaze. And very soon the swimmer has disappeared under the overhang of the dark rocks below. The muted, wind-scattered shouts continue. Standing in the bow of the lifeboat, a yellow-jacketed figure with binoculars keeps watch.

'Come away, my dear,' says Professor Tregeagle.

'No, no. I must know,' says his wife.

And so they all see the life-ring come into view again, with something green tied across it.

'They'd better hurry,' mutters Paul. 'They'd just better.'

'What's on your mind?' asks Andrew.

'The weather is getting nasty, and there's not much light left,' says Paul.

The progress of the swimmer and his burden seems agonizingly slow. Then suddenly a huge wave heaves up, burying the lifeboat completely, and breaking right over everything, crashing up the cliff in a tumult of foam, spraying the faces of the onlookers high above, and retreating in a violent and deadly backwash, leaving waterfalls of foam and hanging mists of spray across the cliff.

The lifeboat reappears, breaking out of the water in a flurry of foam, draining the sea off its sides, floating, netted in a huge web of white cast by the waves, a mesh of spume on the sea. But nothing can be seen of the swimmer or his life-ring.

The stricken onlookers see the crew wind in the broken line. They see, biting their lips, breath held, the anchor cable paid out another chain or so, the boat strain nearer yet to the mouth of hell. They hear broken cries; see the desperation with which the seas are scanned by the men below. Suddenly Paul spots the life-ring, floating a little way to the right. He shouts in vain; the wind whips his voice landward. He and Mr Jones run along the clifftop with his homemade flag, gesticulating.

The coxswain sees. The boat is eased sideways; a movement of the swell sends the ring towards it; they lean, they drag it on board. It had appeared to be empty, floating, but a spot of the bright green colour of Molly's dress is visible as it is heaved on board.

The boat stays for another minute or two. Half its crew are anxiously watching the water. But the others are winching in the anchor cable, hauling the boat out against wind and tide into the deeper water away from the cliff. Painfully, slowly, the boat is inched back. The light is fading; the gleam of the steely sky thrown back off the water is the brightest thing in sight.

At last the boat's engines roar into life again; it swings round, breaking the hold of its anchor, and roars away seaward at last. It goes wide round Godrevy as the light comes softly on, and disappears into the darkening distance.

A clamour of voices, none loud, but many, rises from around Madge as the boat goes off. A crowd of people have gathered unnoticed around them. There are the cars that brought them, in the field below. They surround the reading party.

'Please,' says Madge to Professor Tregeagle, 'help me with Patrick,' but he hardly seems to hear her. He is leading his wife away, jostling through the crowd of spectators. Jake and Mr Jones help. Patrick seems to be in a state of collapse. He does not answer or speak, and is unsteady on his feet. He has to be helped back towards the cars. A stranger is asked to give him a lift; he is driven away.

'A bad business. Ought not to have been tried, that's

212

what,' Madge hears someone saying.

'Who was it in the water, then?' asks another. They are local voices, soft-spoken, concerned.

'It was Stevens, I'm near sure,' says someone else.

'Oh, my God, it was Jeremy!' cries Paul, hearing.

'Oh, no!' wails Madge. Let it not be, let it not be, she cries inwardly. Oh, dear God, let it not be anyone Patrick knows!

'Well, 'twould be,' the voice is saying. 'It would be him, likely. All the others are married men.'

People are trooping down from the cliff's edge. The wind has become so boisterous it is hard not to run before it, as it drives them back.

It seems to Madge that she cannot possibly ride her bicycle home. Her knees feel like water, and her rib cage is full of a choking leaden sensation. But there seems to be no alternative. She waits with Paul, while the last few cars drive off. When all is quiet they begin their unsteady ride. Patrick's and Matthew's bikes are left behind.

They start back. The golden light of Godrevy shines out behind them. But it is a flashing light; dark for nine counts in ten. In the twilight they see the curious colour change on the waters of the bay, the rusty-pink cloudy staining where the Red River runs out, where the land bleeds silently into the sea. Half way to Hayle a car coming up the road stops by them; Matthew has come back to bring them home. They load the bikes on the roof rack, and Matthew struggles with a strap to keep them secure.

'Oh, Paul, what will happen to him?' murmurs Madge, as they gratefully get into the car.

'They'll go and look for him when the wind drops. Most likely he'll be washed up somewhere in a day or two,' says Paul, huskily. He takes her hand, and holds it.

But it was about Patrick that Madge had meant to ask.

                              *   *   *

There is a policeman in the drawing-room. He has a
notebook. He is speaking kindly. 'I am very sorry to
intrude on you at a time like this, but if you could just
tell me what happened exactly . . .'

'I wasn't there, I saw nothing; my son was with
the child,' says Professor Tregeagle. 'And you cannot
speak to him now, I'm afraid. He is in a state of shock.
What he says is not making any sense at all, and the
doctor has given him sedation. Tomorrow, if you really
must.'

'Perhaps I need not insist,' says the officer, 'for among
so many of you, surely somebody saw what happened?'
But everyone is looking blank.

'I saw,' says Paul. 'And so did my sister.' At once
all eyes are on them. Madge feels the ground sway
beneath her. How terrible of Paul to offer . . . she
should have spoken to him on the way home, even
with Matthew listening, should have begged him not
to tell . . . but she knows it would have been useless
to ask Paul to deny the truth.

'Patrick was walking with Molly along the cliff-edge
path,' says Paul. 'We could see them ahead of us. Molly
went very near the edge after some flowers growing
there, and Patrick tried to grab her, but he just didn't
catch her in time, and she fell off the edge.' Madge's
head swims. She can hardly believe . . . Paul *is* lying!
He is lying, unasked, out of sheer good will.

'Patrick Tregeagle tried to catch hold of Molly, and
just missed her . . . are you certain of that, young
Fielding?' asks the policeman.

'Oh, *quite* certain. I saw his arm go up and stretch
towards her. Madge will tell you; she must have seen it
too.' And it is borne in on Madge that Paul is not lying;
Paul is telling the truth according to Paul. He tells
what he saw; it is what she saw that is untellable.

'I saw the same as my brother,' she says. 'It happened just as he says.'

'Well, then, we shan't need to disturb the young man,' says the policeman, putting away his book. 'Two witnesses will do for tonight. There'll be an inquest, sir, a double one I shouldn't wonder, when they find poor Mr Stevens's body. Your son will have to give evidence at that, sir, and so will you, and the two young Fieldings. Would you bear that in mind, sir, when making plans for the next week or so?'

Madge escapes, and clambers up the stairs. She sits down in the window seat of her attic, facing the sea. She is miserable and confused, and dazed. Paul did not lie, she tells herself; he saw – since he says so – Patrick try to save Molly and fail. But I saw Patrick push her over; there's no denying that's what I saw. And I can ask myself over and over if I'm not just nasty-minded, if Paul isn't probably right, and I know he isn't. He has such a loving nature, such an open, unclouded sort of mind, he would never see evil unless he had to. I am the one who saw . . .

The wind is roaring now, rattling the window. Madge leans forward to open it and slam it tight shut, and in with a gust of cool air comes the sound of the sea, the voice of angry surf, and angry wind. She shivers. A moon is rising, masked in bright-margined cloud. Godrevy light shines out. Keep away, it says. Don't come here. And somewhere in the dark waters around it there is a brave man drowned . . .

I saw Patrick commit murder! Madge cries to herself. And I lied about it. I said without any hesitation that I had seen what Paul saw, and I will lie again, and again, and swear false oaths about it. I am the one who lies to protect the fugitive from the madman, and who, Matthew said, in a corner would lie, kill, maim, cheat, fornicate, to gain some good end or other. Patrick is a murderer, and I am his next of kin.

Outside, the wind frets and howls.

*   *   *

To entertain the burglar Gran has spent the morning making seedcake, and scones, and fresh lemon curd. She is still amused at having invited him, and he is another cup to pour; the more there are, the more she feels queen of the teapot.

The burglar is indeed, as she had been promised, distinguished and handsome. He is tall, with grey hair and a slight trace of transatlantic accent.

'This is my ancient mother-in-law,' says Tom, bringing him into the living room. 'Dr Henderson, Mother.'

'How nice,' says Gran. 'Do sit down. This is my daughter, Harriet, and this is Emily, my niece, and Jim, her young man.'

'Your niece?' says Dr Henderson, surprised at Emily.

'Yes indeed,' says Gran. People are often surprised, and she likes to tell them. 'My brother is a little younger than me to start with, and then he married for a second time rather late in life. Emily is the only child of that second marriage. And that . . . sugar? . . . milk? . . . is how she comes to be so deliciously young for her aunt. Or, contrariwise, how she comes to have an aunt so inordinately *old*. Do have some curd on your scone, Mr Henderson, I made it myself, and it really is very nice indeed.'

'Thank you, I will,' says Dr Henderson, settling comfortably into a chair, and arranging his plate and cup on the little table beside it.

'And now you must tell us why you have been lurking around our gate,' says Gran.

'Lurking? Oh, hardly that! Just passing by and looking in.'

'*Lurking*. We have even christened you the burglar, so full of intent was your loiter.'

'Damn me!' he says. 'What do you know!'

216

'What we want to know is, what do you mean by it?' says Gran sternly.

'I'm on a visit from Toronto,' he tells them. 'I was returning to the scenes of my youth, in a way. You see, I once spent a summer vacation here, and I've been trying to decide if it was in this house. But I promise I'm not a felon of any kind.'

'Of course not; you hardly look the part!' says Tom.

'Now I wonder when that could have been?' says Gran. 'Odd, that. It must have been a very long time ago, Dr Henderson.'

'Oh, it was. I, too, am inordinately old.' He smiles at Emily. 'And I don't remember a thing about the inside of the house I stayed in. All gone.'

'Come outside, and see if that helps,' says Gran. She leads the way into the garden.

Standing on the terrace, looking at the wide lovely view, he says quietly, 'You know, I had forgotten the sea.'

'Forgotten the sea?' says Gran. 'Then it can't have been this house.'

'I don't mean I have forgotten whether you could see the sea from where I stayed; I mean I had forgotten what the sea is like to look at. All these years I've kept away from it. I had remembered that it is frightening, and forgotten how beautiful . . . There. I must remember that I am now in England, where people don't talk like that.'

'Don't talk like what?' says Emily, arriving.

'Don't much say what they feel, I think,' he says.

'Oh, it always depended *who*, however far back you remember,' says Gran.

'I'll bet!' says Emily. 'Can't imagine *you* tight-lipped, Aunt, at my age.'

'Cheeky monkey! Go and get me some more tea, Em, will you? And for our guest, too.'

'There was a dramatic lifeboat incident the year I was here,' says Dr Henderson.

217

'That hardly serves to distinguish one year from another in this place.'

'A dreadful thought.'

'It *is* beautiful,' says Gran, looking at the horizon. 'Never more so than when it is terrible. It takes a fool not to be afraid of it.'

'Yes.'

'But you have kept away from it for years. I wonder why?'

'I hardly know. I'm not afraid of heights, or of spiders.'

'Well, well,' says Gran. 'I think one cannot know what one is afraid of until a crisis arises. When it does, like as not, one manages to do what is required.'

'You mean that kindly,' he says, shaking his head. 'But I *do* know the sea is too much for me.' She says nothing. In a while he says, 'I was staying once in a seaport, in terrible weather. It was a small town, with only two hotels, and the hotel porter was the lifeboat secretary. I had signed the register as Dr Henderson – it's an academic doctorate, you know, nothing to do with medicine. By and by the lifeboat coxswain came to me and asked me to go out in the boat with them. They had to get a fisherman with an injured spine off a deep-sea trawler, and they needed a doctor. The local man was delivering a difficult baby. I said no, I wasn't a doctor . . .'

'But for Christ's sake,' says Tom, arriving carrying the extra tea, and followed by Emily, 'if you weren't, you weren't.'

Dr Henderson looks ruefully at Gran. 'I had been trained in mountain rescue,' he says. 'I would have known how to get a man onto a stretcher and give scratch first aid. I could have told them that, and gone with them.'

'But if you were only a visitor, passing through . . . it had nothing to do with you,' says Tom.

'That's what I thought at the time. Not my problem.

218

But I've thought about it now and then, since. And when you think about it, why should the hotel porter go? Or the greengrocer's second son? Or the fisherman who has had the sense to get his own boat in out of the storm? Or the local doctor, who, if he could have finished his breech delivery in time, would have cleaned up hastily, got into oilskins, and gone into the teeth of the easterly without a moment's thought?'

'They go because drowning in raging water is so horrible a fate,' says Gran. 'And going, they risk it for themselves. It has a terrible symmetry.'

'I should have gone,' says Dr Henderson.

'Yes,' says Gran.

'What happened to the fisherman, Dr Henderson?' asks Emily suddenly.

'Oh, he was all right. They managed very well without me, as it happened. But that doesn't make any difference to me.'

'Made plenty of difference to him,' mutters Emily tartly.

'Are you spending long in this country?' asks Tom, brightly. 'And what's Canada like?' He steers the conversation on to safe English subjects for another half an hour.

When Dr Henderson takes his leave, Tom sees him to the door. 'What do you do in Toronto?' Tom asks, as he hands the departing guest his coat.

'I teach philosophy,' says the burglar.

*   *   *

The storm wind sobs and moans over the night roofs of Goldengrove. It tears itself to shreds on the gutter corners and sharp gable ends, and howls with pain. Lying in the attic bed one is submerged in a tide of sound, a cockle on the ocean floor, listening to the fury above. Closed safe and tight in a shell of sheet and quilt, Madge listens. The banshee wailing of the wind cannot drown the other sound: the sound of Patrick sobbing. Madge listens for a long while before getting up and going into Patrick's room. She sits in the battered cane armchair under the window, and folds her hands in her lap, and listens. A little moonlight makes ghost outlines in the room. Of Patrick she can see only the shadowy darkness of his tousled head on the pillow.

'I loved her,' he says, chokingly, after a while.

'Yes,' says Madge softly. 'Of course you did.'

'Oh, God, how horrible. Oh, God, I'm mad, mad. I killed her!'

'You're not mad, Patrick.'

'I wanted . . . Oh, how could I?'

'Are you *sure* you did anything? You know, Paul and I saw her fall, and Paul is usually the calm observant one. I thought you had pushed her, but he thought you had grabbed to stop her falling, and just missed. Couldn't you perhaps have done that?'

'I don't know,' says Patrick, miserably. 'The awful fact is I just don't know. The moment I had done it, I didn't feel quite certain, couldn't remember — Oh, God, Madge, do you think one could murder someone and forget it instantly?'

'Hush, Patrick, try to keep calm. If I got you some hot milk, would it help you sleep?'

'I'll never see her again,' he says. 'I murdered her!'

*   *   *

In the morning comes the first of five bleak, dreadful days. The reading party disperses as rapidly as possible, catching the lunchtime train, with cases and boxes of books. Unasked, and making no comment, Matthew stays, and waits quietly in the background. And those who will be needed for the inquest must stay until the sea spews up the missing body. Six of them in the suddenly quiet house, and each with a raw spot that the others fear to touch.

Mrs Tregeagle bears the waiting best. She keeps to her room for three days, is seen red-eyed. But then she is tranquil, and more than tranquil. Madge thinks she is slowly unfurling, like a florist's rose freed from cellophane. She is more herself – well, more like somebody. She goes for walks. She asks Madge what the heights are called, and where the funny street names in Downalong come from. People are kind to her when she goes out; she finds she can say to them, 'Molly cannot have felt anything. If it weren't for that poor man . . .' A great burden has rolled from her, and the future no longer hangs over her like death. It isn't, Madge perceives, that she didn't love Molly; it isn't that she isn't grieving, for she is. But grieving for Molly is a good deal easier than living with the thought of her there forever, growing larger, stronger, more unruly . . . and it's a good thing, really, that Mrs Tregeagle feels like this, Madge thinks, for it is the only small good effect to flow from Patrick's great attempt at action, at manipulating the universe, at refusing to leave things be and blame God.

Madge listens while Mrs Tregeagle talks of a large gift to the Lifeboat Funds. Unasked and unnoticed, she removes Molly's things, a few clothes, a few battered toys, and gives them to the Methodist sale.

*   *   *

'I *expected* to feel dreadful. I expected to feel crushed by guilt,' Patrick tells Madge, in the dead of night. She is sitting in the chair beside his bed, where he lies face down, his voice half muffled in his crumpled pillow. 'I knew I would. And I thought that was nothing, nothing compared to what she would suffer as she grew to know dimly what other people felt about her. She wasn't as bad as they thought, Madge, she was going to partly know . . . she had a mother who just despaired about her, and a father who thinks the intellect is

221

immortal, and souls resemble bodies . . . and me. I couldn't see how one protected her forever. I hated that doctor more than anyone in the world, that man who kept his own conscience clean by keeping her alive at *whatever* cost to her and everyone else. I thought I ought to be willing to suffer guilt for her sake. Doesn't that sound right? Is that so wrong?'

'I don't know, Patrick,' says Madge. 'I can't tell. It isn't how I think.'

'I'm still not sorry about her!' he says defiantly. 'I'm not! But I hadn't expected to harm anyone else . . . Jeremy . . . Oh, I didn't mean to . . .' He is weeping again.

But unexpected things happen every day, thinks Madge. How can one not expect them? How can one leave them out of account?

'You didn't mean to hurt Jeremy, Patrick,' she says. 'And people usually feel guilty only about what they meant, don't they? Try to sleep.'

'I shall pay,' he says. 'I shall tell the inquest I pushed her, and they will lock me away, safely, where I can't do any more harm.'

'Oh, God, Patrick, no, you mustn't!' says Madge. 'Go to sleep. Think it over in the light of day.'

*   *   *

Paul grieves very quietly. Only Madge knows he is doing it at all; but then, Madge always knows what Paul feels.

'It makes you see how shaky things are,' he says to her, as they roam together along the golden shore, 'when a person who has always been there suddenly isn't. The world seemed safe and solid, and as though it had always been what it is; now I feel it's paper castles.'

And Jeremy had always been there, Madge reflects, as certain as the scenery. Not quite fixed, but recurrent, like the blue and green swathes of nets that drape the quay, organic, an emanation of the local ecosystem. And, Madge sees, he was Paul's root here, Paul's more than hers, but hers also; he was the one whose friendship picked them out of the hordes of visitors and made them belong, gave them not-strangers' faces. Once, a year or so back, there was an upcountry tripper on one of Jeremy's fishing tours around the bay. He was throwing his weight about, showing off his local knowledge. 'Have you been to Hell's Mouth? Have you climbed Trencrom Hill? You ought to, you know . . .'

And, in a while Jeremy cut in past Paul's patient, 'Yes, actually more than once . . .' and said, 'Young Fielding's been coming here since way back. Good as local, he is.' And the man was silenced. Now Jeremy is gone, we are just trippers, Madge thinks, sharing Paul's pain; like any visitor who comes and goes, and prefers Mevagissey, or Helford.

'He was the only real person I have ever known,' says Paul. 'The only one who earned a living in a proper way in the world. I wish he had kept his boat. If he still had his boat I would buy it, somehow.'

'What would we do with it?' murmurs Madge.

*   *   *

'I am damned . . .' says Patrick, with his teeth chattering in his head. 'Oh, God, I thought that if there was no hell, one couldn't be damned . . . I was wrong . . . I am in hell . . .'

And he really is, Madge sees. *Where is the head that hath no chimeras in it?* That a harpy is not a centaur can be as certain knowledge as the propositions of Euclid. And Patrick can be damned.

'Hell is just true in a different way,' he says, lying still enough, but staring horribly at the ceiling. 'In a nearer and more dangerous way, and I am . . .'

Madge, shivering a little in her thin nightgown,

searches desperately for a thought with which to wrestle for Patrick's soul. 'I don't think a person could be damned,' she says, 'while there is still something more awful than anything they have done, which they still shrink from doing. That's what I think.'

'I keep seeing faces staring in the shadows on the ceiling,' says Patrick. 'They keep me awake . . .'

'Come on, then,' she says. 'Try my bed, the ceiling's different.' She leads him to the other attic, and tucks him into the warm hollow in her bed which she left when she went to see him minutes ago.

'There,' she says. 'Better?'

'What is left?' he asks. 'What could be worse?'

'Telling your mother what you did would be worse,' says Madge. 'That would be really damnable.' She sees the stare go out of his eyes as he begins to think about that. 'So you can't tell that inquest *anything*, Patrick,' she says. 'You tell them just what Paul said. You have to. Now I'll get you a drink, if it would help you sleep.'

Later she climbs into his vacant bed. The sheets are all tangled up, and a faint skin smell lingers on the pillow.

*　　*　　*

'Miss Fielding,' says Professor Tregeagle. 'Can you spare me a moment alone with you? Thank you. We are, that is, my wife and I are very grateful to you for being so kind to Patrick. You seem to be the only one who can calm him.'

'There's no need to thank me,' says Madge, blushing, and wanting at once to escape.

'I understand how Patrick feels – at least I think I do. He was the one in charge of Molly when it happened. But of course it could have been anyone. It is impossible to be alert a hundred per cent of the time; it was always in the cards that something terrible would happen to her. It is Patrick's misfortune that he was the one . . . That is what's upsetting him, Miss Fielding, isn't it?'

'Why don't you ask him?' says Madge.

'Of course. I, er, just meant . . . Madge, is there anything you know about what happened, that I ought to know?'

'There is nothing I ought to tell you,' says Madge carefully, after a moment.

'My dear girl, why, after all, should you trust me? But believe me, I love my son dearly, and I am very concerned about him. Half the time he seems out of his mind over all this. He called himself a murderer in my hearing . . . I take it he is raving when he says that.'

I am almost sorry for him, floundering around like this, thinks Madge. Almost, but not quite. Still, he is Patrick's father.

'I think he felt like killing Molly,' she says at last. 'And then the accident happened, and because he had felt like doing it, he thinks perhaps he did do it.' And how plausible that sounds, she thinks as she says it. I must try it on Patrick.

'Why did he feel like killing her?' asks Professor Tregeagle. 'We loved her in spite of . . .'

'Oh, you *wouldn't* know!' cries Madge. 'You wouldn't know anything. Actually sitting there, going on about children and idiots, about how pure intellect is the immortal part, and a person's soul resembles their body – actually saying that in *front* of everyone, actually while Molly's ugliness is being guyed. Don't you think people have feelings, or do you just think they don't matter?'

'Oh, my God,' says Professor Tregeagle. He sits down abruptly, and his tranquil clever face suddenly wears an expression like Patrick's. 'But that's absurd . . . Madge, that isn't what we said. What we said doesn't *mean* that . . .'

'Whoever are you to say what it means?' she asks him. 'It means what it does mean, and you can't stop it. You can sit around all you like, like a stage army muttering "Wittgenstein" instead of "rhubarb," and saying to words, "Thus far shalt thou mean, and no further, and here shalt thou break thy swelling waves." It doesn't make any difference. The words mean what they mean to Patrick as much as they mean what they mean to you.'

'Patrick never could be clear and cool. Never could grasp an accurate definition. It's just like him to make a vast emotional mess of an intellectual discussion. If we ever gave him a gun he'd point it backward.'

'Do you know something?' Madge says, regarding him coldly. 'Do you know why you are here? Because my headmistress thought clever company might do me good, might help to make me decide to try for an Oxford scholarship. But that was a big mistake. I've just decided to be a hairdresser, or work in Woolworth's.'

'My dear, whatever you think of us,' he says, suddenly recovering a little calm, 'don't spite yourself because of it. You are quite clearly a clever girl. You mustn't waste that.'

'Oh, Christ,' says Madge. 'Can't you think of anything else at all?'

*   *   *

Patrick on the fourth day, quite calm, walking around the house and garden with a waxwork face. 'I have accepted it now,' he tells Madge. And when he says it they are standing below the garden gate, on the last turn of the path up to the house, looking down at the beach and beyond. Against the deep-blue ocean, Madge sees as he says it, the grey and white, tawny-white, gullfeather-coloured town, nestling like a folded wing on the curved back of the hills, on the green slopes of the Island, and in a downy drift around the bright shore, so that forever afterwards whenever she remembers what he said, until she is an old woman, she remembers also the soft light of one warm hazy summer day.

'You can stop worrying, Madge,' he says. 'I have accepted what I did. I won't own up at the inquest.'

'Good,' she says. 'It wouldn't do any good.'

'I am a murderer,' he says, quite calmly. 'I shall be in hell till I die. And alone. For my true self, my nearest self, is the one that killed Jeremy. So unless I deceive them about who I am, no-one will ever love me.'

'Oh, no, Patrick,' says Madge. 'No, no. They will. I will.'

*   *   *

Paul on the fourth day insisting on taking Madge off with him, insisting on getting her alone, walking her off to Carbis Bay on the lizard-baking rocky path between the railway and the sea.

'I like him, too,' Paul tells her. 'I can see. He is interesting. And then you've always been a goose about our suffering brethren, haven't you, Sis? Do you remember that perfectly frightful blind man you got taken up with one summer? You're a sucker for wounds, Madge, like a tin of Elastoplast.'

'I thought you were going to say like a vampire, after that!' she says, trying to make him laugh.

'Huh, huh,' he says. 'No, you must listen. Because I have to say this to you. You can't do anything about Patrick. When he's got over this, it will be some other damn thing. He's just the sort of person who leads an unhappy life. You do know that, don't you?'

'Like his namesake, you mean, driven and hounded and condemned for ever to weave ropes of sand on the shore?'

'Do I sound melodramatic? Well, I can't help that. I don't do it often. But you do know, Madge, don't you? You know you can't make him happy, and very likely he'll make you as miserable as he is.'

'Yes, Paul love, I know,' says Madge. The rocks run out under the sunshot shallows of the sea's edge below

227

them, blotching green and turquoise with patches of purple. On the grass where they sit, the thrift grows, and the yellow vetch. And far out, in the distance, the lighthouse in a tissue of haze is just visible.

Madge sighs. She does know. She sees ahead of her a life on the brink of the abyss. It will be all in Patrick's troubled mind, the terrible precipices on whose knife edge of nightmare fall she will have to tread – *Hold them cheap may who ne'er hung there* – and for a moment she wavers, and thinks longingly of the shadowless tranquillity of being with Paul.

'Look! There's a cormorant,' he says. Patrick wouldn't have seen it; he doesn't much notice where he is, she muses.

'I do know, Paul,' she says.

'But it doesn't stop you?'

'No.' For when someone needs love and comfort, one has to go. Hasn't one? Would Paul really turn his back? Could there be much to choose between counting the cost, as he recommends, and that insane calculation of good and evil that brought Patrick where he is? She remembers Jeremy once showing her a picture in a lifeboat manual of the gold medal, the highest award for gallantry of the Royal National Lifeboat Institution. It showed a naked man being drawn out of the water into a boat. *Let not the deep swallow me up*, it said.

'I could explain to Jeremy better than I can to you,' she says, her eyes suddenly full of tears.

*   *   *

Matthew on the fourth day, trying to calm an agitated Paul. 'Don't worry. Come for a swim. No, of course you can't reason with her, she doesn't work like that. She works on instinct. And there's nothing wrong with that.'

'I thought thinking was a good thing. At least

228

according to you,' says Paul.

'It's all right for some. Madge doesn't need it. Her feelings lead her right.'

'Christ, another nutter!' says Paul. 'Damn being led right. I'm afraid she'll be led unhappy.'

'Oh, I don't know,' says Matthew. 'She might well cheer Patrick up. Wouldn't anyone be cheered up? I wish she felt sorry for me!'

'Feeling-sorry-for isn't the same as loving, you poor fool,' says Paul.

'Oh, one thing leads to another, often enough,' says Matthew. 'I'm leaving on the evening train. Tell your sister, in case I don't see her again, that I'll call on her in London sometime and take her out to tea.'

* * *

Patrick on the evening of the fourth day, pacing his room, still unable to sleep.

'God, it's hot in here!' says Madge, arriving in her dressing gown. 'Let's go out.'

'My mother will fuss like anything if she hears me go down,' he says. 'She's *concerned* about me.'

'Out here,' says Madge, opening the little door.

In the roof valley they stand side by side, under a thick sky pierced with stars. The sound of the sea comes clearly to them from far below, in the hushed night.

'You can't, you know,' Patrick says after a while. 'You just can't mean what you said.'

'I can.'

'Any minute you'll see through me, and go away in disgust.'

'You don't have to worry about that,' she says. 'I see through you now, I think.'

'And you don't mind?'

'Don't mind what, Patrick, dear? Who are we to mind each other?'

229

'My horrible bleeding self-pitying soul.'

'The human body is the perfect image of the human soul,' she says, and puts her arms around him.

*   *   *

On the fifth day Jeremy's body is found washed up under Gurnard's Head, and the ordeal is about to be over.

*   *   *

Emily comes, running lightly down the garden, jumping the lavender hedge instead of going down the steps, her long hair swinging down her shirt, to find Gran dozing in a deck chair specially set in a sheltered spot and facing the lovely view through the garden gate left open. She likes that prospect; it reminds her of a painting called *The Blue Door*, or was it a window? but anyway . . . She wakes when Emily's shadow casts coolness on her face.

'Please, Aunt,' says Em, 'the rain came in through the belvedere roof in *floods* during that storm, and all Jim's things are wet. I don't think he ought to sleep out there another night, or he'll catch his *death*. And I don't like to tell Harriet, because she made such a bother about it when we got here . . . so I was wondering if I could clear a space in the attic, just a small space. Would you mind?'

'No, dear, of course I wouldn't,' says Gran. 'Can't have him catching cold. And I think I'll come too, you know, and help you. What fun! We never know *what* we might find!'

'Ah, no, Aunt, it's a pity to spoil your rest. You must snooze off again, and let me do it. And I promise to bring you the three most fun things we find there. Will that do?'

'Yes, Em dear, that would be lovely,' says Gran,

230

settling back into her chair. It seems only yesterday she would have leaped up and climbed up the stairs two at a time, and gone rummaging joyfully through dusty boxes. And one's mind takes it hard, she thinks; one's soul is as lithe as ever, and as volatile, and is amused, patronizing, and irritated by the body's decrepitude.

An aged man is but a paltry thing . . .

yet inside I feel no different; I feel the same as ever, or rather, which is more important, as many different things as ever . . .

A tattered coat upon a stick, unless
Soul clap its hands and sing, and louder sing
For every tatter in its mortal dress . . .

though it isn't monuments of magnificence for me (yet Santa Sophia is more like a vision than a building, I do remember), it's more the brightness falls from the air, the eternally changing sea, and the view of Godrevy light. Yet what could this be inside me, that feels unchanged, through so many and so great revolutions of matter? And, do you know, in all the talk I ever heard about the immortal soul, I never recall the eternal youth of the inner self brought in evidence against us being all bodies . . . odd that. Well, not so odd, really, for it's the old in their ramshackle frames who know it so clearly, and it's young men who bother about the immortal soul . . . I ought to know better at my age. Ghosts in machines, indeed – whoever believed in ghosts? And I think after all I'll take myself upstairs and help Emily. I shall go very slowly. I'll get there.

Little by little. Up the stone steps Emily by-passed, one by one. Past the straggling overgrown bush of Rosa Mundi, past its best long ago, should have been cut down, but Gran likes it. And slowly along the narrow terrace, between the catnip and pinks and lavender, towards the corner of the house where the view is best, because it is easier to go right round than to climb the steep flight of steps to the french windows of the dining-room. And as she goes, here behind her come pattering sandalled footfalls. Young Peter, and Sarah, and small Beth racing after her, calling 'Gran! Gran!' and eyes shining.

And Madge turns round, and stoops, and picks up her grandchild, and holds small Beth up to look at the view, just for a moment, for even this slender, bird-boned child is heavy for her to hold now.

'I like how this place cuddles the sea,' says small Beth.

'Why, yes, Beth, so it does,' says Madge, smiling. 'I like it too.'

'Gran, Gran,' says Sarah. 'Listen to the bell counting one. Why is it?'

'It's tolling, dear. For somebody's funeral.'

'Who's dead?' asks Peter.

'One is not supposed to ask for whom it tolls,' says Madge.

'Sorry, Gran,' says Peter solemnly. 'I didn't know that.'

And, oh, Lord, thinks Madge, now what have I said? Misleading the poor child . . .

'About death,' Peter continues. 'I think it's all a bit crummy, you know, Gran . . .'

But here comes Emily, arriving, laughing, wearing a Paisley shawl rotted into ladders all over, and a huge pink garden-fête straw hat with a moth-eaten white rose that Madge wore decades back, one summer, and holding in her hand a little brown bottle. Behind her comes Jim, her attentive shadow.

'Wow! Hey, how do I look, everyone?' cries Emily, dancing around them.

'Like a prehistoric lady,' says Sarah.

'Can I have the bottle, Aunt?' asks Emily.

'Goodness!' says Madge, taking it. 'That's been lost

for ages. I'm very glad to see it again; it always did make me feel special. And no, Em love, I think I'll keep it. You can have it when I'm gone, if you like.'

'Heavens, Aunt, it's only an old brown bottle with no cork!' says Emily.

'Don't worry, Em, you won't have long to wait,' says Beth. 'She's awfully old.'

'You shouldn't *say* that, Beth,' says Peter.

'Tell me about the bottle, dear funny Aunt,' says Emily, taking Madge's hand. And for all I'm so different from Paul, and always was, thinks Madge, his daughter is quite like me.

'The sea gave it to me, dear,' she says. 'And in all the years I walked on its edge, and watched it, it's the only sign it ever gave of liking me.'

'It washed it up at your feet, you mean?' asks Jim.

'Three times. Twice I threw it back. The third time I kept it. It's a very *nice* bottle, you know.'

'Yes, Aunt, it is,' says Emily, smiling. 'I would very much like it when you're dead. Thank you. I'll put it in your room for now.' And off she goes, whirling Jim after her, around the house, out of sight.

'You see, Gran, what I want to know about death is,' pursues Peter remorselessly, 'is what's the point? I mean, it does make it rather pointless, doesn't it, people just getting born and then dying all over the place? I mean, I don't believe all that stuff about resurrection, because people rot, don't they, when you bury them? And it seems if they just keep on dying, millions of them, well, what's the point of being alive in the first place?'

What can I say? thinks Madge. Of course, he's right. We die, and when we die we rot, and that's an end of it. I have never had any doubts of that. And yet . . . it's an odd thing, but it's not the romantic opinion about the departing soul that is shaken in the actual presence of death . . . in the actual presence of death it is the rational belief in mortality that is shattered. I do remember that quite clearly. Twice I have seen it. It was my dear Patrick once, but before that, long before, it was my own grandmother . . .

There had been a journey. A night journey, in a train with prickly plush headrests that indented my leaning cheek. It was very early in the morning, only just after dawn. The train chugged under Carrack Gladden, and not a single footprint on the wide, wide open sands, only the white waves moving. From the station to the beach, my footprints on it first, winding along the waves' edge. When I reached the house, when I turned my key in the door of the shuttered silent house, I had taken off my shoes. My naked feet left ghost prints on the polished floor. I stretched out my hand to the polished doorknob, and went into the living room. It was darkened, the curtains drawn. A table had been brought into the middle of the room, with a white cloth on it, and my grandmother was laid out on the table under a white sheet. Her face was uncovered. There was an unutterable silence in the room. One would believe it was slowing one's own heartbeat, stilling one's own pulse. I cannot recall anything I thought or felt, except that appalling stillness.

I had come too late. Had I expected to be in time? I don't know. Travelling to a death would always be undiscovered country, from which no traveller returns unchanged. I have never forgotten how it dislocated my certainty. It was my grandmother on the table. Can one have any idea how intensely local, how particular to one person a body is, till one has seen a not-living one? And yet, how totally, how overwhelmingly, how absolutely, I knew *she is not there*. This 'her' is empty of her utterly. It has nothing whatever to do with her, is husk, shell, having her shape in every detail. Here, where she always was, she is not now. The stillness so complete it quenches out of me everything, every flicker of feeling or thought, except awe. And – how can one help it – since she is not here, one wonders where, then, is she? Where has she gone? *Where is she now?*

I sat in a straight-backed chair beside her for a long time. Until the morning sun ruled golden lines across the room from between closed shutters, and Amy, my grandmother's maid, found me there, and tutted and fussed over me, and made breakfast, and wept a little. I was dry-eyed, and with an immortal calm upon me. And I have never forgotten it. That the survival of the soul is a commonplace deduction from the sight of a dead body. In the presence of death it is mortality that seems preposterous. I am still puzzled by that, still awestruck. Who could believe in souls? I am a foolish old woman. But then I was a foolish young one too. I think it was Matthew who said it; nice Matthew, who loved me just *because*, not needing anything, not wanting rescue, and who tried so hard, and at whom I did not look seriously for a moment. He said, 'You are a fool, Madge, but a nice fool.' It was probably true. And goodness, who was the other one on the stairs that first day of the reading party – *I* know who it was: Andrew Henderson – how could I have forgotten him? – who would only climb alone. *That's* who the burglar is! What was I thinking? . . . I remember also looking at my grandmother's face; how that absence seemed not only absolute, but irrevocable. It is just another mystery, like everything else. Not how it is, but that it is, is the heart of things.

And Peter beside her is saying, 'Gran! Gran!' trying to bring her attention back to his question. 'Gran, will you mind dying?'

'I shouldn't think so, dear,' she says. 'It isn't our own death that troubles us. We have enough to do surviving other people's.'

'Gran, you see, first we grow up and have a lot of worries. And then we die, and I don't see the point.'

Heavens! the things children say! They certainly come trailing clouds of metaphysics. 'It's like going on a holiday journey,' she says at last. 'It's not where

235

you're going, it's what you see on the way.' *When you set out for Ithaca, ask that the voyage be long . . .* what's that from? Oh, I forget so much!

The other two have melted away, back to running in the garden, hiding on the thick leafy floor of the shrubbery, climbing the lilac tree, but Peter is remorseless. 'Like what things on the way, though?' he says. 'Do you mean birthdays?'

'Well, yes, Peter, birthdays and other things . . .' She smiles. Patrick, for example, lying asleep beside me in rumpled sheets, every muscle in his body slack, and on his face that shining serenity that never came to him awake. And knowing that was my doing. One can't tell such a thing to a child . . . A piano playing in a downstairs room; Harriet in a cot beside my bed . . . a car going over the top of Exmoor; I am singing: *But not so deep as the love I'm in; I know not where I sink or swim* . . . And something made us laugh so much we couldn't stop, and Patrick had to stop the car. I picked a handful of dark heather. . .

'Well, we all die, but first we all live,' she tells him. 'Don't worry about what's the point. Just take your share. Take it two-handed and in full measure. You have to clap your hands and sing.'

'Oh, yes, *I* will!' cries small Beth arriving, dancing and clapping around them. 'What shall I sing?'

'Anything, anything.' Madge smiles, clapping for her. We leave our mark even on our grandchildren, she thinks, small Beth more like me, Peter more like Patrick.

'And the older you get, Peter dear, the louder you must clap and sing.'

'What shall we sing about?' he asks her, but his solemnity is tripping over into laughter, is getting too much for him. And, what shall we sing about? Madge asks herself. Why, whatever brute or blackguard or random chance made the world, was surely a marvellous conjuror, a dab hand at spectacle! What shall we sing about? Fish to eat fresh from the salt sea, sweet berries from the thorn, bread from the brown furrow, and the orient wheat. We shall see every day, if we just raise our eyes to the hills, the movements of wind and water, and the fall of the light. There are never two moments the same, what with sky and weather, and tide, the passage of time, and the random fall of the rain. To be alive is to be bodily present, to notice where and when one is. Here we are: like amateur actors on some magnificent stage, dwarfed by the cosmic grandeur of our setting, muffing our lines, but producing now and then a fitful gleam of our own, an act of mortal beauty.

'What shall we clap?' she says to Peter. 'The lifeboat in the storm. What shall we sing? The beauty of the world!'

THE END

KNOWLEDGE OF ANGELS
Jill Paton Walsh

SHORTLISTED FOR THE BOOKER PRIZE 1994

'AN IRRESISTIBLE BLEND OF INTELLECT AND PASSION . . .
NOVELS OF IDEAS COME NO BETTER THAN THIS
SENSUAL EXAMPLE'
Mail on Sunday

It is, perhaps, the fifteenth century and the ordered tranquillity of a
Mediterranean island is about to be shattered by the appearance of
two outsiders: one, a castaway, plucked from the sea by fishermen,
whose beliefs represent a challenge to the established order; the
other, a child abandoned by her mother and suckled by wolves,
who knows nothing of the precarious relationship between
church and state but whose innocence will become the subject of a
dangerous experiment.

But the arrival of the Inquisition on the island creates a darker,
more threatening force which will transform what has been a
philosophical game of chess into a matter of life and death . . .

'A COMPELLING MEDIAEVAL FABLE, WRITTEN FROM THE
HEART AND MELDED TO A DRIVING NARRATIVE WHICH
NEVER ONCE LOSES ITS TREMENDOUS PACE'
Guardian

'THIS REMARKABLE NOVEL RESEMBLES AN ILLUMINATED
MANUSCRIPT MAPPED WITH ANGELS AND MOUNTAINS AND
SIGNPOSTS, AN ALLEGORY FOR TODAY AND YESTERDAY
TOO. A BEAUTIFUL, UNSETTLING MORAL FICTION ABOUT
VIRTUE AND INTOLERANCE'
Observer

'REMARKABLE . . . UTTERLY ABSORBING . . . A RICHLY
DETAILED AND FINELY IMAGINED FICTIONAL NARRATIVE'
Sunday Telegraph

0 552 99636 X

BLACK SWAN

A SCHOOL FOR LOVERS
Jill Paton Walsh

'AN INGENIOUS CELEBRATION OF MOZART . . . AN
ENTERTAINING DANCE THROUGH SELF-DECEPTION TO REAL
FEELING . . . ARTFUL IN THE BEST SENSE, ENRICHED BY THE
FINE DESCRIPTIVE WRITING'
Guardian

Against the idyllic background of a labyrinthine country house in
need of restoration, two friends are dared by their manipulative
tutor to try to seduce the other's lover. As the two young women in
question restore the paintings and revive the gardens of the
mansion, they are pursued unobserved. In the absence of their
lovers, each begins to weaken . . .

All too soon, idealistic love is beset by misunderstanding and
irrational desire. And what begins as a game soon becomes a far
darker pursuit . . .

'AN ELEGANT AND WITTY TRIBUTE TO THE GENIUS OF
MOZART . . . THE BEAUTY AND GRACE, ARTIFICE AND SKILL
OF THE WORK . . . A CHARMING RENAISSANCE CONCEIT'
Opera Now

'PACY NARRATIVE, STRONG VISUAL SENSE, DIRECTNESS OF
TONE, CLARITY OF STYLE'
The Times Literary Supplement

'A LIGHT, WITTY NOVEL ABOUT THE RISKS OF FALLING IN
LOVE. THE NOVEL WORKS AS SHAKESPEAREAN COMEDY, AN
OPERETTA WITH MAJESTIC SETTINGS, QUICKSILVER
CHANGES IN EMOTION, AN AMUSED BUT SYMPATHETIC TONE
AND THE BELIEF THAT YOUNG LOVE IS TOO NAIVE AND
TRANSITORY TO BE TRAGIC'
Financial Times

0 552 99646 7

BLACK SWAN

May '99
Chapters

A SELECTED LIST OF FINE WRITING
AVAILABLE FROM BLACK SWAN

THE PRICES SHOWN BELOW WERE CORRECT AT THE TIME OF GOING TO PRESS.
HOWEVER TRANSWORLD PUBLISHERS RESERVE THE RIGHT TO SHOW NEW
RETAIL PRICES ON COVERS WHICH MAY DIFFER FROM THOSE PREVIOUSLY
ADVERTISED IN THE TEXT OR ELSEWHERE.

99588 6	THE HOUSE OF THE SPIRITS	*Isabel Allende*	£6.99
99618 1	BEHIND THE SCENES AT THE MUSEUM	*Kate Atkinson*	£6.99
99648 3	TOUCH AND GO	*Elizabeth Berridge*	£5.99
99531 2	AFTER THE HOLE	*Guy Burt*	£5.99
99628 9	THE KNIGHT OF THE FLAMING HEART	*Michael Carson*	£6.99
99587 8	LIKE WATER FOR CHOCOLATE	*Laura Esquivel*	£6.99
99602 5	THE LAST GIRL	*Penelope Evans*	£5.99
99599 1	SEPARATION	*Dan Franck*	£5.99
99616 5	SIMPLE PRAYERS	*Michael Golding*	£5.99
99681 5	A MAP OF THE WORLD	*Jane Hamilton*	£6.99
99538 X	GOOD AS GOLD	*Joseph Heller*	£6.99
99605 X	A SON OF THE CIRCUS	*John Irving*	£7.99
99567 3	SAILOR SONG	*Ken Kesey*	£6.99
99542 8	SWEET THAMES	*Mathew Kneale*	£6.99
99580 0	CAIRO TRILOGY I: PALACE WALK	*Naguib Mahfouz*	£7.99
99392 1	THE GREAT DIVORCE	*Valerie Martin*	£6.99
99709 9	THEORY OF MIND	*Sanjida O'Connell*	£6.99
99536 3	IN THE PLACE OF FALLEN LEAVES	*Tim Pears*	£5.99
99667 X	GHOSTING	*John Preston*	£6.99
99130 9	NOAH'S ARK	*Barbara Trapido*	£6.99
99643 2	THE BEST OF FRIENDS	*Joanna Trollope*	£6.99
99636 X	KNOWLEDGE OF ANGELS	*Jill Paton Walsh*	£5.99
99647 5	LAPSING	*Jill Paton Walsh*	£5.99
99646 7	A SCHOOL FOR LOVERS	*Jill Paton Walsh*	£6.99
99673 4	DINA'S BOOK	*Herbjørg Wassmo*	£6.99
99592 4	AN IMAGINATIVE EXPERIENCE	*Mary Wesley*	£5.99

All Transworld titles are available by post from:

Book Service By Post, PO Box 29, Douglas, Isle of Man IM99 1BQ

Credit cards accepted. Please telephone 01624 675137, fax 01624 670923
or Internet http://www. bookpost.co.uk for details.

Please allow £0.75 per book for post and packing UK.
Overseas customers allow £1 per book for post and packing.